FACING THE GIANTS

Screenplay by
Alex Kendrick and Stephen Kendrick

Novelization by
Eric Wilson

THOMAS NELSON
Since 1798

NASHVILLE   DALLAS   MEXICO CITY   RIO DE JANEIRO

Aug 2017

Published in Nashville, Tennessee, by Thomas Nelson. Thomas Nelson is a registered trademark of Thomas Nelson, Inc.

Thomas Nelson books may be purchased in bulk for educational, business, fund-raising, or sales promotional use. For information, please e-mail SpecialMarkets@ThomasNelson.com.

Scripture quotations are from THE NEW KING JAMES VERSION, © 1979, 1980, 1982, Thomas Nelson, Inc., Publishers; and the HOLY BIBLE: NEW INTERNATIONAL VERSION®, © 1973, 1978, 1984 by International Bible Society. Used by permission of Zondervan Publishing House. All rights reserved.

Publisher's Note: This novel is a work of fiction. Names, characters, places, and incidents are either products of the author's imagination or used fictitiously. All characters are fictional, and any similarity to people living or dead is purely coincidental.

ISBN: 978-1-4016-8526-3 (repackage)

Library of Congress Cataloging in Publication Data

Wilson, Eric (Eric P.)
    Facing the giants / screenplay by Alex and Stephen Kendrick ; novelization by Eric Wilson.
        p. cm.
    ISBN: 978-1-59554-432-2 (trade paper)
    ISBN: 978-1-59554-519-0 (hardcover w/ dvd)
    1. School sports—Fiction. 2. Football coaches—Fiction. I. Kendrick, Alex, 1970– II. Kendrick, Stephen, 1973– III. Title.
PS3623.I583F33 2007
813'.6—dc22   2007031957

Printed in the United States of America
13 14 15 QG 5 4 3

To our earthly father, Larry Kendrick. You are a hero and an inspiration to us! We could never thank you enough for living out a faith that led us to Jesus Christ. Your drive to glorify Him even from a wheelchair is amazing!
You are a "giant" of faith in our eyes.

To Sherwood Baptist Church. When a group of believers holds nothing back from God, He can do the impossible. We have watched you do that time and time again. Your faith, prayer, and service is evidence of your love for our Lord. May God's hand stay with you.

—ALEX KENDRICK *and* STEPHEN KENDRICK

Dedicated to my childhood friend, Tim Johnson. I'll never forget the hours we spent throwing the football in the street, playing basketball side by side, practicing the high jump . . . and eventually serving the Lord together in Europe and Asia. Your friendship meant the world to me.
Keep the flame burning!

—ERIC WILSON

CONTENTS

THE PRESEASON

CHAPTER 1
On Eagle's Wings

GRANT

Okay, the car wasn't his style. If he were still single, he'd be driving something low and muscular, with a big V-8 rumbling under the hood. And a few dents, as well. A spot or two of rust. Just enough to show that this baby had seen some action, put in some miles, and wasn't to be messed with.

Instead, he was at the wheel of a blue Chevy Celebrity.

Not a bad car. It'd been their first big purchase as a married couple, and Brooke had won him over with her argument that a four-door would soon be a necessity.

He agreed. This was no longer the Grant Taylor show. He now had a wife to think about, and children somewhere down the road.

Wow. There's a wild thought.

First things first, he decided. That was the way he liked to do things—in order, with a specific plan.

Moderate success as a college quarterback? Check.

Bachelor of science, with a minor in sports management? Check.

A beautiful bride of eight months? Check.

God had been good to them. And now, after years of athletics and studies on both their parts, they were en route to his first coaching position. They were leaving behind some fond memories at Georgia Southern University, ready to create new ones amid the tilled farms and pecan groves of little Albany, in the state's south-western corner.

"This is the exit, Grant." Brooke leaned forward in the passenger seat and looked up at the US 80 road sign. "We're still gonna stop, aren't we?"

"If that's what you want."

"Don't you wanna see it? The thing was built in 1880."

"Sounds old."

She brushed blonde hair back over her ear and looked sideways at him.

"Okay," he said. "We'll stop."

A scenic detour. Another small concession on his part. And why not? They had their whole lives charted out in front of them. According to MapQuest, the trek from Statesboro to Albany would take less than four hours. With the small U-Haul trailer, they might lose a little time, but not much.

Soon they would pull into the driveway of the house they had purchased two weeks ago, unload boxes, and begin making it into a home. If things went as planned, if he had the sort of long-term success that Coach Dooley had in his years at the University of Georgia, Coach Grant Taylor would become a household name and have hundreds, even thousands, of boys who would point back to his influence in their young lives.

He was going from the GSU Eagles to the Eagles at Shiloh Christian. For him, that had been a good sign. He was flying high. If Brooke wanted to take a little side trip, then that's what they'd do.

BROOKE

"Ahhh," said Brooke. She took one skip toward the covered bridge, then spun back around. She'd been hoping to visit George L. Smith State Park for years. "Just look at it. It's so *sweet.*"

Grant put his hands on his waist. "It's a bridge. With a roof."

"Built over a hundred years ago. Just think, people used to ride their carriages along there. Let's go walk through it."

Her husband looked unimpressed.

"Come on," she said. "I thought I married a hopeless romantic."

"Tell me one football player you know who's a romantic."

"You."

He glanced at his watch.

"You don't fool me, Grant Taylor." She slipped her arm into his and pulled him along, nearly skipping again. "We're going on a walk together."

The Parrish Mill Bridge was made of dark weathered wood, with double doors opened on both ends. Beneath the structure, a mill worked in conjunction with a dam. Inside, they found it to be cool and quiet, except for the sounds of Fifteen Mile Creek cascading beneath them.

Brooke stopped and let go of Grant's hand. "Can you see what I'm doing?"

"No, it's too dark."

"Let your eyes adjust."

"I . . . You're . . ."

"I'm waiting for you to give me a kiss."

He didn't need any more prodding than that.

On the other side, they found a bench swing. They sat side by side, rocking in the afternoon warmth. The sun was making a slow descent into the west, outlining the shapes of trees and turning the sky a ripe peach color.

"What's this remind you of?"

"Our first date," Grant said. "At the Brooklet Peanut Festival."

She had nothing to say after that. The fact that he remembered was enough. On their trip to this point, they'd passed spook houses, courthouse squares, and antebellum mansions that looked like sets from *Gone with the Wind*. But this was her favorite place so far. Even Grant seemed to like it, though he hadn't said so out loud.

Men, Brooke thought. *They're just like little boys sometimes, trying to act so tough.*

The mere thought of having their own son one day brought a huge smile to her face. Would he have Grant's same adorable gap between his teeth? Would he get her eyes? If they had a girl, Brooke just hoped the poor thing wouldn't inherit those bushy Taylor eyebrows.

"What're you thinking about?"

"You and me," she said. "Our future together."

"Must be good, judging by your smile."

GRANT

"Albany, here we come."

Grant drove along Highway 300, his elbow propped out the driver's window. Only a few more miles to Dougherty County. The route took them past peanut farms and occasional stands of cypress standing in black swamp water. Pines lined the road most of the way.

Despite the wear of their trip, they felt a burst of excitement as they pulled into town. This was it. On Monday, he would tour the grounds at Shiloh Christian Academy, meet his new team, and start putting them through daily doubles in preparation for the first game of the season.

And their first victory.

Soon, winning would be the norm at SCA.

After unhitching the U-Haul at their house on Old Pretoria, they headed up North Westover to grab a bite to eat.

"Sonic sound good?"

"Anything," Brooke answered. "I'm starved."

They pulled into a space at the Sonic Drive-In. This couldn't beat Brooke's fried sweet potatoes and homemade biscuits, but it would do. In the next weeks and months, they'd have plenty of opportunities to start filling the house with the smells of life and hard work and good home-cookin'.

Grant took Brooke's request, then hit the red button and waited.

A man's garbled voice: "Good evenin'. You ready to order?"

"Yeah. We're new in town, so be easy on us." Then, because he couldn't help but brag a bit, he added, "I'm taking over the coaching job at Shiloh Christian."

"The Eagles football team?"

"That's right."

"Woohoo! Thank goodness. We've been waitin' on ya, Coach Taylor, been prayin' too."

"You hear that?" Grant mouthed to his wife.

"An answer to their prayers," she whispered back.

Still wearing a silly grin, Grant placed their order.

His wife slipped her hand into his. "Guess they know a good thing when they see it, *Coach* Taylor."

"I guess so."

"Of course, we haven't won any games yet."

"Hey."

"But we will," she assured him. "Lots of them."

FIRST QUARTER:
TRYING TO STAND

CHAPTER 2
Six Years Later

GRANT

Everything came into focus.

With the clock ticking down, Grant watched his team in red jerseys step up to the line of scrimmage. The defense dug in, waiting for the snap. Fans were roaring from the stands. Along the opponent's sidelines, cheerleaders lifted girls into the air in front of a banner that read "Beat the Eagles."

Would it happen again? Another heart-wrenching loss? Under his leadership, the Shiloh Eagles had gone five seasons without a winning record.

That was about to change, though. They'd won their last three games in a row, bringing them to 5 and 4.

"C'mon," Grant called out.

They needed this. He needed this.

"Blue 18. Set. Hut, hut!"

Sophomore Zach Avery took the snap, turned, and handed off the ball to his fullback. The offensive line surged forward, trying to create a hole for him to run through, but the Tigers were too strong. A linebacker bulldozed into the gap and wrapped up the ballcarrier, taking him down hard.

Shiloh fans groaned.

"Hurry back!" Grant barked. "Time for one more play."

Against the Friday night sky, the scoreboard showed the Eagles were behind by a touchdown with less than a minute to go. The board also indicated they had time-outs left, but the referees had assured Grant it was a mistake. Most likely, the kid manning the clock had been distracted by his buddies . . . again.

Seconds were slipping away. It all came down to this.

Through the pulse pounding in his ears, Grant could hear parents and booster club members screaming from the bleachers. He could feel their expectations pressing down upon his head like heavy hands. Brooke was up there too, probably nervous and praying.

Grant paced. His jaw was set. He was in the zone now, focused. *This is our year! It's time, Lord.*

It was fourth and long. They had one last chance to stun their opponents. They'd send a message to the entire league that the Eagles were no longer the bottom of the heap.

As his players huddled, he called for his quarterback's attention. "Zach. Zach!" He crossed his arms, with one hand in a fist, the other holding up three fingers. "Crossbuck 30. Crossbuck 30!"

Zach nodded. "Crossbuck 30," he told his guys. "Crossbuck 30. Ready?"

"Break." With a united clap, they left the huddle.

Grant stopped breathing. There'd be time for that during the celebration. Nothing less than a touchdown here would do. Along the stands, Shiloh students had draped a hand-painted sign that read "Our Team Don't Take No Mess."

Time to prove it, boys. Let's show 'em what we got!

Shiloh set up in an I formation, with two players in the backfield directly behind the quarterback. This would keep the Tigers guessing. They'd have no idea who was getting the ball.

"Move it, team," the quarterback ordered. "Set. Hut!"

Zach took the snap, pitched it back to Jacob Hall. Jacob ran to the right, creating time for the wide receiver to sprint down the field. Jeremy streaked past his defender and signaled with his hand that he was ready for the pass. Just like they'd done it in practice. This was going to work.

We're gonna win this ball game. It's really gonna happen.

Jacob hesitated.

"Throw it, Jacob!" Grant yelled.

Jacob had only a split second to set his feet and launch the football, but a lanky black kid, Number 1, was charging at him. Jacob spun away, escaping the defender's clutches. Already, another Tiger was coming his way.

Mr. Bridges

Excitement clamped a vise around Mr. Raymond Bridges's chest. Beside him on the sofa, his wife, Martha, was asleep, and he worried he would wake her if Shiloh pulled out a victory. He'd gone through a triple bypass last year and, by the grace of God, he was still here, still cheering for the school where their daughter worked.

From the ancient radio standing guard in the corner of the den, the announcer called the game's conclusion: "The Eagles will have to go for it on fourth down, with just forty-two seconds left in the football game and no time-outs. Coach Grant Taylor can get his first winning season for the Shiloh Christian Academy—*if* they can pull this play off."

The radio emitted a high-pitched whine. The dial's glow wavered. For a moment, Bridges thought it'd given out and he would have to phone around to get the final score.

A loud crackle. Then the signal returned, clearer than before.

Well, don't that beat all? he thought. *Thing's 'bout as old as I am.*

The announcer's voice echoed through the den: "Zach Avery will take the snap. He pitches back to Jacob Hall. Jacob's going to try to pass it. He's got Jeremy Johnson going down the field!"

Bridges rocked forward, rubbing fingers over his gray facial hair.

"But here come the Tigers. Jacob's gonna try to tuck it and run, and he's gonna be taken down at the forty-yard line, stopped there by Lewis Slaughter. Jeremy Johnson was wide open down the field," the announcer explained. "If he'd only had a few seconds more to throw the football, this game might have had a different outcome."

Taking a deep breath, Bridges felt his heart tap against his ribs.

"As it is," the voice rambled on, "the Tigers will take over now and will no doubt take a knee to run out the clock, thus ending Coach Grant Taylor's bid for his first winning season in six years. Now he'll have to wait until next season for that all-elusive winning record."

How much longer, Lord? I keep prayin' for a change.

Bridges reached for the radio knob and listened to the big wooden thing purr itself to sleep. Martha's eyes fluttered and she looked up at him.

"Did they . . . ?"

He shook his head.

"It's all right, Raymond. Maybe next year."

GRANT

It was over?

That couldn't be. They'd practiced that play again and again. It should've worked. It was the right call. Why had Jacob hesitated?

Grant grabbed his head and turned. Brooke was there, looking down at him, her hands steepled over her mouth. The fans wore expressions of shock, disappointment, and disgust. In the radio booth, the announcers were delivering the news to the entire county.

Another loss. Another failed attempt at a winning record.

Amid dejected players and groaning fans, Grant put his hands on his hips and stared at the final score. He would have the long off-season to think about redeeming himself next year.

"If they let him come back next year." That's what those announcers were probably muttering to each other up there. Under his leadership, they'd seen this scenario time and again.

He pulled his hands over his head. He felt alone.

No, not fully alone. Brooke was here. In his time at SCA, she had stood by him, refusing to listen to the whispers of mutinous parents. He appreciated her encouragement but hated to be the object of her sympathy yet again. When would he be able to show her what he was made of? To back up their hopes with some results?

"Coach?"

Grant turned from his view of the emptying bleachers to junior Darren Moore, the team's leading scorer for the season. The kid wore a defiant look, with his helmet clenched in his hand.

"Why didn't you put me in, like I told you?" Darren said. "I woulda run it all the way in for a TD."

"The Tigers would've been looking for that."

"Yeah? Well, I guess you had it all figured out."

Grant felt a rush of heat along his neck. "The world doesn't revolve around you, Darren."

The player stomped off, bouncing his helmet against his thigh pads.

Stanley, the waterboy, came alongside. He was a big, lumbering kid with an active brain. "Statistically, Coach Taylor, you made the right decision. In a fourth-and-long situation, a pass play has a higher percentage of success."

"Thank you, Stanley."

"Of course, statistics are an inexact science, and a screen pass to Darren might've provided a more concrete shot at a victory."

"Okay, Stanley. Don't you have stuff to take to the locker room?"

Grant watched him go. The only numbers that mattered at the moment were those in the win-loss columns: 5 and 5. When would he get this program over .500? Or was he destined to remain mediocre?

Hanging his head, he blinked twice and saw everything turn foggy.

BROOKE

Brooke waited in the car for her husband to arrive from the locker room. What sort of speech had he given the boys? She hoped he'd found the strength to highlight the season's successes. Three wins in a row, at one point. That was a first under Grant's leadership, and something to build on for next year.

The parking lot was empty, save their blue Celebrity. The evening was turning cold, and a chill was seeping through the cardboard slab Grant had taped over the rear passenger window. This past summer, someone had thrown a rock that splintered the glass. They'd never caught the person responsible, but her husband suspected it was the irate parent of one of his players.

This was south Georgia. Former greats like Deion Sanders had come from this area. When it came to football, even some of the Christian school parents had little forgiveness.

"Oh, Grant."

Brooke knew just where to find her husband. She climbed from the car and crossed the pavement. She spotted him in the stands, wearing his blue coat and a ball cap. She walked toward him, passing the players' bench where empty cups surrounded a lone watercooler.

He hardly moved as she climbed into the bleachers, no doubt replaying the game in his mind. Beating himself up.

She looked out at the chalk lines and the chipped orange goalposts. The field lights shone down where the Eagles and Tigers had battled for supremacy thirty-five minutes earlier.

Grant met her eye, then shook his head. She sat beside him as he slapped at the football in his hands. She leaned against his shoulder and prayed. What else could she do? Six years running they had ended the season sitting in this spot. She'd said everything there was to say. There was nothing left.

High overhead, the lights flicked off and plunged the field into darkness.

"Yep," Grant muttered. "That's about right."

CHAPTER 3
The Jury

GRANT

Summer was over. School was back in session.

Grant marched across the Shiloh Christian Academy parking lot, wearing slacks with a belt, and a collared shirt. He'd licked his wounds, healed, even given himself pep talks in the bathroom mirror when no one was around.

This year things were gonna be different.

To his left, a student blew her horn and veered into a parking space. A boy dived out of the way as though he'd been hit. Grant wasn't sure whether to laugh or scold the new driver. He continued forward into the building.

Wide-eyed freshmen milled within the school's cinder-block halls, searching for their lockers. Upperclassmen elbowed through the mob. The smell of fresh paint hung in the air, symbolic of new things to come.

"Good morning, students," a teacher greeted the throngs. "Let's get to class."

Grant pressed through the crowd. "Get 'em, Claire."

"Hey, Grant." Then: "Come on, y'all. Quit talking. Let's go, let's go, let's go. Hurry."

On the way to his office, Grant walked by the glass display case where SCA's previous athletic successes taunted him in the forms of ribbons, metals, and gleaming trophies. He looked straight ahead and entered the small room that was his as head coach. His assistants were waiting inside. Normally, they would be cutting up, but today they were silent.

"What?" He closed the door and took the rolled sheet of paper that Brady handed him. He read it over. "What? You gotta be kidding me. This had better be a joke."

J.T Hawkins was the offensive coordinator, a black man with a trimmed goatee, a shaved head, and a proven sense of humor. Brady Owens was defensive coordinator, a heavyset white man with hopes of being a head coach someday. He too had a mischievous side.

But neither man was smiling.

"Nope," Brady replied.

J.T. folded his arms. "Mandy said he came in this morning, got his papers."

"Wait," Grant said. "A player can't just transfer to another school to play football. He's gotta make a change of address."

"He did," Brady responded. "He's moving in with his dad."

Grant glanced around his office with its framed certificates, the scale against the wall, and the "We Support SCA Eagles" sign on a chair. This was supposed to be his HQ for a victorious new season, not the site of his first setback.

He wadded up the paper and threw it against the window blinds. "I can't *believe* that. This is the third time this has happened. We spend three years pouring into them, and what do they do when they get to their senior year? They transfer to a rival school. *Why?*"

"Well." Brady held up his hands. "'Cause at the end of the season, no one wants to be on TV going, 'We're number six, baby. We're number six.'"

Grant gave him a withering stare.

"Well, you asked."

Worried about what might come out of his mouth, Grant turned to leave. At his back, he overheard J.T. chiding Brady. "Just had to go there, didn't ya?"

GRANT

That afternoon Grant found Stanley, the waterboy, strolling beside him toward the practice field. The boy's freckles were more abundant than ever, brought out by the summer sun. His head was a mop of curly black hair.

"Hi, Coach."

"Stanley."

"I filled the team coolers, but that locker room tap water isn't very cold to start with. My calculated guess is seventy-one, seventy-two degrees."

"Water's water."

"Technically speaking."

"The guys'll take what they get."

"I could drive down to the store and pick up some ice, if you'd like. At one-nineteen each, I could get three bags for under five dollars."

Grant thumbed a bill from his wallet. "Here ya go. Bring me back change and a receipt."

That'll buy me a few minutes of quiet anyway.

On the grass, players were stretching out in their white practice jerseys while others adjusted their pads. Oak and pecan trees stood outside the fence, branches swishing in the breeze.

Brock Kelley, the defensive captain, jogged toward him with helmet in hand. "Coach, is it true that Darren switched to Tucker?"

"We'll talk about it in a minute, Brock."

"So it's true?"

"We'll talk about it in a minute." Grant moved into the middle of the field and called to his players. "Huddle up."

"Coach," Matt Prater asked, "is it true that Darren transferred to Tucker?"

Grant lowered his head and brushed his hand back over his cap. He was going to have to face this issue right here, right now. He looked at his team. "I got word this morning that Darren *did* transfer to Tucker."

Some moaned. Others rolled their eyes.

Brock tossed down his helmet. "There goes the season."

"The season hasn't started," Grant cut in, "and will be whatever we make it."

"Who's gonna take his place? He scored a third of our points last year."

"You let me worry about that."

Another player said, "Coach, maybe if you go talk to him, he'll come back."

"He's not coming back."

"It's worth a try."

"No. Darren's heart is no longer at Shiloh, and you wouldn't want him on this team. Anyway, we're not starting off the season as if it's doomsday. Nobody's irreplaceable."

"Darren is."

"Darren is not," Grant insisted. "There's more to a good football team than a running back. If anything, this oughta push you to take up the slack." Grant turned to Brady. "Coach Owens, is this season over?"

"This season's just starting," Brady fired back.

"Coach Hawkins, is this season over?"

"We ain't lost yet," said J.T. "So we still got a perfect record, Coach."

Grant nodded to his team. "I agree. Stop worrying about Darren. Get out there and start your drills. We've got a game to play this Friday night."

"All right," Brady said. "Let's go, Shiloh! Come on. Let's go."

The boys pulled on their helmets and followed J.T. toward the goal line.

Grant turned and noticed two fathers in the stands wearing solemn faces. Great. The jury was already in session, evaluating his every move.

"Grant." Brady looked around to make sure they were out of earshot of the players. "Who *is* going to take Darren's place?"

"I don't know. Lord knows, we need somebody."

CHAPTER 4
Freight Train

BROOKE

Brooke Taylor stood at the bathroom sink, wearing sweatpants and a yellow top. She stared down at the pregnancy test in her hand, willing a second pink line to appear.

Nothing. Negative. For the umpteenth time.

She dropped the test into the trash can, then pulled back her hair to study herself in the mirror. She and Grant had been married over seven years. Friends still accused them of being two lovebirds. So why couldn't she conceive a baby? Although she'd studied child and family development at Georgia Southern, she seemed incapable of having children of her own.

She turned her head. Those were tires crunching over the gravel lane.

Grant was home, and he didn't need this news. Not now. She would meet him with a smile and a plate of food, and she'd listen to his first-day excitement about this year's prospects for a successful football season.

Would he only end up being crushed again? She hoped not.

Brooke combed a hand through her hair on her way to the front door. From the window, she saw their car coast to a stop at the far end of the drive. The duct tape on the grille and the missing hubcaps were reminders of how things had gone downhill of late.

They still loved each other, though. That was a good thing.

From the front porch, between the white pillars of their modest brick home, she watched her husband climb from the car and slam the door. His shoulders were down, his gym bag in hand. His feet dragged through the dirt.

"Why'd you park all the way out there?"

"Had to," he said. "It died again."

"Why don't we get a new battery?"

"I'll get Brady to help me tomorrow morning. I don't wanna think about it now."

"Do you want me to take a look at it for you?" she teased.

Grant lifted his chin. "Stop it."

She followed him into the kitchen. She'd redone the walls last spring with a blue-and-white-checkered pattern. It was her way of keeping hope fresh. On the counter, boxes of Cheerios and Honey Comb still sat from this morning. Near the sink, apples filled a bowl next to a gallon of sweet tea.

Grant came to a halt and wrinkled his nose. "*Ohhh*, sweetheart . . ."

"Grant, I don't know what that smell is. I've scrubbed everything I can."

"It's terrible."

She shook a container of mayo and returned to sandwich makings. "I know it is, but what else can I do? I don't even know where it's coming from."

He dropped his bag to the floor and started thumbing through the mail. "This day stunk. Why shouldn't my house?"

"What do you mean?"

"Darren transferred to Tucker."

"What? He did *not*!"

"Yep. Came by and got his papers. Didn't even say good-bye."

Brooke drew her question into two syllables, Southern-style: "*Whhhy?*"

"Why do you think? Didn't see a chance of winning at Shiloh. But . . ." Grant set down the bills and pointed a finger as he turned away. "It ain't like Tucker's gonna guarantee him a scholarship."

"Oooh. I bet the boys are *frustrated.*"

"More than you know," Grant replied.

GRANT

Grant stepped into the bathroom to wash up for supper. After finding a box near the sink basin, he noticed a matching plastic object in the garbage.

Could this be a . . . ?

He walked back into view and held up the box for Brooke to see.

She stared at it as though he'd whipped out a surprise piece of courtroom evidence. She dropped her knife onto the sandwich plate and planted her hands on the counter. "I meant to throw that away."

"Did you think you were pregnant?"

"I don't know." She returned to her work. "I just wanna be pregnant so bad that my mind plays tricks on me."

Grant understood. For a moment, hope had brushed by him as well. Like everything else in his life, though, good news seemed to avoid the spot in which he was standing. He set down the box and headed to the wood dining table, where early evening light shone through white shutters onto glasses of tea.

"You know," Brooke said from the other side of the kitchen bar, "it's been four years since we started trying."

Grant nodded. Looked down.

Can't we talk about something else right now?

"Would you be opposed to me going to see a specialist?"

He leaned back. "No."

Brooke slid plates onto the table. "I'd just like to know what she says."

"Okay." He stared at the apple and sandwich on his plate, then lifted his hands. "I thought we were having spaghetti tonight."

"The stove's not working."

"You are kidding me."

Brooke shook her head.

"So we've got a leak in the back room, the dryer only works half the time, the car's dying on us, and now the stove's broken. That's about right." Grant screwed his eyes closed and pulled his hand down over his thinning scalp. "No wonder I'm losing my hair."

She grinned. "I love you."

He gave her a questioning look, then smiled and covered his face as he laughed. After the day's collective bits of bad news, he was afraid that something in him might break. He knew if he kept looking into those round blue eyes she would see right through him—and he couldn't risk that. Not now.

Brooke needed him to be strong. He needed to hold it together.

GRANT

After dinner, he plopped into his living room armchair and turned on WTOL Channel 15. He waited through the TV's depressing news updates. At last, a collage of sports action pieces signified the show's change of direction: "And now your Georgia Sports Break with Alicia Houston."

The camera cut to a gym, where Ms. Houston stood before a weight set and a chalkboard. She spoke into her microphone, "The Richland Giants have started football practice as the new school year gets under way. The team will be defending a three-year GISA state championship run. Now they prepare to fight for a fourth."

The screen widened to include a large man with a crew cut, dressed in a black coach's shirt. He had a sucker in his mouth. In the background, a player was doing bench presses.

Ms. Houston turned. "I'm here with Bobby Lee Duke of the Giants. Coach Duke, how does this year look for the team?"

"Alice . . ." He paused to pluck the sucker from his lips.

Alice? Grant thought. *Her name's Alicia.*

Coach Duke said, "We've grown real fond of the state title, and we don't see any reason to give it up this year. I've got most of my starters coming back and I've got a strong bench, so I've only got one thing to say." He faced the camera and pointed with his sucker. "Get off the tracks, 'cause the freight train's comin'."

Grant slapped at the remote. He'd had enough.

"Yes!" From the laundry room, Brooke cheered as the dryer kicked into action. "We're gonna have some dry towels tonight."

Well, that was something. But Grant needed this season to kick into gear. One more losing record, and he'd be sent packing. This was America. Nobody cared if the coach had issues to worry about at home. Second place meant you were just the first-place losers, and parents didn't go to games for that.

Neither did he, come to think of it.

If he wasn't here to help this team win football games, then what was he here for?

CHAPTER 5
Your Secret's Safe

DAVID

David Childers was shy. Always had been. He was new to Shiloh Christian Academy, still feeling out of place. At his dad's prodding, he had ended up here for the first football game of the season in hopes of getting to know some people from the school.

He climbed into the stands, saw an empty seat next to a black woman with small kids beside her. She was up on her feet, cheering as the Eagles took the field and began pregame warm-ups.

"Anyone sitting there?" he asked over the blaring of the school band.

"Nah," she answered. "All yours."

"Thanks."

David slipped into the spot, ready to hide behind her enthusiasm. He noticed that two elderly men, one row over, were frowning at him. Was there something on his shirt? He looked down and winced, realizing he was wearing the opposing team's colors.

Perfect. I'm such a loser!

All around, people were chatting, munching on snacks, and calling out to players on the sidelines. There was nothing lonelier than a bleacher full of strangers.

"You want some?" the woman said, offering him her bag of popcorn.

"Uh, no thanks."

"You skinny enough. It ain't gonna hurt ya."

"Well. Okay." David took a small handful. "Thank you."

At that moment, one of the assistant coaches came bounding up the steps, wearing an SCA ball cap turned backward. David had seen the guy around school. Everyone called him J.T.

The man leaned in toward the lady. He was wearing a wedding ring. "You made it." He gave her a peck on the cheek.

"Wouldn't miss it, babe. Let's see some points on that board tonight."

"Tha's the plan." J.T. tossed a skeptical look over his shoulder at the band in the bleacher's lower section. The director was trying to coax something melodic out of his ragtag group, with little success. "You know, wavin' his arms that hard ain't gonna make 'em play any better."

"They's tryin', J.T."

"What? To scare off the other team? See ya after the game." He jogged back down to the field.

David couldn't help but smile. This man reminded him of his soccer coach in Athens, full of energy and playful sarcasm. He already liked the guy. Too bad they didn't have a soccer team at SCA. David had played since he was in second grade, with his dad always there on the sidelines, rain or shine, working his wheelchair through the mud and the grass.

Maybe he could suggest starting a soccer team.

Forget it. This was the South. Most of these boys had been playing football for years already. He'd only make a fool of himself.

Turning his head, David spotted kids from a few of his classes. Then he recognized one of the Shiloh cheerleaders down below, a girl with almond-shaped eyes. She was in history, two desks ahead of him.

I wonder what she's like? Would she even talk to me?

"Friend of yours?"

"Huh?" He looked over at J.T.'s wife.

"Shortie on the end, with the straight brown hair. You was starin'."

"I, uh . . . Well, no, not really."

"She's been lookin' up here."

"She's just leading the cheers."

"Nah. She was lookin' at you. And don'tcha argue about it, 'cause we girls know these things."

David felt blood rush to his cheeks. "You won't say anything to her, will you?"

"Do I look like her mother?" The black woman started laughing. "Stop worryin'. Your secret's safe with me."

The crowd roared with anticipation as both teams lined up against each other. In white uniforms and dark blue helmets, Pineview kicked off. The Eagles, in red jerseys and pants, tried to slow the onrushing opponents but were thrown back. The returner was taken down inside the fifteen-yard line.

A moan went up from the stands.

"C'mon, Eagles!" J.T.'s wife cheered. "It's all right."

As the Shiloh offense lined up for their first drive, the cheerleaders shook pom-poms and called out to the crowd. One of the girls was launched high into the air. Student-made banners read "We've got spirit" and "War-Win!"

The fight was on.

DAVID

By the end of the first quarter, the score was Pineview 14, SCA 0. The Eagles ran a few plays, then tried an option on third down that got stuffed at the line of scrimmage. They were forced to punt again.

David watched the head coach, Grant Taylor, pacing the sidelines. The man was intense, his eyes dark beneath his hat. Must be tough, carrying the weight of a team and all these fans.

Near the end of the third quarter, the Eagles broke a big play to the eight-yard line and the crowd went crazy. They might just have a comeback on their hands. During the moments of pandemonium, the brown-haired cheerleader caught David's eye.

Only for a second. But a definite connection.

He looked down. Why was he so nervous? Why couldn't he be more bold, like his biblical namesake? His heart pounded with an excitement separate from the game.

Just as the fans' hopes were renewed, a holding penalty on third down moved the Eagles back to the eighteen-yard line. They set up for a field goal, then bumbled the snap, thus erasing any shot at putting points on the board. Soon after, the Pineview quarterback completed a short wideout that gained good yardage. Number 17 carried the ball, spun, and stretched for a first down.

Time dwindled away as the opponents scored a field goal, followed by another touchdown.

Final score: 23-0.

On the Eagles sideline, Coach Taylor hung his head. David heard people grumbling about the man as they filed from the stands. Didn't seem right. Would they be saying those things to the coach's face?

Beside him, J.T.'s wife rounded up her young ones. "The season's not over yet," she said. "Some of these folks just don't know how to believe."

FACING THE GIANTS

"You sound like my dad."

"Bring him along next time. We could use a little faith out here."

"Yeah."

David looked down as he joined the exodus of disappointed fans. Well, at least he was wearing the winning team's colors.

CHAPTER 6
No Juice

GRANT

Grant sulked through the parking lot to their old Chevy clunker. Brooke walked beside him, her arms crossed. He pulled off his hat, slapped it against his leg, and opened the door for her. He got in and turned the key. The engine tried to kick over, the ignition fluttering like a bird with clipped wings.

How fitting.

Fans strolled by, muttering and avoiding his eyes.

Another try. Another flutter.

A middle-aged couple, booster club members, approached on Brooke's side. The man leaned down and spoke through the window: "I hope that's not a sign of the way the rest of this season's gonna go, Coach."

Grant watched them head away. "Now why'd he have to say that?"

"Just let it go," Brooke said.

"I hate this car."

"Let's find someone with jumper cables and let's go *home*."

"It's bad enough you lose your first game. Now I can't even start my own car."

"This happens to everybody," she said. "Don't be embarrassed about it."

Brooke was right. Her example, as always, was a reminder to

keep the right perspective. If she could handle minor setbacks such as this, he could too.

Grant got out and found a man in an Old Navy T-shirt, about to climb into a glimmering Ford SUV. Grant hated seeking help yet again for his decaying car, but it was his job to rescue his wife—and that's what he would do.

"Excuse me. Would you happen to have any jumper cables?"

"Sure," the man answered. "I've got a set of cables. Where's your car?"

Grant motioned back to the Chevy, to his wife at the passenger window.

Except she was gone. Vanished. Just like that. He did a double take and stared at her window with amazement. She was *hiding*!

"I'll pull around," the man said.

"I really appreciate it," Grant responded before heading back to the car. Still no sign of Brooke. He stood at the duct-taped grille and knocked on the hood, waiting for her head to appear, for a wry smile that said she was sorry and that she supported him—juice in the battery, or no juice.

He waited. The hood popped open with a rusty twang.

Brooke had released the latch from inside the dark cockpit, but she still refused to show herself. Could he really blame her?

BROOKE

Grant was hounding her as she moved into the kitchen. On the counter sat a bottle of Sprite and a bag of homemade pecan cookies, gifts from a neighbor, good wishes for a new season. They remained unopened.

"Why?" Grant demanded. "Explain to me what you were thinking."

"Grant, I wasn't that embarrassed."

"So why did you hide?"

The smell hit him then, right in the face. He threw his head back, closed his eyes, and wrinkled his nose again. "Ohhh, why's this house have to stink so bad?"

"You'll get used to it . . . after a couple of hours."

Her husband groaned.

Brooke pulled mugs from the cupboard and opened a container of Folgers. "Honey, we gotta do something about the car. The only thing it does faithfully for us is break down."

"That's about right." He tossed his cap onto the counter. "Would it not be better to just get a small new car?"

She looked back over her shoulder, while her hand grabbed a paper coffee filter: "You know we can't afford that."

"How do other people do it?"

"Other people make more than twenty-four thousand a year."

"You make six thousand." He reached for a bottle of water. "That takes us to thirty."

"Which is enough to help with repairs *occasionally*, not with a new car payment. Besides, there's other bills we don't normally have to pay."

He took a swig of water. "Like what?"

"Like my doctor bill."

"You saw her today?"

Brooke nodded.

On the other side of the kitchen, Grant braced himself against the counter. "What'd she say?"

"She said that I'm *fine*. My numbers are normal, and she saw nothing that gave her concern."

"That's good."

Brooke put away the supplies and turned to face her husband. They'd always confronted things together. "It doesn't mean the problem is with you."

"What else could it mean?"

"We just may not have given it enough time."

"Four years?"

"Are you still hoping we'll have a baby?" she asked.

Grant's forehead furrowed. "You know I am."

"Me too. I catch myself thinking about it more and more. Don't you want to know if something's preventing it?"

He swallowed.

"Are you afraid of getting checked out?" she pressed.

"Yes."

She admired him for that. Despite everything else that was going on, he was man enough to admit his fears.

She said, "Grant, I'm still clinging to a hope that one day we'll have children." She could see that hope was alive in his eyes too. She looked toward the ceiling, her mind full of the dreams she'd held on to since their wedding day. "I imagine 'em running in this house. I hear 'em playing in the backyard, or . . . running to our bed in a thunderstorm. And I think about reading 'em stories and teaching 'em songs. And I just keep thinking"—her chin quivered as she looked down and mustered the strength to put this into words—"how can I miss someone *so much* that I have never met?"

Grant glanced up, and she let him see her tears. For better or for worse, they were in this together.

"I'll go," he said.

She nodded. Either way, they couldn't hide from this any longer.

CHAPTER 7
Sparkle and Shine

BROCK

Monday mornings were the hardest.

Brock Kelley had survived three losing seasons as a Shiloh Eagle, and he always dreaded coming to class after a weekend of mulling over another loss. He would carry himself through the halls, head held high, daring anyone to say a word. Inside, though, he felt his dreams of college ball melting away.

Math class. First period. Could it get any more boring?

From the front, Mrs. Carter said, "Class, please continue reading chapter two of your workbooks. I'll be back in a minute with your graded quizzes from last week."

He frowned. He was pretty sure he wouldn't like the results.

Once the teacher was gone, he checked around the classroom and noticed a big kid with his head down on his desk. Stanley the waterboy. Was he asleep? Oh, this was too good.

Brock got the attention of the guy next to him. They were on the football team together, and they'd both endured Stanley's statistical outbursts. Without a word, they slipped back to the waterboy. Carefully, they lifted his desk and began moving him toward the front of the classroom. Brock's plan was to set Stanley one inch from the chalkboard, but en route he had an even better idea. Making eye contact with his partner in crime, he motioned with his head and mouthed, "On top."

As classmates watched in wonder, Brock and his friend raised and set Stanley's desk gently atop Mrs. Carter's. The waterboy was now enthroned over the class. Stanley snorted once, then settled into a wheezing snore.

The snickers that passed between the students turned into loud chuckles. Brock gestured for them to keep quiet before returning to his own seat and practicing an expression of innocence. When Mrs. Carter came back, she began handing out graded papers. Halfway up the aisle, she lifted her head and discovered the sleeping king. The class broke into laughter. Unamused by this new development, she circled her desk once, then cocked her head to the side. "Stanley."

Students giggled. Brock tried to hold it in.

"Stanley!"

Blurry-eyed, the waterboy raised his head from his opened mathematics book. Kids were laughing out loud now.

"Stanley," Mrs. Carter demanded, "do you want to tell me what you are doing on the top of my desk?"

"Nooo."

"Do you have any idea how you got on top of my desk?"

"Noooo."

"I suggest you get down immediately."

Stanley nodded and looked around, obviously disoriented. From his peripheral vision, Brock saw a girl behind him stand and point at him and the other guilty party.

Figures. Teacher's pet!

Mrs. Carter approached with graded papers in hand. Her eyes bore into him like ice picks. "You two can tell Coach Taylor that the reason why you're late for practice today is because you've been sitting in detention."

"Oh, come on, Mrs. Carter," he pleaded. "That was some serious humor."

"I'll get serious about your humor when you get serious about your studies." She dropped his paper onto his desk.

He looked down. "55?"

"Well," the teacher said, "if you want to announce your grade to the entire class, you go right ahead."

His partner in crime held up his own paper for Brock to see. He smirked as though he had pulled off an upset in a nationwide academic competition. Pointing at his score, he said: "57."

Brock shook his head. Beaten by an F.

GRANT

With the shame of Friday night's game still in his belly, Grant worried as he poked his head into Principal Dan Ryker's office. Ryker was at his wide desk, with a green accountant's lamp illuminating piles of paperwork. Behind him, a long cabinet filled the wall, stacked with textbooks and framed photos.

"Dan, you wanted to see me?"

"Yeah, Grant. Come on in. Grab the door."

Grant had always had Ryker's support, yet he felt tension as he took a seat across from his boss.

The principal looked up from his work, wearing a tailored shirt and a power tie. He was middle-aged, with red hair and piercing eyes. "So how's practice going?"

Grant tried to sound upbeat. "Well, we're doing all right."

"I was disappointed to hear that Darren was transferring to Tucker."

"Not as much as I was."

"How's that affected our boys?"

"Well, I mean, they don't like it. But they're gonna get over it."

"I hope you're right. Based on Friday's game, I'm not so sure."

Grant opened his mouth, hoping an explanation would spill out.

With raised hands, Ryker spared him the embarrassment. "Let's not dwell on what's happened. You and I both want to see these boys grow, to become more Christlike. That's our top priority here at Shiloh. Of course, I'd love to win ball games too."

"You and me both, Dan."

"The reality is that we're losing students and tuition dollars, due to our struggling athletic department. You know, some of our students have fathers who dream of their boys going to college on scholarships."

"Yeah, but to be fair, this is Albany. Not Athens or Atlanta."

"Agreed. And as a show of support, I want you to know that I've spoken with Alvin Pervis, chairman of the booster club, requesting new helmet logos for the team. The helmets we wore against Pineview looked like last year's leftovers. Let's put some sparkle and shine back on the field."

"I appreciate that. The boys will too."

"I want you to shoot straight with me here, Grant. What kind of season do you see us having this year?"

"Well, I mean, we're gonna do the best we can with what we've got. We've still got some pretty good talent on the team."

"Grant, really." Ryker leaned forward. "What's your gut feeling on this?"

Grant put his head back, sighed, then returned the principal's gaze. "You know, Dan, I hate to say this is gonna be another rebuilding year, but I don't know how else to look at it. We've only got thirty-one boys on the team. Many of 'em are freshmen and sophomores. Our strongest players are going to be playing both ways. It's going to be hard late in the game."

"Is there a chance they'll go 7 and 3? Or even 6 and 4?"

"You know, I wanna say yes to that. But I don't have a lot to work with. We'll have to fight for everything we get."

BRADY

Seated beside his fellow assistant, Brady Owens studied the poster on the wall behind Coach's head. Above the word *Endurance*, an eagle soared on outstretched wings. Nice idea, but it seemed to have little to do with this school's football program under Grant Taylor.

Not that it was all Grant's fault. Sometimes the chemistry was just wrong. And, being a Christian school, they did put more emphasis on scholastic and spiritual development.

Still, it'd been six years, going on seven. Brady had been here with Grant every step of the way. He'd listened to the gripes. Put up with the shame.

Someday, Brady thought, *I'd like to have my own shot at this.*

On the other side of the desk, Grant stared at the season's game schedule with a look of despair. J.T. broke the silence. "So basically, we got the toughest schedule we ever had and less talent than we ever had."

"Well," Brady said, "at least we got Dewey County on Friday night. That'll be a pretty easy win."

Grant swiveled his chair toward the window and put his elbows on his knees. "I'm concerned it might be our only win."

"Nah. We'll pull three or four out," J.T. insisted.

Brady looked up. "That'll give us another average season."

Grant stared across the desk. "I'm so sick of average seasons."

Tell me about it, Coach. This ain't the way I envisioned it.

From the hallway, the school bell rang. Grant glanced at his watch, then stood and collected his keys and wallet. "I gotta go."

"Where ya goin'?" Brady inquired.

"Got a doctor's appointment."

"For what?"

"I have a doctor's appointment."

"For *what*?"

J.T. nudged him in the arm. "Leave the man alone. He don't have to *tell* you." J.T. turned back toward Grant. "So what's wrong with you, man?"

"I'll be back in a couple of hours." Without another word, Grant left.

Brady watched him go, wondering if the stress of the job was causing Coach an ulcer. That sorta thing was an occupational hazard.

"Now look what you did," J.T. said. "You done made him mad."

"Me? You're the one that made him mad."

"No, not me. Besides, I *know* where he's going."

"Where?" Brady stood and shifted his weight over into Coach's chair. He kicked back, getting the feel for this spot behind the desk.

"He's going to the hair doctor. The man is going bald." J.T. circled his hand over the back of his own shiny head. "You hadn't noticed that whole underdeveloped region right up in here?"

"Oh, you're one to talk, Slick."

"Nah. See, when a black man goes bald, he still looks good. Look at Michael Jordan, George Foreman, Samuel L. Jackson. Classy-lookin' brothers. Who you got?" J.T. narrowed his eyes. "Kojak?"

Brady focused on spinning the pigskin in his hands.

"Yeah," said J.T. "Coach is gonna get him some plugs."

"Grant would not get plugs."

"Don't laugh." J.T. pointed across the desk. "You next."

Brady looked up and tightened his grip on the ball. Although he admired Coach's perseverance, he had no desire to follow in his footsteps, whether it came to bald spots or goose eggs in the win column. No sirree.

CHAPTER 8
Something Shifting

DAVID

Wearing black shorts and an orange T-shirt, David juggled the soccer ball in the field behind his home. Pine trees stood guard along the property line, tall and unwilting in the Georgia sun. He dribbled through the grass, from his left foot to his right, around and back again. He could feel a pair of eyes on him from their small stone house. It was an old hunter's cabin, really, but it was big enough for the two of them.

David reached his father's position on the back porch. On the ground, a CD player was plugged in, kicking out the sounds of Bebo Norman. Did his dad really like this stuff? Maybe he wasn't as old as David thought.

David grabbed a water bottle from the white railing and settled onto the steps. His dad reached down and turned down the volume on the player.

"Your soccer skills get better every year, son."

"It doesn't matter, Dad. Shiloh doesn't have a soccer team. They play football."

"So?" Seated in his wheelchair, Larry Childers was peeling an apple with a knife. "Why not kick for the football team? You know, Toni Fritsch was an NFL kicker who started as a soccer player. For decades, he held a record for kicking a field goal in thirteen consecutive play-off games."

"They've already got a good kicker."

"I'm sure they wouldn't mind having two good kickers."

"Dad, I'm too small. I really just don't feel like getting killed."

"Are you saying you're not interested? Or you'd like to try out, but you're afraid?"

"What if I don't even make the team?" David took a drink from the bottle.

"Well, you're already not on the team. I mean, you can't get any more *not* on the team than you are right now."

He rolled his eyes. "Okay, Dad."

"David, you can't be afraid of failure." Larry shifted in his seat and let a strand of apple peel hang over his leg. "Everyone fails at some point. The secret is to fail successfully."

"What's that supposed to mean?"

"If you fail, don't let it be because you didn't try your best."

"So you think I should try out for the football team?"

"Well, if you're waiting around for soccer, it ain't gonna happen."

Although soft-spoken, Larry was never one to mince words. David knew that after nearly twenty years of fighting multiple sclerosis, his dad had come to terms with life's joys and letdowns. Sometimes, though, David just wanted to figure it out for himself. He wanted to know he had strength to face things on his own.

Football? Maybe it was worth a shot.

BRADY

"Coach Owens, have you got a minute?"

Brady heard the voice as he rounded the back corner of the bleachers. He was ready for practice, with a whistle around his neck, an orange cone in one hand, and a clipboard in the other. He looked from beneath his golf visor to find the booster club chairman, Alvin Pervis, coming toward him.

"Yeah?"

"Look," said Pervis. Sunglasses shielded his eyes. "Um, some of the men have been talking. We really want to see this school succeed with our football program, and I know you feel the same way too. But frankly, we don't ever see that happening while Coach Taylor is here."

"Well, you know we're in a rebuilding season."

"Look, I know he's a fine man and all. But he's had six years here, and nothing significant to even show for it."

Brady looked off toward the ballplayers who were scrimmaging in blue-and-white jerseys. The sounds of colliding bodies and football pads carried over the grass. He pursed his lips, unsure what to say.

"You know," Pervis continued, "I honestly believe you would make a better head coach."

Something stirred inside Brady at that point. Pride? Envy?

"Some of us have requested a meeting with Mr. Ryker. If you would just support us, I really believe this could go a lot easier."

Brady shifted on his feet. A glance through the chain-link fencing showed Grant on the sidelines, overseeing the action on the field. Grant turned in that moment and caught Brady's eye, then swung his gaze back to his players.

Brady felt guilty. But why? He'd done nothing wrong. He was hearing out the complaints of a concerned booster, the way any good assistant should.

"Mr. Pervis," he said. "I don't know."

"It's not like we're trying to hurt the guy. What we're doing is for the benefit of the school." The chairman slapped him on the arm. "You just think about it."

Brady waited till Pervis had gone, then meandered toward the sidelines.

"Good hustle, Casey," Grant encouraged one of his players. He folded his arms, glancing sideways as Brady set down his cone. "What was that about?"

"What?"

"Alvin Pervis."

"Oh, we were just talking." Brady put on a pair of shades. He thought of different college and pro coaches known for their sunglasses and individual senses of style. That could be him someday. If . . .

"Everything all right?" Grant persisted.

"Yeah."

Coach seemed like he wanted to say more, but a voice pulled him away.

"Mr. Taylor?"

As Grant strolled off, Brady found himself questioning his own behavior. Only two games into the season, and already his mind was skipping ahead to future prospects. He blamed it on that Mr. Pervis. The man's words were still bouncing between his ears: *"You would make a better head coach . . ."*

In front of him, a cornerback broke up an intended pass. Relishing the chance to lead this practice session, Brady lifted the whistle to his mouth and blew the play dead.

LARRY

With David beside him, Larry Childers wheeled across the track toward the head coach. He could sense his son's earlier bravado deflating. David had embraced for himself the idea of joining the team, but as always his confidence was the issue. Maybe it was part of being an only child. Perhaps a result of having a father in a wheelchair. Either way, Larry hoped his son would see this thing through.

"Dad, why'd we have to stop at Jimmie's Hot Dogs?"

"'Cause you said you were hungry."

"Yeah, and now I've got ketchup stains down the front of my shirt."

"That's not Jimmie's fault," Larry said. "We're here, and there's no sense in leaving."

"I look like a goober."

"Then prove yourself on the field, son." Larry cupped his hands to his mouth. "Mr. Taylor?"

"Yes."

Coach Grant Taylor approached them in dark sweatpants. His strides were long and athletic. Through online research, Larry had learned that Grant once played quarterback at GSU, before a hotshot came along and forced him to play second string. This was a man who knew the roller-coaster turns of organized sports.

"I'm Larry Childers." He shook the coach's outstretched hand. "And this is my son, David. He's a junior, and we're new to the school this year."

"Well, good to meet you. What can I do for you?"

"I just wanted to introduce myself to you, and David wanted to know if it was too late to try out for the team."

Grant looked at David. "You a football player?"

"Well, I've always played soccer, but I figured I could try out as a kicker."

"Okay. Well, I've got a pretty good kicker, but I don't mind letting you try out." The coach turned and gestured at one of his players. "Jonathan, come here for a second." To David, he said, "This is Jonathan. He holds for our main kicker, Joshua Webster."

The kid came closer, helmet in hand. He had strong arms and broad shoulders, but his expression gave no indication that he was a bully or an arrogant jock.

"Jonathan," Grant said, "this is David Childers. He wants to try out as a kicker. Why don't you two go out and try a few kicks, just to get your feet wet a little bit?" He slapped David on the shoulder.

David said, "All right, sure." He jogged onto the grass.

"Thank you, sir," Larry said to the coach. "If you don't mind, I'll just hang around till practice is over."

"No problem. Good to meet you."

He rolled his wheelchair back and squared up with the field. It was hot out here, more humid than they were used to in the mountains of north Georgia.

He watched his son interact with the other kid and thought of the Old Testament story of David and Jonathan, two men from different backgrounds, drawn together by friendship and a love for God.

As a widower, Larry worried about his son's social development. David was courteous. He knew how to interact with adults, since he had no brothers or sisters of his own. At times, however, this alienated him from other boys his age. While they were burping and cutting up, he was reading books about Antarctic expeditions and shipwreck survival on the Pacific Ocean. He'd found some acceptance on the soccer field, at least, leading the team in goals for two seasons straight.

Another aspect of David's social life had recently been coming to light: his interest in girls. Larry welcomed this natural progression, but one thing worried him as a father.

David lacked confidence around women.

The boy had lost his mother at birth, and so he had little knowledge of how females worked, what made them mad, what made them laugh or cry. He always lingered nearby when Larry was speaking with a lady, but he also avoided building any relationships of his own. His natural shyness was compounded by his fear of getting close to a girl and then losing her.

Larry Childers squinted against the sun's brightness.

I've got my own sorrows. Do I have what it takes to help my son?

"Lord," he prayed quietly. "May my son's relationships and actions at this school bring glory to You. He's a good kid. Please give me strength to be the father he needs. Of course, You and I both know I won't be around forever. Lord, help him know You as his heavenly Father, and to become the man You created him to be."

Larry edged farther back, finding shade at the base of the bleachers.

CHAPTER 9
How Long?

DAVID

The sounds of football practice swirled in the air, a heady mix of testosterone and adrenaline. The sun was beating down, already drawing sweat from David's forearms.

"Y'all just move here?" Jonathan asked.

"Yeah, from Athens. My dad got a job teaching at the college."

"That's cool."

"I'm used to kicking soccer balls, but I thought I could at least try out."

"Well, Josh is a pretty good kicker, but he's also a receiver. I think he likes that better than kicking." Jonathan dropped his helmet. "Here ya go." He leaned down to tee up a football on a stand.

David moved back and wondered if there was a wrong way to do this. Best thing to do was just kick it, the same way he'd kick a soccer ball. He stepped forward, planted his left foot, and pivoted his hip so that his full force came through the right leg.

The ball lifted from the tee and sailed wide left.

He hung his head. "I'm sorry."

His second attempt flew off to the right.

"Man, I'm sorry."

Third: to the left again.

"I'm sorry."

On the next attempt, he put one straight down the middle—finally!—but it never got off the ground and went bouncing along the turf.

This was getting embarrassing. He should've known better than to come and make a fool of himself. He was here now, though, with his dad watching from the sidelines.

For this next kick, he knew he'd have to put some lift on it. He leaned back and let his leg connect with the ball late in the downswing, but this time the lopsided pigskin zinged left in a low flight pattern.

Okay. He stepped back and tried to put it all together—height, distance, accuracy. In his fervor, his kick connected with Jonathan's arm. David stumbled to the ground, and Jonathan leaned forward with his head down.

"Owww!"

"Sorry about that," David offered.

"It's all right."

But Jonathan was no dummy. As he set up again, Jonathan scooted far back, his arm stretched out with fingers barely touching the ball.

David made a couple more attempts, to no avail.

His embarrassment turned to frustration. This was it. He had to do this if he was going to have any hope of making the team, winning friends, and fitting in at Shiloh. He drove forward. Connected. The ball launched like a missile to the left, coming point-down into the earth and bouncing forward.

Oh, no. He moaned. *No, no, no!*

The collision was inevitable.

Assistant coach J.T. Hawkins Jr. was walking along the sideline, clipboard in hand, as the football careened toward him. He ducked too late, and the ball ricocheted off his head.

"Hey, watch it!"

David held up his hands. "Sorry."

"Tell me you *didn't* just kick that at me."

"No, sir. I mean, yes, sir. I kicked it, but not at you. I mean, it went at you, but I wasn't aiming it that way."

"You wasn't aiming?" J.T. threw both hands into the air. "Yeah, we in agreement there. You might wanna find a target this time, before you haul off and clobber the thang."

At David's feet, Jonathan was trying to hold back his laughter.

David could see his dad, still seated in the shade of the bleachers. He mumbled, "I'm such a loser."

Jonathan chuckled. "Here, let me help you out." He stood and counted out the field-goal steps, pointing and nodding. Once they were in sync, he gave a thumbs-up and reset the ball.

The next two kicks David drove between the goalposts. They weren't pretty but they went through. With that, he figured it was time to stop. Before things got ugly again.

"How much longer does practice go?" he asked Jonathan.

"Another twenty minutes maybe. Coach'll call us to huddle around one last time as a team."

Jonathan smiled and gestured toward the stain on David's shirt. "Jimmie's?"

"How'd you know?"

"My favorite hot-dog place. I've ruined a lotta shirts there."

David couldn't hide his grin. He knew he had found a friend.

MATT

From the track, Matt Prater watched Coach Taylor rounding up the team equipment. He appreciated the man and the hours he put in with the players, but sometimes he wished he could go back to

Westview, a public school. At least Matt could wear his baggy jeans and T-shirts there, and listen to music he liked. Shiloh was so uptight that none of these do-gooders had a clue how the real world worked. They came from these churchgoing families, all nice and pretty, wrapped up in a bow.

Probably fake, he thought. But what'd it matter? If it worked for them, fine.

I just don't want any part of it.

"Matt!" His father was coming toward him on the track. "Matt, let's go." He looked funny out here, in his business attire—as if the expensive clothes fooled anyone into believing he was a model citizen. Money. Prestige. Those were the things that drove Mr. Neil Prater. Success at any price.

"I'm going with Brock for a little while," Matt snapped.

"Not tonight. You're coming home."

Matt hefted his shoulder pads and helmet, feeling his muscles bulge. "Why?"

"Don't argue with me. Let's go!"

"No, Dad. I'll be home later."

"Matt!"

He spun from his father toward his vanishing teammate. He and Brock liked to play Madden Six after school, imagining the day they'd earn athletic scholarships, maybe even play side by side on the Georgia Bulldogs defense.

As Matt marched away, he noticed Coach Taylor eyeing him over a plastic water cup, with a look of disapproval.

No, not disapproval. Disappointment.

Well, everyone at this school could judge him if they wanted. Matt refused to waste another afternoon listening to his dad rant and rave, while threatening to send his son to a military academy if he didn't shape up.

Nope. Matt had his own life to live.

J.T.

Another sunshiny day. J.T. helped brush his daughter's hair before breakfast, then made pancakes for the family so that his wife could have the bathroom a few extra minutes to herself. In a house full of kids, time alone was hard to come by.

J.T. clipped his pager to his belt on his way to the school. He was on call, working part-time as a locksmith. He liked the job. Never knew when someone would need help getting back into their car or their office.

Of course, your keys were your keys. How hard was that to remember?

In the Shiloh parking lot, J.T. joined up with Grant and Brady. They agreed to a short meeting inside. As they headed through the corridors, they saw a gray-haired man shuffling along and toting a huge, gold-leaf Bible. His free hand traced over the rows of lockers, while he mumbled words barely discernible to human ears.

J.T. followed Grant into his office.

Brady took up the rear, peeking out the door before closing it. "That old man still come every week to pray in the hallway?"

"Mr. Bridges." Grant pawed through the stuff on his desk— memos, schedules, and receipts. "Prays for the students as he passes their locker."

"How long has he been doing that?" J.T. figured he owed the man some respect for his level of faith and dedication. How long had it been since J.T. had gone before God with the needs of this school or this team?

Grant said, "He's been praying for revival since before I got here. Lord knows we need it. The apathy in this school's about as bad as our football record."

Got that right, Coach.

"Oh, that reminds me," J.T. said. "I think you should go ahead and let David Childers on the team."

"You see something there?"

"Well, he's just used to playing soccer. He ain't that strong, but he shows promise."

"All right. I'll give him a shot."

"Coach," Brady interjected, "is it true about the booster club buying us new helmet logos?"

"Where'd you hear that?"

Brady spun the ball in his hands, almost dropped it. "Is it true?"

"Yeah, Principal Ryker told me he put in the request. Says he wants the team to start off on a fresh foot. I guess that means you two'll have your afternoon's work cut out for you, scraping off the old decals."

"Aww, now that ain't right," said J.T. "We gotta do all the work?"

"I got a lunch appointment."

"With who?" Brady wanted to know. "You gonna try talkin' Darren into coming back?"

Grant shook his head.

"Hmm." J.T. rubbed his goatee. "Is it anyone we know?"

"A fine Southern woman," Grant said with a twinkle in his eye.

"Oh, yeah. I see what's happenin' here." J.T. arched his eyebrows. "Coach Taylor's goin' on a date."

CHAPTER 10
Unraveled

BROOKE

"Thank you for doing this," Brooke said.

"Anytime." Jackie slipped into a parking spot at Shiloh Christian Academy. She turned off the engine and looked over at her friend. "You know, you and Grant are one of the only couples I know who seem to still truly love each other."

"We try."

Through her sunglasses, Brooke noticed her husband at a picnic bench, talking to a student. Probably encouraging him to get his grades up, since that seemed to be a never-ending task with some of these athletes. Grant gave the kid a nudge, and the boy shouldered his backpack on his way back toward the school building.

Brooke and Jackie climbed out of the vehicle. Brooke stepped through a gap in the flowers, carting a sack lunch and two cans of Coca-Cola. She saw Grant put his hands on his hips and slap on a playful grin.

She'd always loved that little gap between his front teeth. Kinda cute. She was glad to see him wearing a smile despite last Friday night's game. Maybe two nights from now, against Dewey County, they'd be able to turn things around. Give the boys some hope.

"What're you doing, Jackie?" Grant kidded. "Trying to develop a good reputation?"

Jackie removed her shades. "What're you talking about?"

"Hangin' out with such a classy girl like my wife."

"Well, what I wanna know is, what was a classy girl like Brooke doing marrying a test subject like you?"

"Aaaahh."

"Aaaahh," Jackie growled back. "I'll let you have her for lunch, but I'm coming back to get her in thirty minutes."

"Bye."

"Bye." Jackie walked to her vehicle.

Brooke moved forward. With Grant's arm around her, they found a spot at the table beneath a shade tree. She handed her husband a can of Coke. "Why do you do that to her?"

"Because she likes it. She knows I'm just giving her a hard time."

"She's good to me." Brooke pushed her sunglasses back onto her head. "If she didn't pick me up every day, I couldn't work at the flower shop."

Grant's face fell, and instantly she regretted opening her mouth. This was supposed to be a lunch date. She'd put on earrings, a necklace, some eye makeup—all for his benefit. He didn't need reminders of their junky car and limited budget.

"Any chance they want you full-time?" he inquired.

She flashed a provocative look and added some humor to her tone. "Not unless more husbands start buyin' their wives more flowers."

Grant looked away, disarmed. "Wow."

On the lawn, two boys were heading toward class.

"Hey, David," Grant called out. "Come here."

The students jogged over. She recognized the taller kid as one of the players on the Eagles.

"Yes, sir?" David said in a cautious voice.

"I want you to know I talked it over with Coach Hawkins. I'd like to tell you, you made the team."

"Really?"

"You can pick up your pads and jersey this afternoon," Grant continued. "And Jonathan will tell you about our practice schedule."

"Thanks, Mr. Taylor. Uh . . . I mean, Coach Taylor."

"Welcome to the team. I'll see you at practice."

"See ya later, Coach."

"Oh." Grant held up a hand. "One more thing. Brooke and I have an old barn behind our house. If you want, you can come on over and put in some extra hours, to work on your kicking technique. Just draw yourself a set of goalposts on the barn with some chalk, and you'll be good to go."

"Thanks, Coach, but I don't wanna impose."

"Not at all," Brooke said. "We're just out Old Pretoria Road. Jonathan can show you where we live. Some sweet tea, a little pecan pie, and you boys'll feel right at home."

David and Jonathan offered enthusiastic thank-yous.

As they walked away, she purred like a proud mother. "*Ohh. Did you see the look on his face? You made his day.*"

"Brooke, I've got forty jerseys and thirty-one boys. If you've got two legs and a head, I'd probably take you."

She met his eyes. "Are you ready for Friday night?"

"Hmmm."

"Grant Taylor, tell me that's not the sound of a worried man." She reached out for his hand, which was still cold after gripping the Coke can. "From where I'm sitting, I see a coach who still has what it takes to help these boys win—on the field and off."

"Hope you're right, sweetheart. I really do."

GRANT

Grant was furious. The second game of the season was upon them, only an hour away, and already they'd lost their team identity.

"Look at these." He slapped at a scuffed white helmet on the locker room bench. "We were told we'd get new decals, and what do we get? Nothing! They vetoed our funds. Now why'd they have to go and do that?"

Brady folded his arms, shifting weight back and forth on his feet.

"What is it, Brady?"

"Nothing."

"What?"

"It can wait. The boys'll be in here in a minute."

"Say it. It's just you, me, and J.T."

"Well, I think Mr. Pervis has been unhappy with this program ever since you kicked his son off the team three years ago."

"He was *cheating*. Donnie Pervis thought he was above the rules. I don't care whose son it is, I think it's better to play honestly and lose than to cheat and win."

Brady looked down. "Well, you're getting your wish."

Grant slammed a locker door. "Listen, I'm not gonna keep livin' in the past. Is that clear?"

"That's clear, Coach," said J.T. "Let's move this thing forward."

"Absolutely. Now let's bring the team in here and get ready to stomp the daylights outta Dewey County. We put this win under our belts, and people'll start seeing things differently, I guarantee it."

GRANT

The game unraveled quicker than expected. Despite the energy of SCA's cheerleaders and breathtaking basket tosses that sent the smallest girl high into the air, the results on the field were draining the life from the fans.

On a crucial third down, the defense finally stopped Dewey County and forced a punt. The kick wobbled through the glare of the lights. An Eagle lined up to receive the ball, then let it slip through his hands.

The groan from the stands carried across the turf.

"C'mon, Jake!" Grant yelled from the sidelines. "Catch the ball!"

An opposing player, Number 88, chased down the pigskin, giving his team another chance to turn up the heat on Shiloh Christian Academy.

Grant felt his voice growing hoarse. His frustrations of six years were coming out tonight. They shouldn't be losing this game, not against the league's weakest defense. He looked down the bench and saw Brock Kelley stomping back and forth. On the other end, he spotted two of his players talking over their shoulders to a cheerleader.

"Chick-fil-A," he overheard Jeremy saying. "Yeah, we'll be there."

Grant's blood boiled. He started to head over and cut short the socializing, but the collective gasp of the crowd caused him to turn back toward the gridiron. The Dewey County running back was turning the corner, speeding along the far sideline untouched. He waltzed into the end zone and did a little dance as his teammates mobbed him.

Minutes later, the ball was back in Shiloh's hands and they were driving it down the field. They'd strung together three first downs and now, before the end of the half, they had a chance to put some points on the board.

Quarterback Zach Avery barked out his cadence. "One. Set. Hut!" He took the snap, but it slithered through his grasp.

The defense rumbled forward and one of the linemen fell on the ball.

Great! Just great.

Grant threw his hands up and pulled them over his white cap. Alongside him, David and Jonathan were shaking their heads in embarrassment.

The second half started no better. On the Eagles' first drive, Grant had to jump back to avoid getting hit by an errant third-down pass. Another scoring opportunity down the drain.

"What're you doing?" Grant jabbed his finger. "Concentrate. Stay in the game!"

In the stands, fans were fidgeting. Some had already left. Grant saw Matt's father, Neil Prater, wearing a sour expression.

Preparing to punt, the Eagles took their positions. The center hiked the ball, but it shot over the kicker's head and hopped along the grass. Dewey County was right there, ready to capitalize on the mistake.

Not again. You gotta be kidding me!

"No!" Grant flung his hat to the ground. "No!"

GRANT

In the locker room, Grant smashed his clipboard into the concrete floor and faced his beleaguered team. By the large American flag in the back, J.T. and Brady were trading looks. Beside Grant, on the chalkboard, a diagram showed a play they had never got the chance to use.

Someone had also written an acronym. WIN: *Worship, Inspire, Never Quit.*

Sounded nice, but it seemed disconnected from their play on the field.

"Will someone tell me how we lost to Dewey County, 21 to 7?" Grant's face felt like it was on fire, and he screamed, "*21-7!* Dewey County hasn't beaten Shiloh since you were in *kindergarten.* I don't know what you call that junk out there, but it sure wasn't football!"

Brock looked up through sweaty hair. Zach lowered his eyes.

Grant snatched up the stats clipboard. "Nine dropped passes, four fumbles, three interceptions. Their *defense* scored most of their points! You *gave* the game away."

In the back, J.T. folded his arms, bit his lips, and shook his head.

"You can't win football games if you don't play together as a team," Grant went on. He noticed Zach and Jeremy exchanging glances. "You can't win games when you're more concerned about what you're doing afterward. And you can't learn the plays when you miss practice 'cause you're sitting *in detention!*" He swiped his hat at Brock's head. "I'm sick of the apathy on this team. If we're not here to win football games"—he tossed down the clipboard a second time—"then why are we here?"

He stalked from the room, leaving the team in embarrassed silence.

CHAPTER 11
Take a Swing

LARRY

Larry Childers had experienced a good day at Darton College. His psychology students were beginning to look past his infirmities to find the wisdom in his words. He figured he didn't have much unique to say, but he found that his perspective from this wheelchair added weight to the ideas he proposed.

This was a privilege from God. One he didn't take lightly.

Now, with southern fried chicken simmering on the stove, he'd decided it was time to finish repainting the kitchen cabinets. For him, this was relaxing work. Kept his mind off the burning in his legs.

Beside him, David was in jeans and a gray T-shirt, painting the higher portions of the cabinetry. He was a good worker, attentive to each brushstroke.

"So," Larry asked, "do you agree with him?"

David had just finished recounting Shiloh's loss against Dewey County and the coach's verbal barrage in the locker room.

"I don't know. I guess," David said. "Only a few of the guys on the team really seem to care."

"So, are you ready to play in the game?"

"I don't know why they would use me when they've got Joshua Webster. He can kick a forty-five-yard field goal."

"I bet you could too."

"Dad, I can barely kick a thirty-five-yard field goal. At the end of the game, kinda glad I didn't play. That way, I can't mess up."

"That's fear, son. Sure, a batter that never steps up to the plate won't strike out, but he can't hit the ball unless he swings."

"I just don't want to embarrass the team."

Larry stopped painting. "David, I've asked God since you were a baby that He would show how strong He is in your life, and that through you people would see how good He is."

"Then why would He make me so small? And weak?"

"To show how mighty *He* is."

David ruminated on that, running his brush over the lip of the paint can.

Larry changed the subject. "How's your buddy Jonathan?"

"He's good. Me and him—"

"He and I."

"Right." David dabbed paint at the outer corner of the cabinet. "We're gonna do some kickin' practice tomorrow, over at Coach's house."

"That's awful nice of him to open his home to you like that. I'd say God is already giving you some positive relationships here in Albany."

"Yeah."

"Have you met any nice girls at the school?"

"What?" David snapped his head. "Did someone tell you I did?"

"Have you?"

"Umm . . . well." David's eyes grew dark.

"Listen," Larry said. "Why don't we go ahead and wash up for dinner? We can finish this later."

"All right." David took longer than necessary fixing the paint lid back into place. He gathered up his brush and stir stick, then reached for the front door. He paused. With eyes on the can in his hand, he said, "There is this one girl, Dad."

Larry kept quiet.

"Her name's Amanda. She's in my history class."

This is a first, Larry thought.

"But she's just a friend, that's all."

"Sounds nice. I mean, a good relationship should always be built on friendship. I'm proud of you, David. So, what do the two of you talk about?"

"Ummm . . . We haven't really talked much."

"I see."

"Not to each other anyway."

Larry smiled. The fact his son had even divulged this much was worth a celebration. He watched David head outside to set the supplies on the porch, then ran his eyes over the work they'd done. From his lower position, he saw a place his son had missed far up on the cabinet's right side.

Wonder if I can reach that spot.

The burning in Larry's legs had subsided. Some days he could barely muster the strength to get out of bed and go to work. He'd always had rough spells, since his diagnosis over nineteen years ago. His was the primary progressive form of MS, meaning he'd never had a relapse from his initial symptoms. Sometimes he experienced double vision or troubles with balance. Most often, parts of his body just felt overheated. *I bet I can reach it. Just one little spot.*

He rolled back in the chair, locked the wheels, and eyed the angles of his approach. He had to be careful not to scrape against the bolts jutting from the lower cabinet doors, where the knobs had been removed for the painting project.

He dropped each leg to the floor, then raised the foot pads so that he'd be able to stand without hindrance. He took a deep breath and grunted as he pushed down on the armrests with his hands, lifting himself, defying the deteriorating muscles in his lower body. The chair quivered with the effort, chattering against the wood floor.

To hold his weight, he braced one arm on the counter. Positioned himself. Then he reached down to push against his knees, one by one, and lock them into place.

The pain started to balloon down his spine. Maybe this wasn't such a good idea, after all.

No, I'm not givin' up now.

He lifted the paintbrush from the counter and stretched toward the spot high above. His legs trembled. Then, as he swiped the bristles along the corner, his knees gave out and he tumbled back into the chair.

The clatter brought David rushing through the door.

"Dad!"

Larry was shaking from the energy he'd expended. He felt his son's hands slide beneath his armpits and heft him into an upright sitting position. He'd seen that expression on David's face before—a look of uncertain terror—and it hurt him to think that his son lived in perpetual fear of his father's condition.

"Okay," Larry said. "I'm okay."

"What were you doing?"

He pointed at the cabinet. "You missed a spot up there. Thought I could get it for you. I guess I got a little too ambitious." He wiped the perspiration from his forehead and eyes. "I was just trying to take a swing at it."

DAVID

Saturday afternoon, David met Jonathan in the field behind Coach Taylor's house. The plan was to practice his distance kicking first.

"Did I do it?"

"Almost," Jonathan said. He stood near an orange flag they had tied to a tree, marking the forty yards they'd measured off.

"How close was it?" David jogged forward in his soccer shorts.

"Just shy of forty. It's about thirty-nine yards, but you're still wide left." Jonathan tossed a water bottle to David, and they both found seats in the grass.

"I don't see how Joshua does it. That's about as hard as I can kick."

"Two weeks ago, you could barely kick thirty. That's about ten more yards."

"Now I just gotta figure out how to kick it straight."

"You can kick a *soccer* ball straight. Is a football that different?"

"My dad thinks it's psychological."

Jonathan paused and looked toward David. "Tell me about your dad."

"Well, he's had MS for about twenty years, and . . . thing is, he never complains about it."

"Multiple sclerosis?"

"Yeah. Him and Mom weren't supposed to have kids. I was a surprise. My mom didn't make it through the delivery."

Jonathan tore away a piece of grass and fiddled with it. "So, you help your dad around and all that stuff?"

"Well, he can do a lot on his own. He still tries to stand every once in a while." David's thoughts replayed last night's incident in the kitchen. He wondered what he would do if his dad had a bad fall. Or if he . . .

Stop! Don't even think about it.

Jonathan was talking again. "That's cool that y'all are that close."

"Yeah. He's always been my best friend."

Jonathan drained the rest of his water and said, "You ready to go practice your accuracy?"

"Sure, I guess."

BROOKE

Through the dining room window, Brooke watched little David try over and over again, attempting to put the football between the chalk marks on the dilapidated barn. The poor kid had heart, but his confidence seemed to shrink with each missed kick. She could hear Jonathan trying to cheer him up.

Well, she knew just the cure.

She poured cold glasses of sweet tea, then placed thick slabs of pecan pie onto two plates with forks. Arms full, she walked out to the barn.

Ahead of her, David kicked and slipped to the ground.

"We got any hungry boys out here?" she asked.

"Yes, ma'am!" Jonathan responded.

David picked himself up and nodded.

"How's practice goin'?" Brooke handed each boy a plate and a glass.

"I can't even hit the broadside of a barn."

"It'll get easier, David. You know, Grant tried kickin' once in college, when we were at Georgia Southern. Oooh, that wasn't a pretty sight."

"What position did he normally play?"

"QB. He threw eighteen touchdowns his junior season. But

then this other player came along, and he was bigger than Grant. Real tough to take down."

"He still play his senior year?"

"Of *course*. Grant Taylor is no quitter." Brooke tilted her head, placing a hand on her hip. "If he was, you think he woulda won me over? I was a cheerleader at GSU, and it's not like there weren't other boys on the field."

"A cheerleader?" David echoed.

"From grade school on. Why? Do you need to know how to speak cheerleader?"

He blushed. "Why? Did someone say I did?"

She flashed a smile. "No one had to."

GRANT

He didn't want to go, but he knew it was the right thing to do.

"A sacrifice of praise." Isn't that what the Bible called it?

Grant stared through the Chevy Celebrity's windshield, waiting for Brooke to join him for their drive to Sunday morning service. After Friday night's fiasco, he had no desire to show his face in public. He could imagine the whispers behind his back, the blank stares. Many of his players and their parents attended his church.

"Thanks for waiting." Brooke climbed in beside him.

"Maybe the car'll break down on the way."

"You say that like you want it to happen."

Grant shrugged. "Maybe I do."

"It's not that bad, Grant. It's only been two games."

"Two losses, you mean."

She scooted closer. "So now we have a chance to go 8 and 0."

"I don't think this car'll even go 5 and 0. Maybe on the open highway." It was a weak attempt at humor, but at least he was trying.

BROOKE

After church, Brooke pulled out a coupon she'd found for the Hong Kong Cafe. *Buy one entrée, get one free.* Things were tight, but she'd been saving tips from the flower shop. This would be their first meal out in a while.

"You sure?" Grant said. "What about the shoes you wanted for work?"

"I'm fine with what I've got. Let's just enjoy lunch together."

"Okay."

The hostess seated them at a table in the corner. Facing the window, Brooke basked in the sunlight's warmth. Across from her, though, she noticed her husband's tension returning as he faced the dining area where other churchgoers clustered.

"Here." She pushed back her seat.

"What?"

"Let's switch places."

His eyes narrowed. "Why?"

"It's bright on this side," she said. "You're taller. Maybe the sun won't hit you so directly."

They changed seats, with Grant's back now turned toward the crowded restaurant. Within minutes, his shoulders relaxed. When egg rolls and fried wontons were served as appetizers, his eyes lit up.

"Mmmm." He finished off a roll. "Thanks, Brooke."

"It's fun to be the one who treats every once in a while."

"Yeah, I needed to get out of that house. I don't know why, but it all builds up there. My worries. The bills. That horrible smell."

She took a sip of jasmine tea.

"Sorry I've been stressed. Had a lot on my mind, you know?" As he bit into another egg roll, a shadow passed over his face.

Brooke didn't want to push him, not during lunch. What was he thinking about, though? His meeting with the specialist? When were the results supposed to come back?

"It's okay," she said. "We're in this together, Grant."

GRANT

On Monday, he got the call. The results had come in.

He told the school secretary he'd be back after lunch, and thirty-five minutes later he was seated at Dr. Jordan's desk. He stared down at his lap. The doctor's words crashed over him. His pulse pounded in his ears.

"You're positive, Dr. Jordan?"

The man nodded gravely from across the desk.

"You hear stories," Grant said, "of things getting mixed up. You know, papers switched around. Maybe I—"

"It's been checked and verified, Mr. Taylor. I'm sorry."

Grant stared at this trained professional in the white jacket. The man had tufts of hair poking out from his shirt. A fancy gold pen stood at attention on the desktop. Impressive certificates lined the wall. Even the phone console, with its multiple lines and buttons, implied that this individual was the epitome of success—wanted and needed and capable.

Unlike Grant Taylor.

He tried to stay calm. He was a problem-solver, right? Assess the obstacles, and find a way to overcome them. That'd always been his approach. He looked down at his wedding ring.

To have and to hold. In sickness and in health.

"So, um . . ." He rubbed at his eye. "Uh, what does that mean? I mean, is there a procedure or, uh . . ." He looked up. "I mean, what're my options?"

Dr. Jordan fiddled with his pen. "Grant, first you need to realize this is a fairly common problem for men. There are thousands of couples who are unable to have children. You do have options. Although there's only a 10 percent chance of success, many couples have tried in vitro fertilization."

"We can't afford that."

"Well, the other option is to adopt a child, but it's about as expensive either way. If you're interested, I'll put you in touch with a local agency."

Grant stared at his lap.

"I realize this is difficult for you to hear," the doctor rattled on, "but at least you and your wife can make the best decision—now that you know where you are."

Those words were final nails in the coffin. He'd avoided this for years, but at last he knew. He *knew*. He wrung his hands, his soul staring down into the gaping black pit where he would be forced to bury Brooke's dreams and his.

How was he going to tell her?

Brooke

Brooke stared at the phone, unsure what to do next. She hadn't heard from Grant, and this wasn't like him to ignore her calls. Was he at the school? The office was closed, and she couldn't get anyone on the line.

What if he'd been in an accident? Or maybe the car had died again.

Something was wrong.

Dear Lord, help my husband. Wherever he is, please be with him.

She poured herself a second cup of coffee and sat at the dining table with a copy of *HomeLife* magazine. She'd been reading an article on dealing with strong-willed children. Anything to keep her mind occupied. She flipped through the pages, from back to front, watching words and pictures blur.

GRANT

He paced the empty locker room. He felt numb.

After football practice, he'd busied himself with paperwork and cleaning. He knew Brooke would start to worry, but he had no words to say. Nothing sounded right when he tried it out in his head. And if he said nothing at all, she would suspect something. She would *know*.

He almost tripped as his foot caught on the tall, cylindrical goalpost padding near his desk. He propped it back against the wall upside down. Like it mattered.

The locker room phone rang again. It was getting late.

He sat at the small desk, his head in his hands. Save the glow of a small wall lamp, he was surrounded by darkness.

A rumbling sound came from the hall.

"Sorry," the janitor said. He lifted the bag from the trash can. "I didn't realize anybody was still here."

Grant leaned back, rubbed the back of his neck. "Hey, Steve."

"Putting in late hours tonight?"

"Yeah, I guess so. I can lock up. You can take off."

"All right. Thanks, Coach."

When Grant exited the structure twenty minutes later, the night was warm and insects buzzed in the trees. He trudged across the dirt, then noticed a light on in the adjacent building. Someone had forgotten to hit a switch. He'd better go make sure things were in order. After all, he had made the janitor a promise.

He was shuffling into a moonlit hall when he heard the voices. From a cracked classroom door, a wedge of light fell across the linoleum. These were the tones of grown men, he realized, and they sounded angry.

Someone was speaking his name.

SECOND QUARTER:
THE DEATH CRAWL

CHAPTER 13
Dead Weight

BRADY

Brady Owens nestled in a seat at the far end of the meeting. He flipped a ball from one hand to the other, as fathers and booster members gathered before Principal Ryker. Spread across a desk, last weekend's *Albany Herald* flashed a headline: "Eagles Shot Down."

"Is everyone here?" said Mr. Pervis.

Not Coach Taylor.

"Everyone that's been invited?" Pervis amended.

This just didn't sit right with Brady. Shouldn't Grant be present to defend himself? For years, though, Grant *had* presented his case on the gridiron—with lukewarm results. Coaching was a job, plain and simple. If you couldn't get it done, you were gonna get the boot. You knew that coming in.

All this time, Brady had served as assistant coach while working part-time in audiovisual at a local TV station. He knew J.T. also had a side job, doing locksmith work to help feed his family. While Brady liked the AV work, he was ready to focus his energies on the one thing he really loved, which was football.

Tonight's main question: Who would be head coach?

Brady shifted in his seat. *Well, it's not like I'm grabbin' for it. But if they hand it to me . . . hey.*

GRANT

Grant eased down the darkened hallway. The irate voices were familiar ones. Was this a parent-teacher conference? A club meeting of some sort? He heard his own name a second time. Principal Ryker was speaking.

"Just last week, I told Coach Taylor we'd be getting him new decals. And now we're talking about throwing him out? That's a sudden switch."

Alvin Pervis shot back, "There's nothing sudden about it, Dan. This is about maintaining some respect for your school and what it represents."

"Yeah," Neil Prater chimed in. "And it's about the boys now."

"I'm not asking you to throw him out," Pervis said. "If Shiloh can invest in a winning coach, we don't need to be settling for second best. You can let him go with as much class as you want to."

"Alvin, he's a good man."

Grant closed his eyes and leaned into the wall, clinging to the principal's show of support. He couldn't bring himself to peer around that corner. What if he was spotted? What if they dragged him in there? He was in no condition to stand before them at this moment. They would see right through him, see his incapability on all levels.

Pervis wasn't finished. "I'm not saying he's not a good man. I'm saying he's not a good coach."

"C'mon, Dan," Prater urged. "Just look at the facts. His record speaks for itself. We need new leadership."

"I still think he deserves more time."

"More time?" said another one of his players' parents, Luke Rae. "He's had six years. If he was capable of winning, he'd have done it by now."

"Grant Taylor is not capable of winning," Pervis agreed. "He doesn't have it in him. That's the whole point."

Neil Prater added, "Dan, I'm not for attacking the coach, I'm just saying I want my son to have the best football program possible. My son's got a chance for a football scholarship *if* he's taught by the right coach. Matt's gonna be a senior next year. I don't want to see him lose this opportunity."

A pause.

The principal's voice cut through the air. "Brady, you're awfully quiet. What's your take on this?"

Brady? As in, Coach Owens?

Grant had to look. He squinted through the crack between the door hinges and, sure enough, there was his assistant, his friend, spread out in a chair with his red ball cap on.

C'mon, now. Let's see your loyalty.

"Honestly," Brady said, "I don't know. Sometimes I think Grant could do a better job of building this football program. But then other times I think he's doing just as good as anyone else would in this situation."

"Brady," Pervis said, "you could do better than Coach Taylor."

"You could," said Prater.

"What we need is a change," Pervis insisted.

"Now."

Grant spun away from the classroom door, torn between confronting these backstabbers and fleeing. He placed his hand on the cold wall and stared down at the floor. He could hear them still jawing. Hadn't they said enough?

Alvin Pervis concluded, "We're losing booster support, game attendance is down, and from the looks of it we've already lost this season. Dan, we've got a weak program, because we've got a weak coach. He's dead weight. We need to cut him loose."

Others around the table voiced support of this statement.

Brady remained silent.

With slumped shoulders, Grant retreated toward the exit doors.

It's over. Done. I've given it all I've got, and it's just not good enough.

GRANT

From the dark cockpit of his rattling clunker, Grant stared up at the stoplight. The sky was pitch black. There were no other cars at the intersection. He could drive through the light and no one would care.

But he found himself waiting. Alone.

How fitting. Like every other area of his life, he was at a dead stop, waiting for a sign to tell him it was okay to go.

The traffic light's glowing red bulb seemed to take its time, as if refusing to turn green. And that's when it happened. The engine rattled, gasping for breath—then died.

No. This can't be happening.

Grant turned the key. The engine whined and tried to turn over, but would not crank. In the mirror, he saw headlights in the distance. He turned the key a second time and pressed on the gas.

To no avail.

The light was green—finally. The car behind him was approaching—quickly. He tried again, pumped the pedal twice, but the engine denied his attempt.

"C'mon," he yelled. "Start, you piece of junk!"

Two more turns. Still nothing.

"What're you doing? Why're you acting like this?"

Grant glanced back at the light. Still green. And here he remained, motionless. Behind him, a horn blasted as the car pulled up. He turned the key once more, heard the same whine, then put his arm out the window to wave the car around him. He felt the driver's stare as the vehicle passed, but Grant made sure not to make eye contact.

Watching taillights disappear down the road, Grant sat there, helpless.

Yep. I wouldn't help me either.

Listening to nothing but the crickets, he felt emotion start to well up inside of him. No, not now. Brooke was waiting for him. He had to hold himself together. Staring down at the keys, he turned them in a final effort. The engine rumbled, moaned, then cranked over. He shifted into gear and began to press the gas. But stopped.

The light was red again.

BROOKE

A wave of relief washed over Brooke.

She'd started making calls, even checked with the local hospital about any recent accidents. Now, with Grant heading up the steps, she brought both hands to her face and brushed back her hair. She took a seat at the kitchen table, trying to concentrate on her magazine, anything to mask her concern. Yet as he entered and closed the door, she found herself turning and blurting out: "Grant, have you been at school all this time?"

"Yes."

"I tried to call you an hour ago. Is everything all right?"

The chair scraped on the floor as Grant pulled it out and sat down across from her. She noticed his eyes were grim.

"Grant, talk to me."

He rested both arms on the table, his palms turned up in a show of defeat. "I don't know where to start."

She pushed her magazine to the side. "What's going on?"

"I was trying to lock up for Steve, and I overheard Dan meeting with some fathers. They didn't know I was there. Brooke, they're pushing him to get rid of me."

Brooke didn't know what to say to that. If they lost this job, how would they be able to raise kids? Money was already tight, and she wanted stability for her children, not the upheaval she'd seen in her own home growing up.

Her husband continued. "Neil Prater. Alvin Pervis. Luke Rae. They said I wasn't capable of winning. Called me dead weight."

"They can't make Dan fire you. You've still got support. You . . . you just go get J.T. and Brady and see him tomorrow."

"Brady was there."

Brooke's eyes widened.

"They've just lost confidence in me. You know"—Grant clenched his fist as his voice trembled—"I was so sure I could turn this program around, and I've just sunk it lower. Brooke, I've tried so hard. Why can't I win?"

"You *can* win. Stop beating yourself up, Grant."

He met her gaze. "Brooke, I can't provide you a decent home. I can't provide you a decent car. I'm a failing coach, with a losing record." He paused, rubbing his forehead with his hand. "And I can't give you the children you want."

The words felt like a physical blow.

Brooke lowered her chin, trying to catch her breath. "What?"

"It's me. Like everything else, it's me. We can't have our own children because of me. What's God doing?" Grant's eyes filled with moisture. "I mean, why is it so hard?"

She could barely hold herself together. Across the table, her husband was starting to sob. She knew he needed to feel honored and respected, and instead that was being stripped away, ripping him apart.

She reached out her hand. Slipped her fingers into his.

We can't have children?

She covered her face with her other hand. She wanted so badly to be fruitful, to nurture and care for others, to give love to a precious child.

My baby. Our baby. Is it wrong to wish for that?

Something inside her began to tear as well. Her grip tightened on her husband's hand. She mustered her strength, to let him know she didn't blame him. "It's okay, Grant. It's okay," she said. But her voice was shaking.

Their touch lingered.

Then he pulled away, wrapping his arms over his head as he sobbed harder. She withdrew her hand. Tears rolled down her cheeks. She lowered her gaze as things blurred in the light of the overhead lamp. The stark circle it drew on the table seemed to be an ocean that separated them. They were both floundering, drowning.

Brooke tried to breathe, but she could feel herself going under.

CHAPTER 14
The Right Man

BROOKE

The clock told Brooke it was past three in the morning. She sat up in bed, letting her swollen eyes adjust.

We can't have our own children.

Those words hit her again with such finality. It was like remembering that someone she loved had just died. She'd tossed and turned through the night, finding little consolation between the sheets and the bedspread. This seemed like a horrible joke. Somehow, in a world where many selfish and irresponsible men fathered kids they didn't deserve and didn't want, she and her husband were incapable of producing children who would be raised in a loving home.

It's not right. It can't be right.

Beside her, the bed was empty. She glanced through the doorway and spotted Grant in the living room armchair. Still in his work clothes. Had he been up all night? A side lamp gave the scene a golden hue, illuminating the Bible in his lap.

Part of her wanted to go to him, to give him the comfort he needed—or maybe she needed it. She knew, though, this was something he had to work through on his own. He needed to hear from God. And one thing she'd learned as a child: you didn't interrupt a man-to-man discussion.

She slipped onto her knees beside the bed.

Lord, I'm hurting. My husband's hurting. Why have You taken our children away from us? I've been holding them in my heart for years. I don't understand how You can do this if You love us. Please, Lord, let me hear from You. Let Grant hear from You.

GRANT

Grant wandered into the pecan grove behind the house. The branches were solid and thick, the leaves lush and green. Although morning rays dappled the orchard and offered pools of warmth, he moved through the shadows. His eyes were staring up at the trees, gauging their size.

Who am I? he thought. *I'm nothing.*

The weight of one of these giants could crush him like an ant, and when he was dead and buried, they would still be towering here.

He stepped into a pocket of sunshine and let his Bible fall open in his hand. He loved David's honest pleading throughout the Psalms. The man never put on a front, just let his weaknesses show.

And yet, he always came back to his confidence in God.

Grant didn't feel that right now. But he believed it.

He read aloud from Psalm 18: "'I will love You, O Lord, my strength. The Lord is my rock and my fortress and my deliverer; my God, my strength, in whom I will trust; my shield and the horn of my salvation, my stronghold. I will call upon the Lord, who is worthy to be praised; so shall I be saved from my enemies.'"

Despite the pecan trees that seemed to hover overhead, Grant pulled back his shoulders and stood straight.

"Lord Jesus," he prayed, "would You help me? I need You. Lord, I feel like there's giants of fear and failure just staring down at me, waiting to crush me, and I don't know how to beat 'em, Lord. I'm tired of being afraid. Lord, if You want me to do something else, show me. If You don't want me to have children, so be it."

His voice caught for a second. How could he say such a thing?

From the time he and Brooke had started dating seriously, they'd discussed raising a family of their own. Grant wanted a son named Caleb. Brooke wanted a little Catherine. Sure, the world was a tough place. But they'd hoped to raise godly children, kids who were well-behaved and confident and intent on bringing about change for the better.

Is that too much to ask? I don't understand.

Grant swallowed the lump in his throat. He lifted his fist, as a symbol of his commitment, and pressed on. "But You're my God. You're on the throne. You can have my hopes and my dreams."

What do I do now, though? Where do I go from here?

"Lord, give me something," he pleaded. "Show me something."

BROOKE

Brooke's pillow was still damp with tears when she reawakened at 6:30 a.m. Her husband's side of the bed remained undisturbed.

"Grant?"

She wandered through the house, then spied him through the back window, beneath the huge pecan trees. The dew glistened on the grass. In years past, he'd gone out nearly every morning to meet with God and spend time in His Word, but school and team responsibilities had gnawed away at his energy and his time.

It was good to see him out there again.

She pulled on a robe and house shoes. With arms folded, she walked out to join him. He must be tired. She would offer to make him something to eat.

Grant closed his Bible as she neared.

She drew alongside him and felt a teardrop prick the corner of her eye. This was her man. He was going through a lot right now. He needed to know she was still with him, through thick and thin.

He met her gaze and asked, "If the Lord never gives us children, will you still love Him?"

The question caught her off guard, pushing tears down her cheeks.

Brooke couldn't speak.

Will I? No matter what?

Grant pulled her in with his arm, and she pressed her head against his chest. Her heart felt swollen to the point of bursting with unrealized dreams.

Without another word, they watched sunlight and shadows play tag through the orchard. Ready or not, another day was upon them.

Grant

Grant decided to make something happen. With sinking support at the school, maybe it was time to check out other possibilities. He'd walk out of here with what little dignity he had left.

During his lunch break, he skipped eating and scanned through job possibilities on the computer instead. One immediate opening perked his interest, a coach's position in a neighboring county.

Could this be God's way of opening another door?

He dialed the number and spoke to a Mr. Foster who seemed distracted. The man told him to call back in a few hours. That, at least, seemed like a good sign. It gave him some hope.

The minutes moved at a turtle's pace.

Finally, after tending to some school responsibilities, Grant picked up the phone for the follow-up call. A female voice answered.

He cleared his throat and said, "Uh, Grant Taylor for Mr. Foster, please." A pause. "Thank you."

He leaned forward to peek through his blinds into the school corridor. He wasn't sure if he felt guilty for searching for another position, or if he expected a squad of fathers to come marching from Principal Ryker's office with his official dismissal.

"Hello?"

"Mr. Foster. Grant Taylor. Uh, you said to give you a call about your coaching job, so I just wanted . . . Oh, I see . . . No, I understand . . . Well, if you found the right man, I understand you moving quickly . . . Thank you." Grant tapped the receiver against his mouth, then set it back in the cradle. He ran his hand across his lips, wondering where to turn next.

The right man.

Wouldn't it be nice to hear someone say that about him?

CHAPTER 15
Chalk Lines

DAVID

David and Jonathan met at Coach Taylor's house after school. Their third game was only days away, and David's heart tripped faster at the thought of being sent in to kick a field goal.

Brooke greeted them at the door.

"Mind if we do some more kickin' against the barn?" David asked. "You know, I need all the practice I can get."

"Have at it. I'm home early today, and I'm fixin' to make some sandwiches for when Grant gets here. You want some?"

"No, thanks," Jonathan said.

"What about you, David?"

He caught himself looking away from her eyes, turning his head down. Brooke Taylor reminded him of the photos of his mother. She had the same understanding eyes, the same easy smile. He wondered what it was like to grow up with a mom in the house. He would give anything to have experienced some of that as a kid.

"No. I, uh . . . I mean, I really shouldn't—"

"Now don't be shy," Brooke told him. "If you don't eat 'em, they'll just go to waste. I'll bring a plate out, and you two can help yourselves. How 'bout that?"

"Yeah, okay."

David followed his friend around back. The chalk lines taunted him from the weathered side of the barn. He started tentatively, then grew more aggressive as his sights zeroed in on his target. Several balls went wide right, causing groans from Jonathan. David lined up again, determined to center his kick, but he over-compensated and sent it left of the barn.

"Hey, man." Jonathan stood up. "You got any personal objections to kickin' it between the lines?"

"I don't know what my problem is. Are the goalposts really that narrow on the field?"

Jonathan turned and looked at the chalk lines drawn on the barn. "We measured 'em out, didn't we?"

David knew his friend was right. He could kick it anywhere but in the center. He gazed at the ground in frustration.

Jonathan picked up the stick of chalk they'd used, then grabbed the ladder leaning next to the barn.

"What're you doing?" David asked.

Without a word, his friend climbed the rungs and began drawing new goalpost lines three feet farther out on each side. Once finished, he stepped back down and placed the ball for David's next attempt.

"Hey, you can't do that," David protested.

"Just kick the ball."

Though he knew his friend was trying to build his confidence, David felt like he was being given training wheels. Well, he needed all the help he could get. He stepped back, took aim, then lunged forward and nailed the ball. It sailed up and hit the barn, barely inside the newly drawn left post. A puff of white dust wafted into the air.

"Sweet." Jonathan stood to give him a high five.

He returned the gesture sheepishly. "You know that would still be wide left on a real field."

"In a football game, yes, but it's worth ten points in barn-ball. Dead center would've got ya nothin'."

David laughed. "You're such a goober." He shook his head, marveling at his friend's tireless encouragement.

DAVID

Would he even get to play? David had worried about it all week.

Another Friday night game. Another loss in the making. The stands were only half full, and the crowd was less than enthusiastic. Amanda was here, the almond-eyed cheerleader, but David knew what his head coach thought about unnecessary distractions.

Keep your head in the game, he told himself.

The Eagles, in their blank white helmets, had shown some heart against their bigger opponents, but the scoreboard read 28-0. Coach Taylor and his assistants worked the sidelines as though the game were tied. Brady strutted, while J.T. shouted encouragement to his offensive unit.

Once again, the blue helmets kicked off and their special teams unit sped after the ball, looking to squash an attempt at a decent return.

From the middle of the pack, an Eagles player spurted forward and cleared the first onslaught unscathed. He dodged another blue helmet, spun to his right, and churned ahead with the ball tucked in his arm. Fans jumped to their feet, cheering until he was chased out of bounds at the opponent's forty-eight-yard line.

Shiloh's best field position of the night.

The clock kept ticking as they marched the chains down the sidelines. A pass play for a first down. Two big runs. A few miscues. They found themselves just inside the twenty, facing third and eight. They were in field-goal range.

David's hands turned clammy. Was he gonna get called in?

Zach Avery took the snap and rolled left, looking for a receiver downfield. He started to throw, but a defender was upon him. He tucked the ball to avoid a fumble and got taken down behind the line of scrimmage.

"Field-goal unit," J.T. called out.

"Man, we're getting killed," Brady told Coach Taylor. "You might as well put in the second string and give 'em some playing time."

Grant grabbed the starting kicker as he was about to go onto the field. "Hold on, Joshua. I wanna give David a shot at this one."

Me? Was that my name he said?

The coach was beckoning. "David, come here! This is your field goal. Put us on the board."

Wearing number 15, David felt a slap on his back as he jogged onto the gridiron. He slipped his helmet on. Peering toward the bottom of the stands, he saw his dad in the wheelchair. And there was Amanda, walking along the track between them. Was she watching this? What would she think if he missed?

His dad's advice, the hours of practice . . . It all came down to this.

Jonathan slapped him on the chest, but David still felt small out here under the lights, with everyone watching to see how he would perform.

"Red 19. Set. Hut, hut!"

The center hiked the ball. Jonathan caught and set it. David's foot hooked and sent the kick high to the left, stirring sighs and sympathetic applause from the bleachers. His dad held his chin in his hand.

David leaned forward, hands on his knees. He wanted to

shrink into his uniform and disappear. Wasn't there a way to leave the field without everybody staring down at him? He should've never gone out for football.

Jonathan patted him on the helmet. "It's all right, man. It's all right. You'll get it next time."

"Yeah."

"Against the barn, you know that woulda been good."

GRANT

Stanley, bless his heart, regaled the locker room with facts about winning teams who had started seasons this way. Nobody wanted to hear it. The boys showered and took off, with cleats and pads dragging the floor behind them. Grant was alone. He unzipped his gym bag, searching for his keys.

On the table beside him, one white helmet still sported an SCA decal. That was about right. Did he have even one player who understood the concept of a team? Was there anyone who deserved to wear that logo?

He thought about Zach Avery, who played tough and took hits without complaint. And Brock Kelley. His attitude had soured some this year, but he had the potential to be a first-rate linebacker. The kid could play ball, no doubt about it. He just had to learn to step up when things got tough. As for Matt Prater, no one wanted to go one-on-one with him, even in practice. And when it came to running tight patterns and catching the ball, Jeremy Johnson had more talent than most—even if he did get distracted by his girlfriend on the sidelines.

Then there was rookie David Childers. He'd answered the call tonight, even though he had hooked the ball.

Okay, so there were some deserving kids on this team.

Maybe *he* was the problem.

Grant closed his hand over his keys. In his ears, he could still hear the complaints from that late-night meeting: *"Coach Taylor . . . he's not a good coach . . . He's dead weight."*

The locker room door swung open and J.T. strode in. "Hey, man. Something wrong? Other than the fact that we 0 and 3?"

"Why?"

"Ohh. Just ain't been yourself. Something I should know about?"

"Just pray for me."

"I can do that." J.T. lowered his chin and smiled. "But you better watch out. The Lord's been movin' on my prayers lately. I'm a dangerous man."

"Is that right?"

"Hey, that ol' gray-haired dude, he's been puttin' me to shame, praying through the halls every week. 'Bout time I started takin' this stuff seriously."

Grant was thankful to have at least one assistant coach on his side. He tossed up his keys, grabbed them, then stood and headed out the side door toward his car. He was rounding the corner of the bleachers when he spotted something that wiped the grin from his face.

CHAPTER 16
Face-to-Face

DAVID

After the game, his teammates patted David Childers on the back but most stayed quiet. What was there to say? He'd flubbed his first opportunity and made a complete fool of himself. He'd let the guys down. He showered and changed, then left the locker room with his head lowered.

And what about Amanda? She must think I'm a loser.

He bumped into someone outside the door.

"Sorry. I didn't even . . ." He stopped. The girl standing before him was still in a cheerleader's uniform. Her hair was light brown, draped around a soft face and a timid smile. "Amanda?"

"Oh, hey."

"Hi."

What's she doing here?

David shifted the gym bag on his shoulder. They'd been in a history work group together and passed each other in the halls, but he'd never actually stood face-to-face with her. For a second, their eyes met, and he noticed hers were dark green, turned up at the corners, with lighter rings around the irises that made them seem to glow.

He wanted to say something, but his mind went blank.

"Good try out there," she said.

"I missed, like I knew I would."

She shrugged. "We'd already lost the game. Don't worry, David."

She remembers my name?

"There's always next time," she added.

"If they keep me on the team."

"Well, I'll be there cheering for you if they do."

"Thanks."

"I gotta go. See you Monday in class."

"See ya."

As David headed the other way, he peeked back over his shoulder. Amanda never turned to look at him, and he decided he was reading too much into the whole thing. She was being nice, that was all. Just trying to cheer up the team's weakest link.

He found his father waiting by the van in the parking lot. Larry lowered the hydraulic wheelchair ramp with a switch, and David dropped his bag through the passenger-side window.

"Dad, I don't even know why they let me on the team."

Larry rolled himself in line with the ramp. "Did you do your best, son?"

"I knew I was going to miss it before I even kicked it."

"Your actions will always follow your beliefs, David."

"Dad, I can't even kick it straight."

"And I can't walk. Should I stay home and pout about it? If you accept defeat, David, then that's what you'll get." With a shove of both hands, his dad wheeled himself up the ramp.

David stared across the lot. Here he was, feeling sorry for himself, when his own father would never again have a chance at kicking a football, or running the hundred-meter dash, or reaching the top shelf in the library. Everything about his dad's life said not to quit.

He's right. I've gotta start kickin' like I mean it.

Tomorrow, he decided, he would move those lines in on the barn. He would stop worrying about green-eyed girls who probably cared nothing about him anyway. It was time to narrow his focus.

GRANT

Rounding the corner, Grant caught Mr. Pervis talking to Brady in the shadows. Neither man seemed to notice him. He waited, hoping to hear his assistant shut this man down. Or at least walk away.

Instead, Brady put his hands on his hips and listened, as though this talk was beginning to make some sense.

"Well, Brady. Another fine example of Grant Taylor's *wonderful* coaching abilities. Look, the kids don't deserve it. The fans don't deserve it. When you gonna get a bellyful of this guy?"

Brady nodded his head. He was *agreeing* with this man.

Grant stepped back out of view. His blood coursed through his veins. At the moment, he wanted nothing more than to plant his fist in Alvin Pervis's face. This was the man who'd stolen away their logos. Their team identity. He wasn't here to help, unless it was to make himself feel important and in control.

Get a grip here, Grant cautioned himself.

He'd once heard his pastor read a verse about how the anger of man could not accomplish the righteousness of God. Still, there came a time to make a stand. To choose sides.

No more playing the victim here.

Grant strode into view, hoping to be noticed as he caught these men in their act of backstabbing. Yet they were too involved in conversation to pay him any mind.

"What's it gonna take?" Pervis stood in a dark Windbreaker and a cap. "You got a chance, man. You got a chance to step in and take over this program, and carry it up for a while. When're you gonna get sick and tired of it?"

Grant headed toward the pair.

"You've got an opportunity here," Pervis continued while Brady's head bobbed up and down. "This program's going in the tank. Ryker's gotta—"

As Grant approached, Pervis stopped talking. Grant stepped between the two men and stood face-to-face with Mr. Pervis, staring him down. Their noses were almost touching. His jaw was set and his mouth closed, to keep him from unleashing the choice words on his tongue. But he wouldn't give this man any ammunition against him. They were at a Christian school. He had an obligation before his team, his employers. Before God.

His fingers rolled into a tight fist. Fury throbbed through his limbs, begging to be released.

Just one punch, just one. Gimme a reason!

Pervis was growing uneasy.

Grant's stare remained hard as flint. He wasn't backing down tonight.

The other man fidgeted, then turned and walked away.

Smart move, Pervis.

He swiveled toward his assistant, who now looked equally nervous.

"Grant." His voice cracked. "He came to *me*."

"Brady, you're not doing anybody any favors sitting on the fence. You determine which side you wanna be on—and stay on it!"

He walked off, letting Brady think that one over.

BROOKE

Brooke had been waiting patiently. Game nights ran late. It was one of the hazards of being a coach's wife.

The driver's door clicked open and her husband dropped into the seat. He looked at her. "How long've you had the engine running? It's wastin' gas."

She arched an eyebrow. "Since J.T. came over and jump-started it."

"Oh, I'm sorry. Dead again, huh?"

"Least we weren't stranded in the middle of nowhere."

Grant guided them out of the parking lot. The corners of his mouth were turned down. Brooke knew tonight's loss had magnified his burden. She'd seen parents in the stands shaking their heads, avoiding her eyes. In the concession line during half time, Alvin Pervis had made an obvious effort to put some distance between them.

She scooted across the seat and nuzzled against her husband. She said, "That was nice of you, giving David a chance to kick."

"Not that it did much good."

"He'll get better. Give him time."

After that, they drove in silence to the house.

Inside, they changed into comfy clothes, grabbed snacks, and settled down on the living room floor to catch the TV sports update. They watched an abysmal assessment of Shiloh's loss, followed by an in-your-face interview with Bobby Lee Duke after his third straight win, this one by thirty-two points.

"Once again," Alicia Houston commentated, "I'm here with the Giants' head coach. Coach Duke, with your team's continued dominating performances on the field, how do you intend to keep motivating your players?"

Duke said, "Two words, Lisa . . ."

"Her name's *Alicia*," Brooke corrected, pointing at the screen.

"State championship," Duke carried on. "I just wave the carrot in front of their noses"—he plucked the sucker from his mouth and let it swing from his meaty fingers—"and they're ready to go. Winning's what football is all about, and that's all my boys know how to do."

Alicia turned back to the camera. "There you have it, from the state champion head coach three years running."

Brooke let out a huff, then pushed the remote's Off button, but the television remained on.

"You know," Grant said, "he used to be a pro wrestler."

"Bobby Lee Duke? That doesn't surprise me one bit." Brooke kept tapping at the button, pointing the remote at the TV from different angles. The screen still flickered with sports highlights.

"He was part of a tag team," Grant explained. "Called 'Destruction Inc.'"

Brooke stared at the controls. "Now *why* won't this thing work?"

"Must be the batteries."

Grant snatched away the remote and wandered down the hall to find fresh double AAs. Brooke rolled her neck, then crawled forward and hit the TV's manual Off button. From the end table, she collected hers and Grant's Bibles. He came back, shaking his head. "Guess I'm buying batteries tomorrow."

"Don't worry about it now," she said. "Can I show you a verse I read?"

"Anything's better than watching Coach Duke run off at the mouth."

He plopped down on the floor rug beside her. They leaned

back against the couch, and she pressed into him, wearing a soft red sweatshirt. He opened his Bible on his lap and crossed his ankles.

She found the Scripture she'd been looking for, and read it to her husband: "'And my God shall supply all your need according to His riches in glory by Christ Jesus.'" She looked at him. "Does that mean we can ask Him for a better car and more income?"

"Huh." Chuckling, Grant contemplated her question. "Well, I think we can ask, but He wants us to be content with what we've got, so . . ." He turned a page, then lifted his hand. "If He wants to bless us, He can. I mean, He's sovereign."

"Can we ask Him anyway?"

Grant jutted out his chin. "I already have." He scratched at his neck. "Several times."

Brooke grinned. She moved closer with a kiss, but felt him stiffen. "What?"

He shook his head.

She wasn't going to let him off that easy. "Talk to me."

He looked off to the side. "It's already tough trying to keep my head up, without being reminded of my inadequacies at home."

"Your inadequacies? What are you—?"

Grant cut in. "I don't like our financial situation or our car any more than you do."

She took his face in her hands. "Grant Taylor, I love you. When I said 'yes' to you, it was for life."

"Why, Brooke? Tell me that much."

"Because," she said. "You were the only man for me. You were the *right* man."

CHAPTER 17
Currents and Rain

GRANT

A soft splat of water awakened Grant. He looked up. The second drop landed in his eye, causing him to jump out of bed. It must've rained last night, causing the roof to leak again. He'd hoped last week's moisture on the ceiling was only humidity. He should've known better.

He propped a bucket on the bed, surrounded it with a thick towel. He dressed, gave Brooke a kiss, then grabbed his keys. As he opened the front door, a draft of air stirred the house's odor.

"Ohhh, what *is* that?"

He would have to investigate later. He'd be late for work if he didn't take off now. The Celebrity's engine turned over after a few sputters, and he headed into town. Soggy with rain, the cardboard in the rear passenger window fluttered open as he drove along Old Pretoria.

He gritted his teeth. One more thing to add to the list.

At Shiloh Christian, Grant settled into his leather desk chair. The start of a new week. Though the halls were quiet and kids were in classrooms, his thoughts were restless. Out in the orchard, he'd asked the Lord to show him something, give him something to work with. Since that time, things had continued to nose-dive.

Puttering footsteps neared his office.

Mr. Bridges.

Grant realized he'd only had brief conversations with the man. Bridges always came into the building, prayed, shuffled back out. Where did he work? Did he have a family? What motivated him to come to the school each week?

The man entered Grant's office without knocking.

Okay, that's a first.

Grant glanced up at his visitor. "Mr. Bridges."

The gray-haired man wore a blue vest over a checkered shirt. Without segue, he started paraphrasing: "Revelation chapter 3 says that we serve a God that opens doors that no one can shut, and He shuts doors that no one can open."

And that's why you can just barge into my office?

Bridges continued, unconcerned with the reaction of his audience.

As he did so, Grant felt something begin to switch inside him like a breaker that had been tripped and reset. He sat back in his chair. A current tingled through his limbs.

The words kept coming. "He says, 'Behold I have placed before you an open door that no one can shut. I know you have a little strength, yet you have kept my word and have not denied my name.' Coach Taylor, the Lord is not through with you yet. You still have an open door here. And until the Lord moves you, you're to bloom right where you're planted."

Not through with me? Grant wanted to believe that.

"I just felt led to come and tell you that today," Bridges said. He turned and shuffled from the room.

The electricity was buzzing in Grant's head, an unnerving sense of power. He needed to know more, to understand what to do with this. He stood and hurried down the hall, along the row of lockers.

"Mr. Bridges?"

The gentleman turned.

Grant hesitated, pushing his hands into his pockets. "You believe God told you to come tell me that?"

"I do."

"I admit to you, I have been struggling. But I've also been praying. I just don't see Him at work here."

"Grant, I heard a story about two farmers who desperately needed rain. And both of them prayed for rain, but only one of them went out and prepared his fields to receive it. Which one do you think trusted God to send the rain?"

"Well, the one who prepared his fields for it."

"Which one are you?"

Grant was stunned by the question.

Mr. Bridges continued. "God will send the rain when He's ready. You need to prepare your field to receive it."

The messenger turned to leave, and Grant found himself standing motionless in the hallway. The short illustration spoke volumes, and the answer thundered in his heart. He had prayed for God to move, but he'd never prepared his fields as an act of faith. It made perfect sense.

Why would God answer my prayers when He knows I'm not even ready?

GRANT

Grant sat at home that evening with a Bible and a notepad on his knees. What was it that drove him as a coach? Where did God fit into his priorities? For too long, he'd relied solely on college-knowledge to shape his leadership.

Sure, it'd been a good education. He'd learned the way an

athlete's psychological makeup could be converted into a winning attitude. In fact, he believed that was part of God's nature at work in people, responding to sacrifice, discipline, and confidence. Even self-absorbed Coach Bobby Lee Duke had discovered that if he tapped into the right vein, he could bleed success from his players.

There had to be more, though. Football wasn't life, only an analogy of it.

Grant scratched at his neck. He smoothed the notepad on his knees and wrote across the top:

WHAT'S THE PURPOSE OF THIS TEAM?

He held his pen in his mouth while he flipped to various verses. He scrawled out answers to his question, excitement building as he tapped into truths that seemed bigger than football or dead batteries or conniving parents. These were concepts he had let fall by the wayside. It was time to change that. Time to lead by example.

After two hours of praying, searching the Scriptures, and writing, Grant looked over his notes:

Concept 1: We are here for God's glory, not our own. (*Revelation 4:11: "You are worthy, O Lord, to receive glory and honor and power; for You created all things, and by Your will they exist and were created."*)

Concept 2: Loving God and others is the most important thing we can do. (*Matthew 22:37–39: "'You shall love the Lord your God with all your heart, with all your soul, and with all your mind.' This is the first and great commandment. And the second is like it: 'You shall love your neighbor as yourself.'"*)

Concept 3: Give God your best in every area. (*Colossians 3:23: "Whatever you do, do it heartily, as to the Lord and not to men."*)

Concept 4: God deserves our worship and praise whether we succeed or fail. (*Job 1:21: "The Lord gave, and the Lord has taken away; blessed be the name of the Lord."*)

It seemed basic, even simple, yet so different from the goals he was used to seeing from coaches. He recalled his prayer in the pecan grove as he begged God to show him something. God was now answering his request.

From the driveway came the sound of Jackie's vehicle, dropping Brooke off from the flower shop. Grant peeked through the living room shutters and saw his wife coming up the path, her purse over her shoulder. He was excited about sharing with her his new manifesto, and he grinned as he opened the door.

"Hey, sweetheart," he greeted her. "How was your day?"

"Fine." She walked up the steps. "What're you smiling about? Did you win a free pizza or something?"

Grant chuckled. "It's actually better than that. After you change clothes, I wanna show you something."

She returned a few minutes later, took the paper from him, and found a seat near the living room window. She was backlit by the waning sun, blonde hair framing her face as she read.

"So," she said, "this is your new team philosophy?"

He pressed his fist to his mouth. "Whaddya think?"

"I think this applies to all of life, not just football."

"Well, that's my point."

She nodded, eyes sparkling.

"Oh, no," he said. "What's with that mischievous grin?"

"I'm just remembering all over again why I fell in love with you."

"That's obvious, isn't it? My chiseled good looks."

"Nuh-uh."

"My sharp wit?"

"Grant, I saw in you a man who wanted to love God. In my house growin' up, I saw the opposite of that. For a long time, I turned to guys like my father 'cause I didn't *know* any different. Until I met you."

"And I just thought you looked good in your cheerleading uniform."

Brooke grabbed a sofa pillow and threw it his direction.

"Oh, and because you had a good pitching arm."

"You are *so* bad."

"Did I mention your radiant smile? And your gorgeous eyes?"

"Hmm. I don't think you did."

"Or that you're the nicest and most forgiving person I've ever met?"

"Are you sure about that, Mr. Taylor?"

Her next pillow toss caught him square on the chin.

CHAPTER 18
The Challenge

MATT

With his dad out of town on another of his business trips, Matt Prater had been up half the night. He'd found things on the Internet that numbed his sense of loneliness—for a while anyway—but now that morning was here, he was dog tired. Feeling guilty too.

Why'd he have to go to Shiloh Christian with its rigid rules?

Was he supposed to turn into one of *them*?

He trudged through the school day, doing his best to avoid the eyes of others. The thought of football practice kept him going. He'd take out his frustrations there. Play some smash-mouth defense.

When he arrived in the locker room, things were strangely quiet. As players pulled on pads and practice jerseys, the message circulated that Coach was sitting them down for a team meeting.

Matt smirked. *Earplugs, anyone? Get ready for some yellin'.*

By the time he rounded the corner, most everyone had found places on the locker room benches. He took an empty spot up front and looked around. J.T. was on his feet, shifting back and forth. To the right, Brady was holding up a wall with his shoulder.

Okay, what was going on?

Coach Grant Taylor entered the room, his face serene, his

shoulders relaxed. He propped himself on a stool, then held up a folded ten-dollar bill. He said, "Ten bucks to the person who can tell me who won the state championship a decade ago."

Matt had no idea.

"Walker Jennings," someone ventured.

"No."

"North Metro."

"Stop guessing," Grant said. "You know it or you don't. How 'bout five years ago?"

"Richland?" tried Jeremy Johnson.

"That was three years ago. You can't remember, can you?" Grant lowered his arm. "That leads me to ask a couple of questions. What's the purpose of this team?"

Matt knew this one. "To win ball games."

"Then what?"

"We get a trophy, and people talk about us."

"Maybe, for a while. Then what?"

"I don't know." Matt's mouth twisted in thought. "Get a scholarship, play for college, and, uh, coach Little League."

His teammates laughed.

"What're you getting at, Grant?" asked Brady. "You think we're just wasting our time?"

"If our main goal is to win football games, then yes."

Matt's jaw dropped. It was all clear to him now, why this team was stinking it up on the field and why his hopes for a scholarship were evaporating. Maybe his dad, for once, was right. "You don't *want* us to win games?" he demanded.

Grant didn't even blink. "No."

Coach has gone crazy. This season's done for!

"Not if that's our main goal," Grant added. "Winning football games is too small a thing to live for. And I love football as much as anybody."

Matt looked to the right for some support. He knew his father and others had been twisting the assistant coach's ear, trying to force some changes. Brady wore a shell-shocked expression.

"But even championship trophies will one day collect dust and be forgotten," Grant explained. "It's just that so far all this has been about us—how we can look good, how we can get the glory."

Matt glanced back a few rows. His friend, Brock Kelley, was staring down into his lap. Was Brock buying into this? Fine, then. Matt figured he'd hear the coach out so that he'd be able to report this entire thing to his father.

Grant lifted up a Bible. "The more I read this book, the more I realize life's not about us. We're not here just to get glory, make money, and die. The Bible says that God put us here for Him. To honor Him. Jesus said the most important thing you could do with your life is to love God with everything you are, and love others as yourself. So if we win every game and we miss that, we've done nothing. Football then means *nothing*. So I'm here to present you a new team philosophy. I think that football is just one of the tools we use to honor God."

Matt repositioned himself on the bench. He felt out of place with all this Christian talk. His father's actions told him the opposite, that life was about glory gained and money earned.

How's that saying go? He who dies with the most toys wins!

"So you think God *does* care about football?" Brock spoke up.

Matt dropped his chin and smiled. *There ya go, Brock. Keepin' it real.*

"I think He cares about your faith," Grant answered. "He cares about where your heart is. And if you can live your faith out on the football field, then yes, God cares about football because He cares about you. He sent His Son, Jesus, to die for us so we could live for Him. That's why we're here."

No, I'm here to play football. Don't know about the rest of y'all.

Grant wasn't finished. "But see, it's not just on the football field. We've gotta honor Him in our relationships, in our respect for authority, in the classroom . . . and when you're at home alone surfing the Internet."

Matt kept his head down.

"I want God to bless this team so much people talk about what He did. But it means we gotta give Him our best in every area. And if we win, we praise Him. And if we lose, we praise Him. Either way, we honor Him with our actions and our attitudes. So I'm asking you"—Grant peered around at his players—"what are you living for? I've resolved to give God everything I've got. Then I'll leave the results up to Him. I wanna know if you'll join me."

The challenge echoed in Matt's ears. He had no solid answer.

J.T.

The team was lined up across the end zone, with Grant standing about twenty yards away. J.T. Hawkins Jr. was liking the sound of this new-and-improved head coach. He wondered if his own "dangerous" prayers weren't beginning to have some effect.

Of course, not all the players were thrilled.

"Your attitude's like the aroma of your heart," Grant told them. "If your attitude stinks, it means your heart's not right."

Brock, Number 54, rubbed a hand over his mouth and muttered to Matt Prater, "He sure is preachy today."

"Mm-hmm."

J.T. folded his arms and approached the captain of the

defense. He sniffed at Brock's chest, made a sour face, and shook his head.

"What?"

"How's your attitude, Brock?" Grant asked.

"It's fine."

"Then you'll be okay with the death crawl, right?"

The entire team moaned. J.T. figured they had it coming.

"All right," said Grant. "Everybody on the goal line. Get your partner. Let's go!"

The death crawl involved two people at a time. One player got on his hands and knees, while the other sat on his back and lay down, facing the sky. The top man reached his arms back to grip his partner's shoulders, then lifted bent legs off the ground. The man on bottom carried both players' weight, moving forward on hands and feet while keeping knees off the grass.

The exercise had earned its name. It was a killer.

"No, you ain't getting out of this," J.T. barked at a player dawdling in the back. "Man, step on up."

Curly-haired Stanley lugged over a watercooler and set it down. He wiped the condensation from his hands, then pulled a book of football stats from his back pocket and thumbed through the pages. "I've been digging, Coach Hawkins, and I've found no references to the death crawl. Does it have any other names?"

"None that's fit for repeatin'."

"All right, let's go!" Grant ordered the first set of guys on the goal line. "Show me something. Ten yards. Move it, move it. Let's go, let's go! Matt, let's go. Let's go, Jonathan. Show me something. Ten yards."

Players advanced across the turf. Gnats swarmed in the heat.

Grant walked backward, goading the boys along. "Show me some power. No knees. Keep your knees off the ground." He clapped his hands. "Show me something. Here we go. Ten yards. Show me some muscle, show me some power. Gimme some heart. Let's go!"

"Next group," Brady called. "Up off your knees."

"Tha's right," J.T. said. "It'll be okay when the pain goes away. Y'all ready?"

Grant congratulated the first group as they crossed the ten-yard line. "Very good, boys. Very good. Let's run it back."

J.T. watched Matt stand and stumble. "How you feelin', Prater?"

"It's hot out here."

"Hot? You hear dat, Brady? The boys think ninety-eight degrees is hot. What you think, Coach?" He turned to see Grant guzzling a cup of water and dragging a forearm across his forehead.

Stanley piped up. "The hottest football game on record was in—"

"Stanley!"

"Yes, Coach Hawkins."

"Wha's the longest any one human being's gone without speakin'?"

"Sir, athletic endeavors are my area of expertise. I'm not sure how that particular record fits with—"

"Oh, it fits. Believe me. We get this team to stop talkin' and start actin', then we got something."

Grant nodded in agreement.

"You find me that stat, Stanley, and we'll let you suit up the last game of the season. If that's all right with Coach here."

"Sure. But no more stats until then," Grant stipulated.

"My investigation's under way, sir." The waterboy lumbered off.

Collapsed on the grass, the players were awaiting Coach's last words before they headed for the shade. These guys were half-cooked, panting like dogs. Good thing practice was coming to an end.

J.T. had no idea things were about to kick into another gear.

CHAPTER 19
Something Burning

GRANT

Grant could see his team was tired. The humidity had a way of sapping a person's energy. He decided to utter a short sentence or two, something to underline what he'd proposed earlier in the locker room, and then he'd let the boys head home.

"Ohhh, man, Brock!"

Grant turned in time to catch his defensive captain dumping a cup of water over Matt Prater's head. The others laughed.

"Oh, man," Matt said again, wiping at his hair. He shoved his friend. "That's not even funny, dude."

"Oh, yeah it is."

Grant put his hands on his hips, waiting for their attention.

"Sorry, Coach." Brock was still chuckling.

"You guys think you're ready to play Westview on Friday?"

"My old school." Matt wrinkled up his face. "Buncha blowhards."

Another player asked, "So, Coach, how strong is Westview this year?"

"A lot stronger than we are," Brock said.

"You already written Friday night down as a loss, Brock?"

"Well, not if I knew we could beat 'em."

Grant glanced away. An uneasy silence settled over the field, save the chirping of birds in the oaks along the chain-link fence.

He wondered how best to handle this first challenge to his new team philosophy. The others looked up to this kid. He was strong, likable, a natural leader.

"Come here, Brock." Grant gestured with his hand. "You too, Jeremy."

Both players looked at each other before standing and moving forward.

"What?" Brock asked. "Am I in trouble now?"

"Not yet."

BROCK

Brock strode toward the goal line. His wrists were taped, and he felt imposing in his shoulder pads. He'd been working on his pecs and deltoids, bulking up. Recently he'd sloughed off some, but it was hard to stay motivated when your team was staring down the barrel of another losing season.

What's Coach got in mind? I want this day to be over.

His teammates were watching him. He rested his weight on one leg, trying to appear cool, unconcerned.

Inside him, though, something had been simmering since that talk in the locker room. He knew his attitude had been going down the toilet. He'd lost his spark for Shiloh football this season, and in the classroom he'd been muttering snide remarks to get laughs instead of worrying about his grades.

Was this really how he wanted to spend his senior year?

Grant faced him at the goal line. Brock raised an eyebrow.

"I wanna see you do the death crawl again," Grant said. "Except I wanna see your absolute best."

The players on the sideline snickered, and Matt pointed a finger at him.

Brock figured he could handle this. Coach wanted to push him, to make an example out of him. Fine, he'd step it up and show the stuff he was made of. "What? You want me to go the thirty?"

"I think you can go to the fifty."

"The fifty?" Brock scoffed, staring at the line halfway down the field. He leaned in. "I can go to the fifty, if nobody's on my back."

"I think you can do it with Jeremy on your back." Grant reached into his own pocket. "But even if you can't, I want you to promise me you're gonna do your best."

Brock shrugged. "All right."

"Your best?"

"Okay."

"You're gonna give me your best?" Grant said again.

Brock was annoyed. "I'm gonna give you my best."

"All right. One more thing." Grant stepped forward and circled a cloth around his head. "I want you to do it blindfolded."

"Why?"

Grant cinched and knotted the material. "'Cause I don't want you givin' up at a certain point when you could go farther."

Brock's world narrowed to the dark strip before his eyes.

Grant slapped his shoulder pad. "Get down."

Feeling for the ground, Brock lowered himself. His teammates were still laughing, but the sound was less obvious than a few seconds ago. He was more aware of his palms pressing down into grass, his knees digging into the soil.

"Jeremy, get on his back."

Brock felt his partner sit on his flattened back, then he lay down, so that they were pressed spine-to-spine.

"Now get a good tight hold, Jeremy."

Jeremy's fingers hooked into the sleeves of Brock's jersey as he situated himself. Brock could feel the guy's back muscles flexing as he pulled his legs up in preparation for the drill.

"All right," Grant said. "Let's go, Brock."

Brock imagined himself on the defensive line of scrimmage. He lifted his knees, pushed his cleats into the turf, and started to drive forward. The initial settling of his partner's weight forced a grunt from his throat.

"Keep your knees off the ground. Just your hands and feet. There ya go."

Brock lumbered ahead like a giant tortoise. The heat bore down on him.

"A little bit left," Grant directed. "A little bit left."

Brock made the adjustment. He couldn't see a stinkin' thing. He envisioned the fifty-yard line, and it seemed like a mile away. But he was determined. He was spurred on by the catcalling of his teammates from the left. "Come on, Brock." "I don't think he'll make it." "Let's go, baby."

Matt's voice cut through the others. "I bet he don't even make it to the thirty."

If nothing else, Brock determined, he would do this to quiet his friend. Tonight, playing Madden Six, he would pound his chest and hold bragging rights over the entire family room.

How far had he gone now? Ten yards, maybe?

"There ya go. Show me some good effort." Grant's footsteps swished through the grass near Brock's head, guiding him forward.

He grunted again. With each pistoning motion of his legs, he could feel Jeremy shift back and forth on his back. His quads were starting to ache.

"Thataway, Brock," Grant cheered him on. "You keep coming."

Sweat was popping out on his forearms, running down and dripping from his elbows. His breathing was getting heavier.

"There ya go."

The players were still heckling. "Come on, Brock." "There's no way."

"It's a good start," Grant said. "Little bit left, little bit left."

Well, I'd know where to go, he thought, *if I wasn't wearing this stupid blindfold. I better be getting close to the twenty, at least.*

His calf muscles began to strain. His Achilles tendons were taut, like ropes about to snap. One leg started to give, causing his knee to dip, and he felt a blade of grass thread through the hair on his shin. He drove ahead, straightening the knee before it could fold on him.

"There ya go, Brock. Good strength."

Matt was still heckling, but quieter now. "You gotta be kiddin' me."

The words registered in Brock's head, but they were less distinct than before. His senses were centering in on his labor. His pulse was pounding in his ears. His eyes were seeing spots dance against the pressure of the blindfold.

"That's it, Brock. That's it." Grant's voice was steady.

"Am I to the twenty yet?"

"Forget the twenty. You give me your best. You keep going. That's it."

Brock felt Jeremy start to slide off one end. Brock's arms locked into place, as though they had minds of their own. They were afraid to move. Afraid to make a mistake. If he went another inch, he might collapse. He tried to roll his hip slowly, to redistribute the weight of his partner, but that only intensified the pain in his back and thighs.

Grant raised his voice. "Now, don't stop, Brock! You got more in you than that."

He took shallow breaths. The air was humid and hot, burning along his throat and into his lungs. "I ain't done. I'm just restin' a second." He moved his right hand a few inches, feeling the grass turn itchy between sweaty fingers.

"You gotta keep moving, let's keep moving. Let's go. Don't quit till you got nothing left."

Brock lunged forward again. He dug in with his legs. In moments, he had rediscovered a rhythm, and he told himself he had to be nearing the thirty. He didn't care anymore what the guys thought. In fact, he hardly even noticed their jabbering now.

"There ya go. Keep moving, keep moving."

Brock's muscles started to protest again. Lactic acid was building up, burning through his limbs. His toes were swollen knots of wood in his shoes, pushing into the ground, shoving him onward as his arms shifted to keep up. His shoulders began quivering beneath the pads.

"Keep moving, Brock. That's it. You keep driving."

Another few steps. A few more.

"Keep your knees off the ground. Keep drivin' it. Your *very* best."

Maybe the forty's my very best. I'm about done!

"Your very best," Grant urged. "Your *very* best! Keep moving, Brock."

Inside his shirt, sweat was running down his chest. His legs were trembling, but he couldn't stop. Only a few more yards. He had to be getting close. Maybe Coach was right. Maybe he *could* make it to the fifty.

"That's it, that's it, that's it. Keep going. Don't quit on me! Keep going."

MATT

In the unforgiving sun, Matt leaned back on one arm and stared across the grass and chalk lines. Around him, the other guys had arms folded on their knees, getting caught up in the drama on the field.

It was a scorcher out here.

The death crawl? Well, that was one way to die.

Matt had to admit he hadn't thought Brock would make it this far. For some reason, the big guy was stepping it up—as if he had something to prove, or actually cared what Coach Taylor thought.

Grant's voice carried over the hash marks. "Keep drivin' it. Keep your knees off the ground. That's it."

Was all that yelling supposed to help? Matt knew what it was like to have his father bark orders, and it didn't make him wanna try any harder, that was for sure.

"Your very best!" Grant kept saying. "Don't quit on me. Your *very* best!"

A few yards over, David Childers stood to view Brock's struggle. Jonathan joined him. Like spectators cheering a weary athlete to the finish line, a few others got to their feet. Or maybe they were more like fans falling into a reverent silence, as they realized they were witnessing something amazing.

"Keep drivin', keep drivin'! There ya go. There ya go."

Matt leaned forward. Actually, this *was* pretty unbelievable. What was keeping Brock up? This exercise was torture. Just ten yards with another person on your back, and you were ready to call it quits.

"That's it. You keep drivin'!" Grant shouted. "You keep your knees off the ground. Keep drivin' it! Don't quit till you've got *nothing* left."

Even if you were the one being carried, the death crawl was no cake walk. Your abs started to cramp as you tried to hold yourself in place. Your thighs strained to keep your legs up, and your fingers felt like they were ready to fall off from holding on in that awkward position.

It was a humbling thing, being carried by another person like that.

Perspiration slid down Matt's forehead into his eye. It stung, and he wiped at his face. He could only imagine the way his friend felt out there, doing all the work, carrying Jeremy along. How was he still going?

Whatever it is, that dude's got something burning inside him.

"Keep moving, Brock. That's it, that's it, that's it!" Even from the sidelines, the urgency in Grant's tone was unmistakable. "Keep going. I want everything you've got! Come on, *keep* going."

Matt climbed to his feet. Forget what the others thought. He had to see this for himself.

Brock's body was shaking now. "It hurts," he moaned.

"Don't quit on me. Your *very* best! Keep drivin', keep drivin'. There ya go, there ya go."

All around, the rest of the guys rose to observe what was going on—Brady, J.T., everyone. If Matt could've bet money on it, he would have said they were all wondering the same thing:

Is Brock actually gonna make it?

CHAPTER 20
Look Up

BROCK

With short raspy breaths, Brock tried to draw in oxygen for his straining muscles. The air tasted earthy and humid on his tongue, then turned to sunbaked sand as it scraped down his throat. His lungs were heaving, bursting with exertion. There was nothing left, no reprieve. His body was feeding off reserves, shaking from his fingers, through his arms, along his torso, to his toes.

"He's heavy!"

Coach Grant Taylor dropped down beside him. "I know he's heavy."

"I'm about outta strength."

"Then you negotiate with your body to find more strength." Coach was right there, moving with him, guiding him along. "But don't you give up on me, Brock. You keep going, you hear me? You *keep* going. You're doing good! You keep going. Do *not* quit on me. You keep going!"

"It *hurts!*"

"I know it hurts. You keep going. You *keep* going."

Brock quivered with each shift of his arms, every step of his legs. Sweat layered his body in hot droplets. Gnats hovered around his mouth. But he was still moving. At the start, his thighs had felt like pile drivers, yet now they were nothing more than used rags, shriveled and stained and good for nothing.

"It's all heart from here. Thirty more steps."

Thirty? I don't know if I can make it.

Brock swallowed a bug, felt the creature suck down his windpipe. That only made him mad. He was not gonna let some pesky insect stop him. Give him a whole mouthful of those things and he was still not gonna quit.

"You keep going, Brock. *Come on.* Keep going."

"It *burns!*"

He was venting now. There was no reason left to put on a front, or act like he had it all together. He was doing the stinkin' death crawl. He was dying. There was no way around it, no pretty way through it.

"Then let it burn!"

"My arms are *burning.*"

"It's all heart. You keep going, Brock. Come on, *come on.*"

Bile rose up in his mouth. He heard his teammates' footsteps in the grass, tracking behind him, but what did they matter? What did anything matter? He was alone, lost in the darkness behind this blindfold. And in pain like he'd never felt before.

"Keep going. You promised me your best. Your *best!*"

Brock blocked it all out. He ached with every moment, but centered it all inward—*all heart now, all heart.* Coach was right here, pushing him to do more, to be something he could not be on his own. He was not alone. He shouldn't even still be up. Yet he was still moving, plodding ahead one jerky movement at a time.

"Don't stop! Keep going."

"It's too hard."

"It's *not* too hard. You keep going. Come on, Brock. Gimme more, gimme more. Keep going! Twenty more steps. *Twenty* more."

Brock was gasping. On the verge of collapse.

"Keep going, Brock! Gimme your best. Don't quit. No! Keep going, keep going, keep going. Don't quit. *Don't* quit!"

Brock felt himself crawling into a long black tunnel, dank and suffocating. He groaned, then let out a loud growl. What was going on here? Coach must want him to die. Maybe Coach had lost it, lost all his marbles. This was *beyond* crazy.

"Don't quit!"

Was Brock nothing more than a numbered jersey to this madman? Why give everything for this? This was insane.

Then, through the hammering of blood in his ears and the bitter taste of swallowed gnats and his disjointed thoughts, a distinct command cut through.

"Brock Kelley, you don't quit!"

His name.

He was known, not forgotten.

He made another lurching step, but this time the pain rekindled more intensely than ever.

"It *burrrrns!*"

"*Keep* going, *keep* going. Go, Brock Kelley! You don't quit on me. *No*, you keep going! You keep going. Go, Brock! Ten more steps. Ten more, ten more, ten more. Keep going. *Don't* quit. Gimme your heart."

His entire being was shaking. "I can't do it!"

"You *can*. You *can*! Five more, five more."

If he had the strength, he would've yelled: "*Have* my heart! Take it all, take *everything*. There's nothing left!"

"Come on, Brock. Come on. *Don't* quit, *don't* quit!"

"*Arrghh!*"

"Come on! Two more. One more."

Brock gasped and collapsed forward, landing on his face. The weight rolled off his back, but his chest kept heaving with sobs. "That's gotta be the fifty. That's *gotta* be the fifty. I don't have any more."

The blindfold was being peeled from his eyes. His arms and legs were throbbing, wasted. Nothing but jelly.

"Look up, Brock." His coach was stretched out on the ground, facing him. "You're in the end zone."

With his last bit of strength, he peeked through sweat-drenched hair and saw orange goalposts straight ahead. He was shocked. He'd gone the full hundred yards, from one end to the other. His body was over the goal line, as though extended to ensure the winning score.

Brock's face dropped back into the grass.

GRANT

Grant was belly-down in the end zone. He could see J.T. and Brady leading the team forward in a stunned shuffle, but he knew he couldn't let this moment pass. What he'd just witnessed, what he'd been a part of, was nothing less than jaw-dropping. To back off now would be to miss the point.

"Brock," he said. "You are the most influential player on this team. If you walk around defeated, so will they. Don't *tell* me you can't give me more than what I've been seeing. You just carried a hundred-and-forty-pound man across this whole field on your arms." Grant saw his player's look of exhaustion, of humility. He'd been broken down and, for the first time, he was truly listening. "Brock, I *need* you." Grant struck the earth with his fist. "God's gifted you with the ability of leadership. *Don't* waste it."

Standing above them, Jeremy said, "Coach?"

Grant kept his eyes on Brock. "Can I count on you?"

Still panting, Brock paused and then nodded. "Yes."

"Coach?" Jeremy said again.

What did the kid want? Didn't he see what was happening here? Grant looked up. "What is it, Jeremy?"

"I weigh one-sixty."

Grant's eyes widened, and he swiveled his head back toward Brock. Then, he pulled himself up, patted his player on the back, and walked off toward the rest of the guys. He looked back once and saw Jeremy still standing at his friend's side. Until Brock Kelley had the strength to stand again, Jeremy Johnson wouldn't be going anywhere.

So this was what it felt like to break in a horse.

With a wry grin, J.T. turned and slapped his hands together. He called out to the gathered players, "All right. *Who's* next?"

CHAPTER 21
A Big Stink

GRANT

J.T. had arms crossed high on his chest, dancing from one foot to the other. His energy was contagious as he encouraged the team. "Good practice, boys. See y'all tomorrow."

Grant moved up beside his offensive coordinator. He gripped the threads of a Wilson football, remembering the love he'd once had for the game, running plays as quarterback for the GSU Eagles. He'd let some of that get buried in the cares of daily life.

"Hey, man," J.T. said. "For the first time in a while, I actually feel good about Friday night."

"Yeah? Why?"

J.T. lifted his shoulders. "I'm just on board with whatcha doin'. If *they* get a hold of it, it'll change their lives." He slapped Grant's arm. "You can count me in."

Grant pressed his lips together and spun the ball in his hands as his assistant walked away.

Wearing a black golf visor, Brady came alongside. "Grant, me too."

"Yeah?"

"Yeah." Brady clutched a set of plastic cones. "I feel like I owe you an apology. I just want you to know that, uh . . . I'm with ya."

Grant nodded. "Thank you."

Brady clapped a hand on his back. "See ya tomorrow."

A glance around the field told Grant that his assistants had collected the supplies into the oversize gym bags, and all he'd have to do was throw them into the pile by the metal bench.

He realized, then, that one player was still sitting in the stands.

MATT

From the edge of his vision, Matt saw Coach drop a pad onto the grass and wander across the track. Was he coming this way? Matt had no interest in talking—not after that sermon in the locker room and the exhibition on the field. He was a guy. He didn't like to jabber when he had a lot on his mind.

What was keeping his father anyway? He was late again. Same ol' excuses, same ol' routine.

Man, I'm so ready for a change.

As Grant got closer, Matt leaned forward with arms crossed over his knees. He kept his head turned toward the parking lot in hopes his coach would take a hint and leave him alone.

"You need a ride, Matt?"

"No, my dad's coming. Or at least he'd better be."

Grant's hands were on the chain-link fence. He peered up from beneath his red cap. "Can I shoot straight with you for a minute?"

"Sure." Matt met his eyes.

"I feel like you owe your dad more respect."

"Why?"

"'Cause he's your father."

"You don't know him like I know him." Matt thought of the phone conversations he'd overhead, between his father and shady county inspectors. Anything to save a buck. Everyone bowing to the almighty dollar.

"I don't have to know him. You need to respect him because it's the right thing to do."

"You know, Coach, my dad doesn't even like you. He thinks the school needs to find somebody else."

Grant looked away, then brought his gaze back to his player. "That's beside the point. Scripture says to honor your parents, and all you do is complain. Remember, it's the attitude of your heart that counts—and yours stinks."

Oh, here it comes. All that holier-than-thou stuff.

"Yeah?" Matt snapped. "Well, when I was a kid, I tried making him happy any way I could. He wanted me to play Little League, that's what I did. Truck needed work, and I was right there with the tools. Wanted me to go hunting with him, we went hunting. And I don't even *like* quail."

"And now he wants you here playing football?"

"Not if we keep losing."

"Okay. Well, for this season, this is where God has you."

"Seems like y'all are trying to control my life." Matt furrowed his brow against the late sun. "My dad, all he does is boss me around. He doesn't even try to understand me."

"Matt, you can't judge your father by his actions, and then judge yourself by your intentions. It doesn't work that way. You're not responsible for him. You're responsible for you. You honor God by honoring your authority."

"You really believe in all that honoring God and following Jesus stuff?"

"Yes," Grant said. "I do."

He blew air from the corner of his mouth. "Well, I ain't trying to be disrespectful, but not everybody believes in that. Religion works for some people, but I'm just here 'cause I got kicked out of Westview."

"Matt, nobody's forcing anything on you. Following Jesus Christ is the decision you're gonna have to make for yourself. You may not wanna accept Him—because He'll change your life and you'll never be the same. I do hope one day you'll realize how much He loves you. I'll see you tomorrow."

With heat beating down on his head, Matt watched him go.

"He'll change your life . . ."

A change. Matt Prater wanted nothing more. He was only seventeen, and he was already sick of this day-to-day grind.

GRANT

In shorts and tennis shoes, Grant kneeled over a floor vent in the dining room. He removed the hardware and peered down into the duct with a flashlight. The smell was overpowering, but at last he'd zeroed in on the problem.

A dead rat.

After this, he planned to climb onto the roof with hammer and nails, some sealant, tar paper, and a few new tiles. No more odor. No more leaks over his head. Things were gonna change around this house, starting with this dead creature.

Uh-oh. Here comes Brooke.

He'd been hoping to get this taken care of before she finished her weeding along the shrubs in front of the house. Maybe if he just stayed quiet she would walk on by to the back bedroom.

Nope.

His wife entered the kitchen, cute and barefoot, wearing coveralls over a tank top. She stepped forward to see what he was doing, then screamed at the sight of the rat he was digging up from the vent. She waved her hands and dashed from the room on her tip-toes.

Grant chuckled and reached out his gloved hand, as though offering support. She stayed far back. "Okay," he said. "I'll get him. Just bring that trash bag over here and set it down."

Still squealing, Brooke shook out a white plastic bag and advanced. "*Ooooh,* don't you let that touch me."

"I'm not gonna let him touch you, Brooke. I'm gonna get him outta here." He leaned toward the vent, struck again by the odor. He sat back up and wrinkled his nose. "Oh, man, he stinks."

"Ohhh, I can't believe that was in my house!"

"Okay, I'm gonna get him out."

"Just make sure it's still dead." She stepped closer, still cautious.

"It's dead. He's probably been dead for weeks." Grant took hold of the tail and lifted the rodent onto the plastic bag. "Ah, there ya go. There ya go."

"You just get it outta here. Out, out!"

"Stop being a . . ."

Grant hesitated as he got an idea.

"Come here." He gestured with his glove.

"Nuh-uh."

"Just look at him."

"No."

"He looks like a big hamster."

"Ohhhh. Nuh-uh."

"Come here, come here. Don't be afraid. Just face your fear. Look." He pointed at the thing, showing that it was lifeless, harmless. Evening light shone through the shutters, spotlighting the rotting corpse.

Legs together and hands on her knees, Brooke took a peek.

"He's got a cute little tail there," Grant tried to reason with her. "He's just got a big stink. Look, see his cute little eyes there."

She moved a little closer.

"See his teeth?"

She was staring down at the thing now, actually intrigued.

He lowered his voice. "Look at his teeth. It almost looks like he's mad . . . Aaahhhh!" he yelled, grabbing the bag and shaking it at her.

Brooke covered her face and screamed. Her feet were trampling in place, her hands quivering, waving. Then she turned and scampered from the room, amid shrieks of terror.

Grant belly-laughed. That couldn't have worked any better.

"*Ohh!* You are terrible!" she scolded him. "I can't believe you did that to me, Grant Taylor."

With tears forming in his eyes, he pounded the wall with laughter, then ducked as a dishtowel sailed from the kitchen. It whacked him in the head.

"You are *so* bad!"

A second towel also hit its mark. Boy, his wife had pretty good aim.

CHAPTER 22
Gates and Keys

J.T.

His mama would've been proud. Ready to put some of Coach Taylor's philosophy into practice, J.T. had spent part of the night looking through Scripture for portions he could apply to the game of football. Now, on an overcast but muggy Wednesday, he addressed the Shiloh quarterback and corps of receivers.

"We been having some problems catchin' the ball, am I right?"

Jeremy and the others hung their heads.

"Am I right?"

Zach Avery spoke up. "You're right, Coach Hawkins."

"Don't I know it. So today, we gonna think about what the Bible has to say regardin' this." He folded his arms. "*You* heard me. You lookin' at me like you got cotton in your ears. See, Jesus asked this question, 'Why do you look at the speck of sawdust in your brother's eye and pay no attention to the plank in your own eye?'"

"You want us to stop judging each other?" Nathan guessed.

"That too. We oughta be encouragers on the field." He whipped out an eye patch and dangled it for them to see. They were probably nervous, after that whole ordeal with the blindfolded death crawl. "I borrowed this drill from the Oregon Ducks' coach."

"A Pac Ten team?" one of the receivers whined.

"Ahh." J.T. held up a finger. "You already lookin' at the sawdust again. Guess you get to go first."

"Yes, sir."

"This one's all about narrowin' your focus. I put this over your eye, and then you gonna run a slant pattern. Zach, you hit him about fifteen yards out. The patch, it'll force you to keep your eye on the ball. Run five from the right, five from the left, then give the patch to the next receiver."

Brady wandered over. "They look like a buncha pirates," he quipped as the first receiver completely missed the ball.

"Gotta stay focused, Nathan!"

"You know, J.T., the boys'll lose their depth perception with one eye covered."

"Don't ya think I know that?" The next pass hit a receiver on the chin, knocking him off-balance to the ground. J.T. waved his arm. "Okay, listen up, y'all. I forgot to tell you to wear your helmets for this drill."

The players pulled on their protective gear, snapping mouth guards into place.

"Where'd ya come up with this one anyway?" Brady asked.

"Coach Bellotti."

"From Oregon? You're talkin' Pac Ten."

J.T. shook his head in a show of disappointment.

"What?"

"Man, I'm just tryin' to bring those ideas out onto the field, the things Grant talked about. Instead, everybody lookin' for sawdust."

"Sawdust?" Brady sounded confused.

DAVID

David got into position while Jonathan teed up the football.

With his cap turned backward as usual, J.T. stood nearby. His hands were on his waist. "David, right down the middle. You got this."

He stepped forward. Swung his foot. Watched the ball fly to the left.

Figures. So much for kickin' it like I mean it.

Around the field, guys were running drills, whistles were blowing, and Grant was giving orders to the running backs. "All right, set it up. Run it again."

David hung his head. "Sorry, Coach."

J.T. faced him. "David. Listen, son. You act like you gonna miss before you even kick the ball. See, we're gonna have to change your whole kickin' philosophy. Now see, you're kickin' wide left or"—he made broad gestures with his arms—"wide right. But that ain't what's gonna get you *home*. The ball has got to go through the middle."

"I know, Coach."

"No. No, you don't." J.T. paused. "Now, what does Scripture say about this?"

David's eyebrows knitted together. Was this a trick question? "Ummm . . ."

"Scripture says, 'Wide is the gate and broad is the way that leads to destruction, and there are many who go in by it.'"

David saw Coach Taylor turning to listen in on this.

"Now to us," J.T. continued, "that's wide left and wide right."

Brady threw out a warbly, gospel-style affirmation. "*Weeeell.*"

"'But narrow is the gate and straight is the way that leads to life, and few there be that find it.'"

"*Weeeell.*"

J.T. seemed to be in a rhythm now, like he was in church back home with a deep-voiced preacher and a purple-robed choir. "Anybody can kick it wide left and wide right," he proclaimed. "My *mamma* can kick it wide left and wide right. But that ain't what's gonna get you *home*."

"Come *oooon!*" Brady responded.

"It don't have to look pretty. It don't have to look smooth." J.T. bounced on his toes, waving his arms. "It can look like a dying duck. But the ball has got to go through the middle."

Brady called out, "Oh, *my* word!"

David felt dazed as he spotted Grant strolling over. Great, now all the coaches were here to eye his performance. His hands felt clammy.

"Now, David," J.T. said. "You're gonna have to choose the narrow way, 'cause that's the only path where you will get your reward. Now send this ball through these pearly posts. Set it up one more time for me, Jonathan."

Grant grinned. "David, I've never heard it that way before, but there's a lot of truth to what he's saying. Let's see ya kick it."

See me miss it, is more like it.

He took a few steps back. Jonathan set the ball. He ran forward and drove the ball up through the goalposts. Grant gave him congratulatory punches in the arm, and he beamed with a sense of accomplishment.

"Yeah," J.T. said. "That's what I'm talkin' about."

GRANT

Practice had been good. The team was coming along.

Grant and Brady picked up the watercooler and carried it back to the locker room. The boys had already gone, and J.T. had left early to answer a service call. The man not only worked hard as an assistant coach, he also showed commitment to his position with Flint River Locksmith. He'd grown up on the south end of town and learned the value of a good day's work.

Though Grant admired the way J.T. saved for his kids' college education, he also found it amusing to watch J.T. slap large company magnets onto the side of his white GMC van, then take off like a superhero to help those in distress.

Let's hope I don't need any help getting myself home.

Grant settled into his car and turned the key, rolling the dice. He groaned as the engine argued with him over whether or not to start. After three attempts, Grant won the debate and rolled onto Old Pretoria Road.

A mile into his journey home, he found a white van on the roadside in front of a small church. As he neared, he recognized J.T. leaned up against the driver's door.

What's he doing out here? Wonder if he's stranded?

Grant pulled in front of the van, left his car idling, and got out. "You okay?"

"I'm good." J.T. glanced down at his watch. "You can take off, man. I'm all right."

"Whatcha waiting for? Someone get locked outta the church?"

"Uh, yeah, but I got 'em in. It's all good. Really, you can go." J.T. glanced down the road, as though waiting on someone with whom he'd rather not be seen.

Grant turned in the same direction but saw nothing. This was so unlike J.T. He was an honorable man with nothing to hide, right? Grant decided to press the issue. "If you've already unlocked the church, then why're you still standin' out here?"

"Man," J.T. snapped. "Shouldn't you be getting on home? Brooke's probably got dinner on the table for ya. You better go."

"Give it to me straight, J.T. Are you outta gas?"

"No, man, I wouldn't let that happen. Look, everything's fine."

Grant couldn't figure this out. J.T. seemed nervous, fidgety.

Why was he brushing away offers of assistance? Then Grant got his answer.

An engine rumbled at his back, and he turned to see a truck pulling up behind J.T. 's van. On the vehicle's side panel, a large business sign advertising Jessie's Lock & Key. A man, presumably Jessie, climbed out and sauntered toward J.T.

Grant put the pieces together and burst out laughing. The two businesses were rivals, and J.T. no doubt hated having to call his competitor to get into his own vehicle.

"Well, well, well." Jessie folded his arms beneath a big smile. "Whadda we have here? Has the other locksmith in town locked his own keys in his van?"

"Would ya just hurry up and do your job!" J.T. shot back. "I ain't got all day."

Grant was belly-laughing now.

J.T. whirled on him. "Man, why'd you have to hang around? I didn't want nobody to see this!"

Grant tried to respond, but couldn't. He held his side and leaned against the van, struggling to breathe as tears of mirth rolled down his face. Beside him, Jessie took his time unlocking the van door, relishing the fact that each passing car could see J.T.'s predicament.

"Grant, don't ya dare tell Brady. I mean it, man! Promise me ya won't say nothin'."

Grant wasn't about to promise anything. This was an ace up his sleeve in case J.T. ever gave him a hard time. He turned and headed back to his car, still trying to control his laughter. From the driver's seat, he could hear J.T. still voicing his appeal.

"C'mon, Grant. Ya gotta promise me. Not a word!"

CHAPTER 23
The Fuse

Thursday. A lazy afternoon. Later, reflecting back, Grant knew that he'd had no clue what he was about to discover.

In his office, with the door open, Grant pored over the stuff on his desk. For years, he had worked his coaching schedule around the same basic format: stretches and team drills, a water break and coach's speech, then separate offensive and defensive drills.

By Tuesdays, he'd have the quarterback rehearsing the game plan.

On Thursdays, he'd run them through a light scrimmage in final preparation for Friday's opponent.

On Saturdays, he'd watch videotape and start drafting plans for the next skirmish.

That was how he'd always done it.

In his years at Georgia Southern, he'd been instructed also in sports finance and management. He dreaded this part, figuring how to keep everything on budget: team travel, equipment, laundry, and all else that was entailed. Principal Ryker had been good to work with, yet Grant always felt pressure to cut expenses. Particularly as the team's record sank, players transferred, and funds trickled away to other schools.

He was ready to see things change. He only hoped his team was on board. The last few practices had encouraged him, but sometimes it was hard to tell with teenagers. They might laugh something off, even while the words were sinking in. They might act oblivious, then respond dramatically on game day.

Had Brock's death crawl impacted the others the way it had Grant?

On his stomach in the end zone, facing his exhausted player, he'd felt something stir in him, a new zeal for God and the game. A new understanding of the Lord's perseverance in his and Brooke's lives.

"Grant?" The science teacher's head popped into his office. "Are you not aware of what's going on outside on the field?"

"What?"

Mr. Layne patted the wall. "You might wanna come check this out."

What now? Grant worried. *A fight between some of my boys?*

Two years ago, a brawl between Donnie Pervis and Robert Catt had nearly divided the team, derailing what had been the start of a good season. It was that fight that had earned Robert the nickname "Bobcat."

Grant stood and followed Mr. Layne out to the football field.

Cutting through an open gate, Layne filled him in. "Mitch decided to bring his Bible class outside today. After he started teaching, Matt Prater stood up and accepted Christ as his Lord."

What? Grant's head jerked up. *Neil Prater's son?*

"It was awesome," the teacher said. "He started confessing stuff from his life. He started asking his friends for forgiveness. Next thing we know, Bob Duke stands up and does the same thing."

Grant had always thought it funny that Shiloh had a student with a name so close to Coach Bobby Lee Duke's, and he found himself wishing Coach Duke was the one out on this field today. But that was just selfish thinking.

No, this was amazing.

And Matt Prater of all people?

"Kids start breaking up into groups. They begin to pray for each other. They begin to ask forgiveness for sins that they've committed." Mr. Layne came to a stop. "This has been going on for three hours. How'd you not know what was going on?"

Grant felt a lump rise in his throat. He walked onto the field—the same place he'd seen victories and defeats, the place Brock had carried his teammate from one end to the other. What looked to Grant like only an athletic battlefield had become God's territory.

Groups of kids were sitting on the grass, praying and talking. There were tears and smiles. Mitch was standing, addressing a half-circle of students.

Was that Zach in the group? Yeah, and Brock was there too.

Grant knew this had not been orchestrated by human effort. If it had, it would've been temporary and ultimately empty. Instead, God's Spirit was moving. He could see it in the bleachers, where a cluster of girls sat together with heads in their hands. These were the same ones he'd heard shredding each other days earlier with their sharp words.

Mr. Layne walked over to speak with them.

As these happenings flashed across Grant's vision, he recalled the fervent and faithful prayers of Mr. Bridges in the hallways. The muttering words. The scuffling steps. The trembling hands that brushed over student lockers at Shiloh Christian Academy.

He could hear the old man now: *"Bless them in a special way, Lord. I ask You to lift them up to You."*

And here they were, these kids scattered around the field.

"*I ask You to bring up a generation that has a heart for You, Lord.*"

Grant heard someone approaching from his right. He turned to see Matt Prater looking up at him.

"Coach?"

Grant's voice failed him. He had no words. His player's gaze was devoid of animosity or bitterness. This was a different kid from the one he'd spoken to in the stands two days ago. A change had occurred.

They opened their arms at the same time, meeting in a firm embrace.

"I'm proud of you, Matt."

Matt stepped back, taking no time to glory in that. He said, "I need to talk with my dad. I'd like to go see him."

Grant considered his obligations, but what could matter more than this?

"I'll take you right now," he said.

Neil

Through large office windows, Neil Prater heard a sputtering engine in the architectural firm's parking lot. That was unusual. Most of his clients and coworkers owned a nice set of wheels. All part of the image one had to portray.

Probably somebody lost, he thought. *Just turning around.*

He ran a hand back through his slick hair, loosened his top shirt button, and leaned over the blueprints on his desk. A local developer, Mr. Jones, stood beside him in a dangling tie and wire-rim glasses.

"So," Jones explained, "what we've done here is we've gained four lots by moving the retention pond down here. We could try and do that through here, if you want."

"No, I like this. That's perfect."

Neil's intercom buzzed. "Mr. Prater, there's someone here to see you."

These interruptions annoyed him to no end. His secretary knew he had Mr. Jones in here, so why did she do this? Did she not understand his request to be left undisturbed?

"Sarah," he said. "I'm in a meeting."

"Uh, it's your son."

That was unexpected. Well, not totally. How many times in the past few years had Matt been in trouble? A rumble in a school hallway. Something stolen from a locker. Westview's principal had ended that by expelling him.

As a last-ditch effort, Neil had enrolled his son at Shiloh Christian in hopes they might be able to do something with him. Neil had grown up going to church, and even though it never meant more than an interruption in his Sunday TV viewing, he believed there was a God out there somewhere.

What is it this time? Has even the Big Guy given up on my kid?

Mr. Jones brought his thoughts back to the present. "Would you like me to step out?"

"No, it's okay."

Neil was done covering for his son. Matt was almost eighteen now—about time he learned that life could bring him to his knees.

"Sarah," he spoke into the intercom. "Send him in."

He faced the door, half expecting to see the boy enter with a bruised eye or a broken nose. It'd happened before. Instead, Matt appeared with a clean shirt tucked into belted jeans, and no sign of that usual chip on his shoulder. He looked mild and almost, well . . .

Meek and mild. Maybe he *had* been brought to his knees.

Neil sat back in his chair. "Matt, you okay?"

"I'm sorry, Dad. I didn't know you were in a meeting."

"What is it, son?"

"Uh, Dad." Matt's arms hung at his sides as he stepped into the office. "I just wanted to say that I'm sorry . . ."

Neil didn't blink. *Did he just say he was sorry?*

"I'm sorry for the way I've been acting. I got right with God today. And I just needed to say that, uh, from now on I'll respect your authority. Whatever you say, goes. That's it."

As unexpectedly as he'd arrived, he departed.

Neil swallowed once. He stared straight ahead.

"You know," Mr. Jones said, "I could come back tomorrow if that'd be better for you."

"No. It's okay. I'm sorry. I, uh . . ."

Neil swiveled and rose from his desk, then stepped to the window. What he saw next was nothing he expected. There was Grant Taylor, the coach he'd been hoping to get rid of, giving his son a slap on the arm before they both climbed into an old Chevy Celebrity. A real heap. Was that all that could be afforded on a head coach's salary?

Well, that explains the noise I heard earlier.

"For what it's worth," said the man at his desk, "I'd give my right arm to hear my son say that to me."

Neil watched the Chevy pull away. He blinked twice. Still gazing outside, he said, "You mind if we finish this a little later, Mr. Jones? I just, uh . . . Could you give me a few minutes?"

GRANT

This was it. Friday night.

Grant gathered his team in the locker room. He felt he needed

FACING THE GIANTS

to seal the things that had happened this week—on and off the football field. The players were attentive. He sensed their eagerness to get out and play. Soon enough. A few more minutes in here would only increase that explosive drive.

"Guys, first I want to apologize that we're still without helmet logos."

"Hey, Coach," J.T. said. "Me and Brady, we just done whatcha told us."

Brady nodded.

"Through no fault of anyone in this room," Grant clarified, "we will be without logos for the rest of the season. But before anyone starts to groan, let me say that I think it's a good thing. For too long, you've played as individuals, focused on padding your own stats. That's all gonna change, starting tonight."

From the back of the room, Stanley cut in. "According to this year's records, no Shiloh player has even broken into the league's top five in any category."

"Well, you sure ain't one to sugarcoat the truth," Brady said.

"Whoa now, whoa." J.T. stabbed fingers against his palm. "Time out, Stanley. You s'posed to be keepin' your stats to yourself. That was our deal."

"Yes, sir. But only until I found the record about staying quiet the longest."

"And?"

"I found it."

"You found . . . Oh, here we go. Well, I wanna hear this for myself."

"Not until you suit me up for the last game, as per our agreement."

"He's right, J.T. Now back to tonight's business." Grant met the

148

eyes of his players. "I want our blank helmets to be a reminder to you that we're here to play with one heart, as one unit. Our identity is not in a decal, it's in the way our attitudes honor God, the way we work together and support our guys from the sidelines."

"Sounds good, Coach."

"Thank you, Brady. I feel like I'm standing before a new team tonight. It's a new day and a new game. What you've experienced in your hearts this week is about to be released on the field. Stay humble, but confident." He tapped his defensive captain's arm. "Why don't you take this one, Brock?"

Brock dropped to a knee. The rest of the team followed. With his taped wrist on Matt Prater's shoulder, he prayed: "Lord, we know our lives are not about football, but we do thank You for allowing us to play tonight. Lord, we're gonna give You our best. If we win, we'll praise You. And if we lose, we'll praise You. We give You all the honor and the glory for this tonight, Lord. Keep us safe. In Jesus' name I pray, amen."

"Amen," the team agreed.

"All right, guys, look at me." Grant watched faces turn his way, full of anticipation, and he knew this was the moment to light the fuse in this team. "Play hard!" he said. "Have fun!"

With a clap of his hands, he led the way onto the field.

Time to set this thing off.

HALF TIME

HALF TIME

NEIL

While spectators around him chattered, Neil Prater fixed his attention on the boys headed into the locker room. Their heads were up, their eyes burning with a new fire. After two quarters, the score was tied.

"Doin' good, Matt!" he yelled down at his son.

Despite a twitch of a grin, Matt kept jogging along with his team.

These boys should've been dead in the water. They were undersized, overmatched. Four years in a row, Westview had beaten them.

Instead, I feel like I'm watching a resurrection, Neil mused.

And why not? For him, football had always been larger than life.

Raised in Decatur, he'd followed UGA games from the time he was a little tyke. He bled Georgia red. Tailgate parties were entrenched in his memory: potato salad and deviled eggs, pimento cheese sandwiches and fried chicken, and lots of loud, rowdy people.

Soon, he was one of 'em. Wildest of the bunch.

And that's the way it went—college games on Saturdays, soul-searching on Sundays. Death and resurrection. From the South's symbolic struggle to rise again, to the barriers of race and skin color, it was all worked out on the gridiron. But he'd never seen anything like what had happened yesterday in his office. His son, apologizing? That would make a believer out of anyone.

BROOKE

Flanked by his assistant coaches, Grant patted his players' backs as he led them off the field. Brooke watched from the bleachers, feeling her heart swell with pride. Her husband cared about these boys.

And he would make such a good dad.

She pulled her hands to her mouth, as though her thoughts would spill from her tongue. She had to stop torturing herself with these ideas. Had to stop running to the pharmacy for a pregnancy test every time she felt queasy.

You just put it behind you, she scolded herself. *And move on.*

"Well, there they go, Brooke," J.T.'s wife said. "Let's hope they find a way to keep them boys inspired."

"Oh, they will."

"You sure about that?" The woman's eyes twinkled. "My husband, the locksmith, he can't even find his own keys."

"I heard." Brooke chuckled. "But at least his van starts."

"Yeah, there's stories about *your* car troubles."

"It's not that bad."

"Nah? It just don't run half the time. We're quite the pair, aren't we? Guess nothing beats the life of a coach's wife."

Brooke caught a glimpse of Neil Prater over her friend's shoulder. Indignation rushed through her, as she thought of the way this man and others had torn her husband down in front of Principal Ryker.

And in secret. Behind Grant's back!

She stared at him for a moment, then decided it was time to give him a piece of her mind. Threading her way across the bleachers, she began silently wording the verbal lashing he was due. A few feet away, though, something stopped her.

No, Brooke. Don't say something you'll regret. Just kill him with kindness.

Although he was turned to the side, she could see a grin on his face as he watched the team run by below.

"Well, you're all smiles, Mr. Prater."

As he shifted around and spotted her, he revealed an expression of surprise. She was the wife of the coach he'd been trying to oust. "Oh, uh . . . Hello, Mrs. Taylor."

Brooke maintained eye contact. "Matt's been playing a great game tonight. He's really stepped it up. You must be very proud of him."

"I feel like I'm watching a whole new team tonight."

"Well, Grant's been workin' hard with the boys."

"So I've noticed."

Mr. Prater still had a slight deer-in-the-headlights look on his face.

"I just wanted you to know," Brooke continued, "that we're praying for Matt, and we're excited about the decisions he's been making lately."

The man nodded, then looked down.

Brooke could tell she was getting to him. *This is torturing him.*

He raised his head and met her gaze. "Listen, I . . . I've said some things, not very nice things, about the direction this program was going. From what I've seen lately, I'd say I was wrong."

"My husband's a good man."

"I'm sure he is."

"And a good coach."

"Well," Mr. Prater conceded, "tonight's definitely a good start."

MR. BRIDGES

"Half time's almost over," Martha called. "They're fixin' to kick off."

"Shiloh's receiving, ain't they?"

"Believe so."

Mr. Bridges shuffled back into the den with a notepad, a pen, and a glass of tomato juice. The game was tied. He could ask for nothing more.

See, this is how it happens, he thought. *Players get inspired, they start workin' together, and a whole season comes back to life.*

From its early days, football in this region had been about death and life. Bridges knew the story of Vonalbade Gammon, a Georgia player who'd died in 1897 from injuries in a contest against Virginia. The state legislature passed a bill soon afterward making it illegal to play football, but before the governor could sign it, he received a letter from Vonalbade's mother, bidding him not to do so. Her son had loved the game, she wrote, and would want it to live on.

The bill was never signed. Georgia football survived.

Though Bridges didn't talk about it much, he took some satisfaction in penning occasional sports features for the *Albany Herald*. He wrote them under assumed names, seeing no need to draw attention to himself.

"Turn it up, would ya?" Martha said.

He reached for the knob, eliciting crackles of complaint from the old radio. The funny thing was, his silver-haired bride usually nodded off before game's end, but tonight she was all ears.

He had nothing but respect for her. She was a hardworkin' woman. During his years of alcohol abuse, she'd kept their finances afloat as an office assistant at the local Pippin's Snack Pecans.

Way he figured it, he was to blame for the hunch in her shoulders.

Bridges lowered himself onto the cushions. The last two decades had been good, at least. He'd finished out his time at Cooper Tire, earned a decent pension, and now flipped burgers as a way of staying in touch with this next generation's concerns.

At Sonic, he saw it all: tattoos and bare midriffs and foul words scratched into tables. Didn't understand it. Didn't like it.

But he loved all them kids just the same. They were his mission field.

"We're back on a balmy Friday evening," the radio announcer was saying. "With the score knotted up at seven apiece, Westview prepares to kick off the second half. The ball is up, and Shiloh lets it bounce into the end zone. They'll start with the ball on their own twenty-yard line, hoping to add some points to the board and take their first lead of the game."

"Can ya even hear that?" Martha asked. "Did ya turn it up like I asked?"

"I can hear it just fine."

"Still sounds awful muffled to me."

Bridges smiled. At least she wasn't snoozing. The radio hissed and snapped as he turned the knob another notch to the right.

THIRD QUARTER:
FARTHER TO FLY

CHAPTER 25
Out of the Nest

MATT

"Matt, you ready to eat some dirt?" growled a Westview lineman.

On the offensive side of the ball, Matt got down in a three-point stance and faced his former schoolmate. Would he be playing for a winning team if he'd stayed at Westview? Would scouts already be calling about college ball?

He'd thrown all that away with a few bad choices. Now, as a Shiloh Eagle, he hoped to rise above.

"Hut!"

The center snapped the ball to Zach Avery, and in an instant the entire offensive line surged forward. Elbows out, hands in front of them, they tried to manhandle the defense in order to create a gap for their halfback.

Things happened fast. A blur of motion.

It was hot in here, rank with body odor and huffing players. Yellow helmets and white jerseys flashed between the wall of Shiloh red.

Matt kept his center of gravity low. He and his opponent collided, pushing and clawing. The defensive lineman poked stiff fingers into Matt's neck. It was an old trick, meant to provoke a reaction.

He wasn't falling for it.

He spun from the guy's other hand, and drove sideways to catch a linebacker coming through the hole. Matt kept his legs moving in measured steps, freezing the defender in place. To his left, Jacob Hall cut through the gap and plowed forward six or seven yards, carrying yellow helmets with him.

Not only was this a new team, Matt was a new person.

Time to lay it all out on the field.

DAVID

David Childers knew this field goal was out of his range. On a crucial third down, Shiloh's quarterback had been sacked and they were facing a forty-three-yarder into the wind. Still, some part of him waited to be called forward by Coach Taylor. He'd been practicing, driving it into the barn with chalk-dust-flying kicks, and this could be his chance to do something memorable.

Grant looked down the sideline, caught David's eye.

Then, just that quickly, the coach tugged at Joshua Webster's jersey and sent him in to take care of business.

David couldn't blame him. The last time Grant had given him an opportunity, he'd pushed the kick to the left and failed to put points on the board.

With his helmet gripped against his chest, David heard old doubts start whispering: *"You're no good. Why do you even waste your time, you little runt?"*

But he was learning, wasn't he? Improving each day.

"For what? So you can look like a loser to Amanda? So you can let down your crippled father who'll never even get a chance to kick a ball?"

Joshua was out on the turf, testing his footing with his cleats. He stepped back, the ball was snapped, and he launched an end-over-ender that skimmed between the goalposts. David pumped his arm in the air and cheered along with the rest of the crowd.

Shiloh had the lead: 10-7.

If they could hold on, they might actually win this one.

After Westview's kickoff return, Shiloh's defensive unit prepared to take the field. David could feel anticipation all around. It filled the warm September night, like one of those high-pressure storm cells on the weather reports.

"We've got this game," Grant told the players. "Stay tough out there."

"Let's surprise 'em, Coach," Brady said. "Let's keep 'em guessing."

"What've you got in mind?"

"Let's blitz 'em on first down."

"Now?"

"I can feel it. Let's just try it, on this series of downs at least."

Grant nodded. "All right."

"You hear that?" Brady huddled his defense. "Let's put some hurt on these boys, make 'em think twice every time they snap the ball."

On subsequent plays, Brock Kelley plowed the Westview quarterback to the ground. The storm cell was gaining strength, and the lanky kid's composure started to crumble. Rattled by the lack of protection he was getting in the pocket, he began hurrying passes and scrambling from phantom shadows at his back.

During one of these plays, however, the Shiloh defense broke down, and he took advantage by dashing forward eighteen yards. The gamble had backfired, and Westview was into Eagle territory.

Not again. David watched from the side. *We can't lose this one.*

"Stay on your toes!" Brady yelled. "Watch for them to air it out."

Brock nodded and relayed the message to his guys. They lined up, showing blitz again, but this time the linebackers fell back to defend the middle.

FACING THE GIANTS

Westview's quarterback stood in the pocket, saw all his short routes covered, then cocked his arm and let one fly. The ball spiraled through the air, arching downfield toward a receiver who had head-faked the cornerback. The pass was a little behind him, but he had good separation and went up high for it. Fingers scraped over leather and threads, bobbling the reception.

David stood on his toes and watched the ball hang there.

Still aloft. Floating in the stadium lights.

Spectators gasped.

Robert Catt was playing safety for Shiloh. Wearing number 81, Bobcat rushed into position for an interception, juggled the pigskin, then tucked it and headed upfield.

Eight plays later, Zach Avery faked a handoff and waited for his offensive line to pull to the right, before sweeping around the left for an uncontested touchdown. The stands exploded in celebration.

"You see that, David?" J.T. said. "Yeah, that's what I'm talkin' about!"

The coaches slapped hands. Players clapped one another on the back.

Westview's final attempt to make something happen was stopped short by a bone-crushing hit by Matt Prater. In a gesture of good sportsmanship, he helped the yellow-helmeted fullback to his feet, but between the whistles there were no gestures of mercy.

This was football. This was war.

And the Eagles were on their way to a 17-7 victory.

David smiled. He'd played on strong soccer teams, so he knew what it was like to win, but this was a whole different atmosphere. The energy, the raw emotion, and the exuberance from the crowd . . .

Okay, maybe I'm glad I tried out.

He could just imagine what the local sports columnist would have to say about this. The Eagles had been pushed out of the nest and found their wings.

Collecting his stuff, David followed Jonathan toward the locker room. In a half hour, he and his father would be meeting Amanda and her parents at Pizza Hut. His dad had even encouraged it.

A voice stopped him. "David."

"Yes, sir?"

"Listen, you be ready next game." Grant set a hand on his shoulder. "You're gonna drill one through. You've got it in you, I believe that."

"Okay."

"Do *you* believe it?"

"I, uh . . ."

Whispers filled David's ears again. What about his size? His inexperience? Then his dad's words broke through, reminding him that his actions would always follow his beliefs. Anyway, if he had the courage to eat stringy cheese pizza in front of a girl he liked, then he could do just about anything, couldn't he?

"Yes, Coach," he said. "It's goin' right down the middle."

LARRY

Larry Childers wheeled himself into Pizza Hut and moved aside a chair so he could fit at the table. Diners watched from the corners of their eyes. This had been one of Larry's rough days, but he refused to let the pain take center stage.

Tonight's about my son. I can make it through this.

David sat beside him, and they introduced themselves to Amanda and her parents. An awkward silence followed. No wonder

David had been so jittery in the van. Of course, children were always embarrassed to have their parents around in these situations, but they never realized how uncomfortable it was for good ol' Mom and Dad.

Sure wish you were here to share this with me, honey. Larry glanced over. *Our little boy's turning into a man before my eyes.*

"Are y'all ready to order?"

"Give us another minute," Amanda's father told the server.

"Would you like me to start you off with some drinks?" she inquired. She went around the table, fielding their requests. David and Amanda exchanged shy looks. When the server came to Larry, she lowered the volume of her voice. "And for you, sir?"

"A Coke."

"Be back in a few minutes. Thank you."

"You get that a lot, Larry?" Amanda's father asked.

"What?"

"Them treating you like you're deaf or . . ."

"Slow in the head?"

"Yes."

Larry nodded. "Oh, there's no doubt that you see things differently from the perspective of this chair. Seems most of us just don't know how to relate to those who aren't like us."

"Well, if that ain't the truth," Amanda's mother responded. "We can see that right here at this table, between our two youngest diners."

"Mom!" Amanda blurted out.

"She's right," David said. "I don't even know what to say."

"See there, Amanda. You're not the only one."

"Mom, please."

Larry felt sorry for the girl. She had pretty eyes and a round face with high cheekbones, but those cheeks were now glowing red. He said, "I bet you two would rather go play video games than listen to a bunch of old people talk." He turned to Amanda's parents. "If, of course, that's okay with you folks."

"Fine by us," the father said.

"You got some money on you, son?"

"Yeah. Thanks, Dad."

Amanda stood and nudged David. "Hope you don't mind getting beat."

"By a girl?"

"Are you already scared?"

Larry watched them walk away, arms brushing, and he felt something twist inside him. He'd raised this child from birth, taught and guided and befriended him. Until now, Larry Childers had never faced the fact that one day he would be living in an empty nest.

CHAPTER 26
The Wildcats

BROCK

In Monday's health class, Brock was still feeling bone-tired and sore. But this was a different kind of sore. These bruises meant they had won a ball game. These were battlefield wounds, to be worn with pride.

The funny thing was, his mind seemed more alert than ever. He'd been going to bed earlier, getting up more rested. No more PlayStation sessions till one or two in the morning.

Brock scanned through his workbook, then marked an answer on his sheet. He tapped his knuckles on his desk. "Matt."

His friend looked up.

"You and me, Saturday," he mouthed. "A Madden rematch."

Matt nodded, then turned back to his work.

Brock put his pencil in his mouth and skimmed down another page. As he filled in more answers, the teacher came down the aisle in a red sweater and glasses. She was distributing last week's tests.

His paper landed on the desk, and he stared down at his results.

A perfect score?

Sure, health class was one of his easier ones, but he'd never done that in here. School had always been a challenge for him, and his parents would stinkin' keel over when he dropped this one in their laps. As for his teacher, she must be in a state of shock.

Brock glanced to his right. Toggled his eyebrows and grinned.

"What?" Matt whispered.

He couldn't resist showing this one off. He poked a finger at his A+. Oh, yeah, he was firing on all cylinders now. Reading assignments, pop quizzes, worksheets . . . He'd take whatever they threw his direction.

After the Mighty Crawl of Death, this stuff was a breeze.

MATT

Matt stared at the chalkboard. What did all that gibberish mean?

"*Fractions.*" "*Algebra.*" "*Rational Approximations to the Square Foot.*"

Standing at the front, one of his teammates was working on a problem. To the right, the redheaded class genius was solving his own. Matt was happy that Brock had scored high in health—good for him—but this math stuff was on a whole other level.

Go, Bobcat. You can do this.

To everyone's surprise, Robert Catt circled his answer first and sauntered back to his desk, tossing his marker to Mrs. Carter on his way. She caught it, shot him a look, then glanced back to the solution on the board: *6.773.*

The redheaded kid peeked over. Did a double take. In stunned silence, Mrs. Carter and Genius Boy turned and watched Bobcat settle into his seat.

Matt felt a grin spread across his face. He figured if his teammate could do it, he could too. The next time the teacher called for a volunteer, he'd pop up his hand and face this challenge head-on.

And if she didn't call on him, fine. He'd rather be back out on the gridiron anyway. Practice was only a few hours from now.

GRANT

Grant was at his locker room desk, reading a collection of Vance Havner sermons, when he got the call from his wife.

"Hey, Brooke."

"Hey."

"I know you're the one who called, but you got a minute?"

"Uh . . . Okay."

Grant figured if J.T. could run offensive drills based on biblical concepts, then he could pull off a defensive one.

"Listen." The idea gushed from his mouth. "You know the story of Nehemiah, right? He wanted to rebuild the walls of Jerusalem, to protect the city from further destruction, but all the people did was gripe and complain about helping him. Well, eventually he overcame their fears by praying, coming up with a plan, and then putting his faith into action."

"Yeah?"

"I think I can apply this to football." He filled her in with the details. "I'm gonna present it to the team this afternoon. Whaddya think?"

"Sounds great, Grant."

"You really think so?"

"I do, but . . ."

"But what?"

"Right now, we need to worry about fixin' a leaky roof."

Grant grabbed his head. "Oh, I even picked up the supplies. I just forgot."

"You've been busy."

"That's no excuse. One good rain, and we'll be sleeping in a water bed."

"Might be romantic," Brooke purred.

He liked this playful side of his wife. After his medical results, they'd gone through a tense period, but their friendship was stronger than the obstacles between them. In some ways, their relationship seemed freer now that the pressure to get pregnant was off.

"Where'd you put the stuff?" Brooke asked. "I can get to work on it."

"Stop it."

"Just offerin'."

"Sweetheart, that's a job that should be done with a spotter. We'll work on it when I get home from practice tonight. Should still be plenty of daylight."

"Should be."

"Why'd you call, anyway?"

She paused. "Have you had lunch yet?"

"No, I've been writing this stuff down. Why? You got some time off from the shop?"

"Enough."

Grant felt his heart rate pick up. "Enough?"

BROCK

Brock downed a cup of cold water. Nothing tasted better after a tough practice surrounded by dirt, sweat, and gnats. "Thanks, Stanley."

"You want more?"

"I'm good."

"Two-thirds of the human body is composed of H_2O, so it's important to keep hydrated."

"Had three cups already."

Stanley moved between the players, dragging his big blue

watercooler and a stack of cups. Although clouds blocked out the sun, they only seemed to hold down the humidity, like a lid on a boiling pot. Most of the guys were dripping with sweat and breathing hard.

From across the field, Grant strode toward them in his red cap and athletic director's shirt. He seemed upbeat, energetic. Even whistling. He clapped his hands once and huddled the team around.

"Coach, whatcha got for us?" J.T. inquired.

"This one's especially for the defense."

"That's me and my boys," Brady said. "Give it to us."

Brock was fine with this, so long as it didn't mean crawling from end zone to end zone again. He'd been there, done that.

"In the Old Testament," Grant said, "Nehemiah had the task of building a stone wall around his city for protection. But he didn't have enough people, or resources, or time. But because each person worked on the stone wall that was in front of their house, they got it done in record time. That's what you're gonna do. On defense, you have to resolve nothing gets by you as an individual. Nothing gets by us as a team. I need you to build me a stone wall."

Oh, yeah, Brock thought. *We can make that work.*

GRANT

Grant paced the sideline, slapping players on their helmets. The season's fifth game pitted them against the Walker Jennings Wildcats. It was an afternoon skirmish. The early October air was still sticky. There were fewer fans than usual, but he could see in his kids' expressions they were ready to play.

C'mon, he thought. *Let's make this two in a row.*

The Wildcats took the field in gold pants, with navy jerseys and helmets. They'd won three of their first four games, with sights set on a play-off run. Judging by their swagger, they considered the lowly Eagles an easy addition to their win column.

The first drive of the game proved them wrong.

"Nothing gets by us!" Brock shouted at his teammates. "Nothing!"

Facing a long third down, the Wildcats quarterback dropped back for a pass. He looked poised, ready to make a big play, but Bobcat flew around a defender and ambushed the QB from his blind side.

"Whooo!" Brady jumped into the air. "Good hustle, defense."

Walker Jennings had to punt, but their kicker was goofing around on the bench and nearly cost them a delay-of-game penalty. He hadn't expected to be called into duty so early.

Or so often.

Grant watched his team swarm to the ball, holding their opponents to only four first downs in the first half. The Eagles were gaining some momentum. A fierce pass rush rocked the Wildcats on their heels, and a blocked field goal held them scoreless until late in the third period.

The stone wall was beginning to solidify.

Offensively, Zach Avery showed better decision-making, but the Eagles failed to convert many of their long drives into points. At least their time of possession was wearing down the Wildcats, softening their front line until bigger gaps started opening for Shiloh's backfield.

A key third-and-one play came up.

Grant called a time-out. "We're tied, with less than six minutes left. This is where we take charge. They expect us to run the ball, so let's catch them off guard."

FACING THE GIANTS

Zach showed no hesitation. He took the snap, dropped back five steps, and lobbed a beautiful pass into the flat. The receiver, Number 34, went up for a sure-handed, big-time play.

With two minutes left, the Eagles scored their second touchdown.

Final score: 14-7.

CHAPTER 27
White Wristbands

GRANT

Grant strolled into the teachers' lounge to grab a drink from the corner machine. Most days, he avoided this place. This was where the women gathered to talk about hairstyles, bargain buys, and nutrition.

All he ever wanted was a Coke.

Today seemed no different. On the small sofa, Mrs. Carter sat with legs crossed, cradling a cup of coffee. At a table, three other female teachers nursed drinks and fiddled with items from a basket of snacks.

Rush in, rush out, and don't get involved.

"I'm just amazed at what's going on around here," Mrs. Carter said.

"Oh, it's unbelievable," Miss Murdoch agreed.

Grant pushed coins into the slot, while eyeing the goodies in the teachers' midst. Was he allowed to take one? As a coach he liked to establish parameters, but he'd never been able to figure out the rules of this lounge.

Miss Murdoch continued. "I have not had a problem out of any of them these past two weeks." She pointed her finger. "And you know, not a sarcastic comment either."

"It's like we're teaching at a different school," Miss Hall said.

He heard his Coke drop into the slot. He was untwisting the cap when his own name was spoken.

"Grant."

Oh, no. He turned toward the voice. *So much for a quick exit.*

Mrs. Dillon was wearing a denim dress and a pearl necklace. Her tone was almost accusatory. "What're you doing with those football players?"

"Whaddya mean?" He noticed a stray piece of candy on the table.

"I mean, Matt Prater and Robert Catt got the highest grades on their history exams yesterday."

"Huh. Bobcat got the highest grade?"

"A 98."

"You know," he pointed out, "we are a Christian school. Shouldn't we expect miracles every now and then?"

Nobody laughed. Not even a giggle.

Tough crowd, he told himself. *Time to make my getaway—with that stray candy in hand, if possible.*

"Grant, you must be doing something right." Mrs. Dillon picked up the goody and began unwrapping it. "If their attitudes weren't so much better, I'd bet the farm they were cheating." She slipped the candy into her mouth.

Treasure stolen.

"Well," Mrs. Carter said, "Missy Claxton is sure upset about all this."

"Why?" Grant asked.

"Because three of your defensive linemen are competing with her for the highest average in chemistry."

"Wow." He shot her a look. "Did you say *three*?"

"You heard correctly."

"Wow."

He fiddled with the Coke bottle cap. What was wrong with

him? While these teachers praised the changes in his boys, he was fixating on sugar. Of course, he deserved no glory for the things that'd happened. God had moved in the students' lives, and they were the ones doing the class work. If anything, Grant needed to get on his knees and give credit where credit was due.

"It's like they're different kids now," Miss Murdoch noted.

"Well, you get your focus right," he said, heading from the lounge, "and everything else seems to fall into place, doesn't it?"

Miss Murdoch's voice followed him out the door: "I am *tellin'* you."

He rounded a hallway corner and spotted venerable Mr. Bridges, gold-leaf Bible in hand. That was no surprise. What was surprising was the image of a muscular teenager engaging the gray-haired gentleman in conversation.

Was that Brock Kelley?

BROCK

Brock's brain was tired, but he was ready for practice. The physical and mental challenge sparked something in him—a rush of testosterone, a will to overcome. The harder he was pushed, the deeper he dug down.

A man's gotta endure to the end. That's what the old guy told me.

In the locker room, he pulled on thigh, hip, and shoulder pads. Laced up his football pants. Pulled on size 13 Riddell cleats.

The white wristbands were his finishing touch.

Matt pointed. "Hey, man, what's that say?"

"What?"

"Your wristbands. Looks like you wrote something on 'em."

"Maybe."

"I'm your friend. What? You can't tell me?"

"It's my own little reminder, okay? Just drop it."

"How 'bout this?" Matt punched him in the arm. "I get more tackles than you against the Generals, and you have to tell me."

Brock smirked. "No problem."

After jumping jacks, hurdler stretches, and push-ups, the team formed rows on the grass. Following Coach Taylor's pointing finger, they shuffled sideways with arms lifted, churning their feet up and down in rapid succession. With each whistle-blow, they switched directions.

Blocking drills followed, with players driving low and hard into the sleds. Once they reached a certain point, they veered to the side and smashed into guys holding Eagles cushions. Next, they took a handoff from Coach and rushed through spring-loaded pads, tucking the football, training themselves to resist opponents who wanted to strip the ball away.

"Turnovers can be backbreakers. Grip that leather," Grant told them. "No changing hands, not unless the ball's pressed into your rib cage."

Brock wedged the pigskin between his hand, forearm, and gut. He charged between the pads, envisioning his own touchdown off a forced fumble.

"Let's go, let's go!" J.T. cheered him on, clapping. "Run through there like you just stole something. Come on now."

Oh, I'm not through. Not even close!

He faced Brady's chiding next. While he threw blocks at padded dummies, the assistant coach shouted in his ear. "Come on, Brock. Hit somebody, son! I wanna see some hittin'. I wanna see some hittin'. Dig those feet. Come on, you ain't on my team yet! You're not on my defense. You gotta dig those feet."

Brock completed the drill and slapped Matt's hand.

His friend dived forward.

"All right, Prater," Brady goaded. "Get in there, boy. Let's go. Hit 'em. Hit 'em, son! You gotta hit 'em a little harder than that. All right, this ain't *ballet* practice. This is football practice."

Brock grinned. Where did Coach Owens come up with this stuff?

"That's not a miniskirt," Brady carried on. "Those are *football* pants! You gotta dig in, Prater. Dig in! Or the Generals are gonna come in here, slap you around, and call you Susan!"

"Man," said J.T. "Why you talkin' like that, Brady? Like you some drill sergeant."

"I'm a defensive coordinator."

"You a wannabe comedian. We'll see who's laughin', come gametime."

Coach Taylor threw a ball to one of his players, oblivious to the movement behind him. The friendly rivalry between his assistants had raised the players' intensity on the practice field, but now it was spilling over onto the sidelines. Big ol' Brady rumbled toward J.T., launched forward, and brought him to the ground. Both men moaned. Then, chuckling, they bounced back to their feet. J.T. cracked his neck once, repositioned his cap, and chased Brady the other direction.

"You think he can tackle him?" Matt asked.

"Oh, yeah," Brock said. "Coach Owens is gonna eat it."

Grant finally realized what was going on. He turned in time to see J.T. drag the larger man down. He just shook his head and smiled.

"Hey, I think that's your dad." Shading his eyes, Brock gestured toward the stands where Neil Prater sat, with sunglasses on a cord around his neck.

"Yeah, he said he might take off early to come watch us."

"I thought he was a real hardnose about his job."

"He was. Still is, I guess. He just, uh . . . said this was more important."

"That's cool."

"Yeah." Matt shoved Brock toward the field. "C'mon, let's go show him the kinda pansy tackler you are. Friday, I'm gonna find out what you got written on those wristbands."

"No. Now you're just dreaming."

CHAPTER 28
Is That All?

DAVID

The glare of the Friday night lights got David's blood pumping. He could see bugs and dust churning high above. He could feel the beams' growing intensity as he moved across the track toward the turf. Fresh chalk measured the battlefield in increments.

"See you after the game," Larry Childers called.

"Thanks, Dad."

"I want you to go out there with your head up, you hear me?"

"Yes, sir."

The Eagles were hosting the Generals. The crowd was bigger than last Friday's, gathered after a long workweek to cheer along sons, students, and friends. Amanda was here also, ready to help lead the chants.

This could get Shiloh back to even. The .500 mark.

"One game at a time," Grant told the guys before kickoff. "Don't think about our record, or your stats, or the people in the bleachers. You think about this game. You focus on each play. That's how we're gonna climb outta the basement, one step at a time. Starting *tonight*."

The Eagles began their first offensive effort from the thirty-two-yard line. David stood by his coaches, intent on the game. Two plays straight up the middle gave them a first down at the center of the field. Fans were on their feet, energized by the cries of the cheerleaders.

But the Generals had come to fight.

After a seesawing effort from both sides, half time arrived with the home team trailing 7 to 10.

The Generals received the ball to start the third quarter. They came out fired up, attempting to tear down the Eagles. Teeth-grinding runs were followed by option plays and short screen passes. They drove the ball from the twenty on one end to the twelve-yard line on the other, eating up over seven minutes on the clock.

Even from his place on the side, David could see the look of determination that passed between Brock Kelley and Matt Prater. Those were two boys he'd rather not tangle with. Sure, they might not be cut out for soccer, but they were tenacious and explosive on the gridiron.

The Generals set up over the ball.

"Hold 'em!" David yelled.

In silver pants and helmet, the quarterback faked a handoff and followed his fullback through an off-tackle hole. He had it. He was going to score. Out of nowhere, Matt sidestepped an opponent and threw himself forward, bringing down the QB. But there was no whistle.

Seconds later, a referee threw his hands into the air, signaling a touchdown. The quarterback had lateralled the ball before hitting the grass, and his halfback had carried it across the goal line.

Shiloh Christian Academy was now behind 7 to 17.

It's not over till it's over, David thought. *One step at a time.*

While they failed to make anything happen on their next attempt, they kept fighting hard on defense, forming their stone wall.

The Generals punted. An Eagle caught the ball, waited for his wall of blockers to form, then followed them upfield. A seam opened and he dashed through, leaving defenders in his wake.

With one quarter remaining, Shiloh had cut the lead to three.

Nine minutes later, Zach passed to Number 11 on second down. Silver helmets surrounded him, but he broke a tackle and churned forward. Grant and J.T. were jumping up and down on the sideline.

"Don't stop!" David waved his hands. "Keep going, keep going!"

On the next play, Zach found a receiver in the corner of the end zone. "We've got the lead?" Brady was incredulous. "Woooo!"

J.T. stared at him. "What'd you expect? We came here to win."

"That's right," Grant said. "But there's still plenty of time on the clock, and we're only ahead by three. We need this extra point to keep them from being able to tie it up with a field goal."

"Coach, I got this one."

The trio of coaches turned toward David.

Did I let that slip outta my own mouth?

He put on his helmet. "I can do it."

"I know you can." Grant slapped him on the back. "Get out there."

David trotted across the turf, heart hammering against his chest. Although Jonathan looked up in the huddle, no words were exchanged. The fact he'd met David's eyes said enough: he believed.

Both teams faced off. Jonathan crouched down, ready to tee it up.

Just like I'm kickin' it against the barn. No problem.

"David. David!"

He glanced over and saw his father at the foot of the bleachers, nodding, both arms raised, signaling his faith that his son would make it. That was all David needed. He turned back. In the glow of the lights, he watched everything come into focus—the ball shooting into Jonathan's hands, its threads spinning around, and its nose touching the ground.

He stepped up and swung his leg all the way through. He raised his fists as the ball split the uprights. From the wheelchair, Larry clenched his fists too. Jonathan lifted David up as Eagles mobbed him with congratulations.

Within minutes they'd won their third in a row, 21-17.

Amid whoops and hollers, the team followed their coaches into the locker room. Grant wiped off the chalkboard with wide sweeps of his eraser, then wrote, *Wins: 3, Losses: 3.*

"We're all even, guys. This is a fresh start!"

BOBBY LEE DUKE

At the wheel of his slate-gray Hummer, Coach Bobby Lee Duke drove into the gated community he shared with other local luminaries. He'd made a good income while tag-team wrestling, yet still saw himself as one of the working class. A regular joe.

He rubbed a hand over his buzz-cut hair and smiled. Tonight, his Richland Giants had played an away game against a fierce rival. After a close first half, the Giants had overpowered their opponents by seventeen points.

"Should be smooth sailin' from here, boys," he said aloud.

They'd won six in a row, with their toughest foes now behind them.

He pressed the remote and watched his garage door retract. Headlights splashed over a weight set, barbells, and an old "Destruction, Inc." poster. His younger image peered at him from the wall.

Ah, those were the good ol' days.

Before two botched marriages, a rocky relationship with his son in college, and a rotator cuff injury that'd cut short his career in the ring.

He parked, disengaged the house alarm, and went inside to his gleaming refrigerator. With an energy drink in hand, he plopped down on the brushed leather couch and turned on his HDTV. He'd TiVo-ed the Georgia Sports Break, hoping to hear their assessment of his team's performance.

But something was wrong.

The sportscaster was talking to a normal-looking guy in a red baseball cap. Text along the bottom of the screen said the Shiloh Eagles had won three straight games.

"Is that all?" Bobby Lee pointed at the TV. "Who is this guy?"

With no one to answer him in his five-bedroom house, he turned up the volume and listened to that dark-haired female sports anchor.

Lisa. Or is it Felicia?

He could never keep her name straight.

CHAPTER 29
Something Wrong

MATT

"Hello?"

Although Matt Prater heard his teacher's voice, his thoughts were on other things. He couldn't believe Brock Kelley had out-tackled him last Friday night—according to Stanley's stats—and that meant he still had no clue what was written on his friend's wristbands.

Of course, with three wins in a row he wasn't gonna complain. Like Coach Taylor said, it was a team effort.

"Matt?"

"Uh." He blinked. "Yes, Mrs. Carter?"

"Are you tapping your fingers to get my attention?" She put one hand on her hip. "Or are you simply hoping for a turn at the board?"

A few days ago he'd hoped for that very thing, to prove he could master ratios and fractions and all that. His resolve melted now, though, under her searing glare. Not only was he worn-out from football, he'd been up till one in the morning trying to wrap his head around his latest math homework. Wasn't it good enough that he'd turned in the assignment on time?

"Sorry," he said, halting his rhythmic taps on the desk. He lowered his head and kept his mouth shut. Maybe she'd forget about him. Or spot a student passing notes. Or someone listening to an iPod, with hidden earbuds.

The classroom door clicked open.

"Matthew," said Mrs. Carter. "Your father's here to see you."

In the middle of a school day?

His head snapped up. Sure enough, Neil Prater stood in the doorway, dressed in slacks and a casual shirt, with a pager clinging to his belt.

"Dad?"

"Let's go," Neil said. "I already got Ryker's permission."

"Why?" Matt blurted out.

It was his default response—questioning everything, creating enough friction that his father would just leave him alone. But it seemed crazy. He'd wanted things to change, and now that they had, wasn't it immature to stick to his old way of handling things?

Lord, help me here. I'm still learnin'.

"Sorry, Dad." Matt gathered his books.

"We don't have a lotta time."

"Is something wrong?" he asked as they marched down the hall.

"Guess you could say that."

Matt's throat tightened. "Is it Mom?"

"No, no, nothing like that. Last I heard, your mother was fine."

"So, what's this all about?"

His dad grinned. "We're going shopping, Matt."

"Shopping? Like, at a store? Man, something really *is* wrong."

GRANT

Grant twisted the plastic rod, shutting his office blinds. The mid October sun was still capable of turning this space into a cooker, and he'd learned to take precautions.

He rocked back in his chair, hands clasped behind his neck. *An ice-cold drink would be perfect right now.*

He stepped out of his office. Headed toward the teachers' lounge, he spotted Mr. Bridges in the hallway, faithful as always, praying for God's intervention in the students' lives.

God, give me a burden to pray like that.

Looking up, the old man made eye contact with Grant, smiled, and walked toward him. Grant met him halfway.

"Grant, how are you?"

"I'm fine, thanks. Good to see someone still covering this school in prayer."

"And it's good to see the right man still coachin' these boys."

Grant smiled. "Well, I don't know if I'm the right man, but I'm sure tryin'."

"You are the right man. I've believed it since I first met you at the Sonic over six years ago."

"Sonic?"

"On North Westover," Bridges responded. "I took your order over the speaker. You said you were the new coach at Shiloh, and you'd just arrived in town."

Grant tilted his head. "Sonic? Are you sure?"

"I've been working there part-time for years, flippin' burgers, watching and praying over all the kids who come by after school. It was my daughter who pointed me to Christ. I'm tellin' you, I was the worst of the worst. A drunkard with a bad reputation. One Easter, she nagged me into going to church with her and her mother, so I went. Just to get them off my back, I reckon. And Jesus met me there in that place. I haven't been the same since."

"So that was you, huh? At the drive-in? I would've never guessed."

"It was me. My prayer is that God'll use the students of this school to have an impact on the lives of others. Just like my daughter did for me."

"Where is she now?"

"You mean Grace?" Bridges pointed down the hall. "Room 118."

"Grace? As in, uh . . . Mrs. Carter, she's your daughter?"

The older man nodded with a smile.

"No one's ever told me."

"Maybe you never asked."

MATT

It wasn't until a few hours later, back in the SCA parking lot, that Matt Prater understood his father's entire plan. With the dismissal bell only forty-five minutes away, buses and cars would soon be lining up out front. They would have to act quickly.

"You sure about this, Dad?"

"I'm sure."

"We won't get in trouble for . . ."

"What? For stealing?" Neil Prater chuckled. "C'mon, jump in and steer while I push."

Matt followed his father's orders, settling into the seat of an old junker. He shifted into neutral, let off the e-brake. Neil pushed against the front grille as Matt looked back over his shoulder and guided the vehicle behind the cover of some trees and kudzu vines.

"You mind if I do the second part?" Matt requested.

His dad tossed him a set of keys. "I'd have it no other way."

J.T.

J.T. was shaking his head. See, this was just as he expected. He'd rattled off a whole list of new plays for Coach Taylor, but Grant showed only passing interest. Clearly, the man's mind was on other things.

"You even heard a word I've said?"

"Sure, J.T. You need me to give you a ride home."

"Yeah, my van's in the shop. I appreciate that, I do. But what I'm talkin' about is these plays. If we keep on winning, we could be goin' to the play-offs." J.T. followed his head coach through the school doors. "That's where these'd come in handy, 'cause ain't nobody expecting 'em."

As they headed for the parking lot, J.T. saw Grant glancing at the notebook opened in his hands. J.T. read from his own list, trying to push the issue. "Double Sweep Pitch Left. Pro 45 Flex. Man, even a 26 Powerhouse . . . Man, these some good plays. When we gonna run these plays, Grant?"

"We're gonna run 'em."

"Man, we got all type of potential on this sheet. When?"

They moved from beneath an overhang, and J.T. saw a glistening red Ford pickup angled along the curb. The thing was taking up two full spaces. Now why did people think that buying themselves some fancy ride meant they got the parking spots to go with it?

Grant was walking ahead. "We're gonna run them. I promise."

"Yeah. See, you always tell me you gonna run 'em," said J.T. "See all my plays? You don't *wanna* run my plays."

"Hey!"

"It's all right," he grumbled. "You don't wanna—"

"Where's my car?" Grant demanded.

J.T. looked up, wondering if this wasn't an intentional diversion from the topic at hand. The lot *was* empty, though, in both directions. He said, "Where'd you park it?"

"Right here."

"You sure? 'Cause there ain't no way it got stolen. Man, you couldn't *pay* nobody to steal your car."

"Did the boys do something with it?"

"I don't know." From the driver's door of the red Ford F150, a sheet of paper flapped in the breeze. "Hey man, there's a note on this truck for you."

"What does it say?"

J.T. smoothed out the paper as Coach came alongside. "Let's see. Says, 'Grant Taylor, the impact you've made on our school means more to us than you'll ever know. The Lord has used you to meet a need in our lives, and now we want to meet a need in yours. You'll find the title of this new truck in your name. Please accept it as our way of saying thank you.'"

Grant looked at the Ford. Looked back. Snatched the note from J.T.

"Nuh-uh," J.T. said. "Somebody done gave you a *truck*?"

Grant stared down at the note in a daze.

J.T. cupped his hands to the window and peeked into the cab, then tried the door handle. It was open. Keys dangled from the ignition, and another paper sat on the driver's seat.

"Man," he said, "this title got *your* name on it."

Grant dropped his notebook to the ground.

"You got to be kiddin' me." J.T. moved to the front of the vehicle, where he saw a plate advertising Jay Austin Motors. He'd seen the dealer in the news a few years back. The place had a good reputation. "Grant Taylor, somebody done gave you a new truck."

"This is my truck?" Grant mouthed in shock.

"When it rains, it pours—that's what my mama always told me. And I'd say God been pourin' it down on *you* this year. Pourin' it down good."

Although Grant's mouth moved, no words came out. He stepped closer and began circling the pickup, running his hand over the waxed paint job.

"Is this just 'cause you head coach?" J.T. said. "'Cause I'm assistant coach. You'd think I'd get a *moped* outta this or *something.*"

Grant completed his inspection. He pulled his hand over his hair, his eyes filling with moisture. "Oh, Lord, You've given me a truck."

"Whatcha think I been tellin' you? Well, it's your truck. Drive it."

Grant climbed in. Fired it up. Pulled forward.

"Tha's right. No more jumper cables." J.T. watched the vehicle pass by and begin to accelerate. It was nice to see his friend being blessed for his dedication to the school. Grant was a good guy. He was . . .

"Hey!" J.T. yelled. "Wait up, Grant. You my ride!"

MATT

From the shelter of draping foliage, Matt sat beside his father in their SUV and watched the entire scene play out. He was wearing a wide grin.

"Not a word to anyone," his dad said.

Matt nodded. "Yes, sir."

192

BROOKE

Brooke closed the oven door and stood to listen.

Who was that pulling into their driveway? Jackie? No. The engine sounded lower, deeper. Maybe one of the neighbors? A few weeks ago, a man had dropped by to say he had an animal loose in their orchard.

And what a sight we must've been. It still made her giggle. *Grown adults trying to corral a frisky goat.*

A horn sounded outside.

"What now?"

Brooke tossed her pot holder onto the counter and went to the front door. Through the glass, she noticed a polished red truck. She had no idea who that belonged to, and she could see nothing behind the windshield's glare.

She stepped outside. Gave a tentative wave. "Hello?"

The engine turned off and the driver's door opened. Out came her husband, wearing a grim expression. He looked her in the eye.

"Grant, what's wrong? Did the car die again?"

"That thing's gone for good."

"Well, whose truck is this? Guess it was nice of them to help you out."

"Very nice," Grant said. "Very, very nice."

She tilted her head and pushed blonde strands back over her ear. "What're you sayin'? Are you gonna tell me who the owner is?"

"Here." He handed her an official-looking document. "See for yourself."

DAVID

"What?" David sat up in the recliner. "A brand-new truck?"

"That's what I heard," Amanda said through the phone. "It was just waiting out there in the parking lot after school. He found the papers in his name, all paid up and everything."

From the kitchen, his father called to him. "Son, it's time to finish up your conversation. Dinner's ready."

"Okay. Almost done."

"You have to go?" Amanda asked.

"Yeah, we're having green-bean casserole. Blah."

"I like that stuff."

"Are you kiddin'?"

"My grandma makes it the best. I'm sure we'll be having some at Thanksgiving, so if you wanna come over . . ."

"Oooh," he said. "No thanks. I mean, uh . . . that's not what I meant. I'd wanna be there, yeah. I just wouldn't want the green beans."

Amanda laughed.

The first time David had called her, he'd had no idea what to say. What did girls like to talk about? Clothes and makeup? Their Facebook accounts? He was more into sports and classic survival stories.

Amanda surprised him, though. He'd already seen her boisterous side at football games when she was part of a group choreography, but one-on-one she was fairly soft-spoken.

Was she nervous too? He'd never even considered that.

"David."

"Coming, Dad." He cleared his throat. "I gotta go, Amanda. So, you think it'll work?"

"The idea I told you? Yeah, as long as we don't get caught."

"I'll be careful."

"See you at school. And remember, don't tell anyone."

"I won't."

Larry rolled into view with a dinner tray, and David hit the End button. He followed his father to the coffee table and dropped onto the couch. They ate here often, sometimes over a game of Scrabble or Yahtzee.

Between nibbles from a mound of casserole, he told his dad about the latest development at Shiloh Christian.

"A brand-new truck?" Larry said. "That's incredible. And he doesn't know who gave it to him?"

"He said whoever did it paid for it in his name. I think he deserves it."

"Well, I think the Lord is blessing him for the way he's leading the team."

David speared a green bean. "Dad, do you ever worry about the future?"

"In what way?"

"Well." He pushed the bean around the plate. "What if your MS gets worse?"

"It might. But that's okay."

"It's okay?"

"Oh, I'm not saying I'll like it. It's already getting harder every year."

"Have the doctors said anything?"

"They don't really know. It's just different for everyone."

"I think you deal with it better than most other people."

"I used to get so frustrated," Larry confessed. "But you know, in some ways it's been a blessing. I believe I'm closer to the Lord and in a position to touch people's lives because I'm sittin' in this chair."

"So, you've accepted it?"

"I won't lie to you, son. I'd still love to stand and walk around, but whatever situation He wants me in, to make the biggest impact, that's where I wanna be."

David took a bite of his meal. With the things that had been going on at the school, he'd been contemplating a lot. "You know," he said, "I wanna do something big. I mean, something significant."

"Why? To impress Amanda?"

"Ummm . . ."

"Significant things don't come through weak choices, David. Your motives have gotta be right, 'cause I guarantee you they'll be tested. You can ask God for an opportunity to be used for His glory, but you better be ready to face some huge hurdles."

He weighed his father's words. He thought about his hours of kicking practice—the missed field goals, the sore legs. He asked, "Does there have to be hurdles?"

"Well, that's how He gets the glory. If it was easy, you'd do it on your own."

"Yeah, I guess."

"He's just looking for faith and obedience."

"You sound like Coach Taylor. He says we have to give God our best and leave the results up to Him."

"And what if you still lose, son?"

"You give God praise."

"That's right." Larry patted the armrests of the wheelchair. "That's the way I choose to see it."

CHAPTER 31
Number 00

MR. BRIDGES

This was Shiloh's year. Mr. Bridges could feel it in his bones. He was sitting in his den that Friday evening, preparing to listen to another radio broadcast, when he made his decision.

"I'm attendin' the games," he told his wife. "Ain't no two ways about it."

"What about your heart, Raymond? You're too old to be in those crowds."

"I'm too old *not* to be."

"Well, you do whatcha gotta," Martha said. "Never could change your mind about much."

"You helped point me to Christ."

"And you're all His." She huffed. "I'm done worryin'."

He slipped into his red Windbreaker and put on a pair of tennis shoes. With pad and pencil tucked into his pocket, he headed for the school. He would slip into the stands and try to remain calm, while basking in the emotions of those around him. Though his heart gave him occasional trouble, his eyesight was still good. He'd be a keen observer. A subdued spectator.

And for the next three weeks, that's exactly what he was.

From high in the bleachers, he chronicled the team's results on his notepad.

"Game seven: Shiloh vs. Ivey Grove . . ."

In solid blue helmets and pants, Ivey Grove looked sharp. The momentum teetered back and forth, a defensive chess match between tough ball clubs. With three minutes remaining, Shiloh clung to a 14 to 10 lead.

Ivey Grove set up for a big third-down play. If they earned a first down, they would have time to march it in for a game-winning score.

"Brock. Brock!" From the sidelines, Coach Taylor yelled at his lead tackler and pointed at the opposing halfback. "You watch him, you watch him!"

Number 54 nodded. Brock Kelley had made four sacks already, and displayed a true instinct for where the ball was going.

The play started, and Brock tracked the halfback as he took the handoff and turned downfield. Brock surged forward on powerful legs and hit the kid between the numbers. With arms wrapped around the ballcarrier, he hammered him into the earth.

Shiloh players and fans screamed with excitement, while the Ivey Grove halfback rolled on the ground, still shaken up.

Shiloh held on for the win: 14-10.

"Game eight: Shiloh vs. Eastland . . ."

Zach Avery put on an offensive showcase, drilling passes between defenders and lofting them over tight coverage. Number 81 reached the hundred-yard mark for receptions. On Bobcat's biggest catch, he turned, tucked the ball, faked one way so that his defender dived and missed, then spun the opposite direction. He waltzed unchallenged into the end zone.

The Shiloh assistant coaches ran the sideline, cheering. Coach Taylor held both fists in the air. Players banged helmets as the crowd celebrated.

But Zach wasn't done. He went on to complete eleven straight passes.

His final throw went to a fast black kid wearing number 23. He made the catch in the flat, dodged one tackler, and literally hurdled over the next. He went in for another six on the scoreboard. Joshua's extra-point kick was good.

With a final score of 24-13, the Eagles had won five in a row.

"Game nine: Shiloh vs. Gracey . . ."

Gracey was a small, athletic team. They matched up well against the Eagles' speed.

Yet they had no answer for Zach.

The quarterback continued his brilliance, flicking short passes over the middle and reading blitzes like a pro. In one critical series, while under pressure, he managed to zip a spiral pass over Jeremy Johnson's shoulder into waiting hands. The Gracey cornerback stretched out to break up a touchdown, but fell short and skidded across the turf.

On defense, Shiloh's stone wall mentality had spread from Brock Kelley and Matt Prater to the rest of the unit. Gracey snapped the ball, and Jonathan Weston wrestled against their noseguard. Breaking loose, he swung around and caught the opponent's quarterback from the blind side.

"Wooo! Wooo! Wooo!" Brady punctuated each yell with pumped fists. He threw down his hat. "Wooo! Wooo!"

Coach Taylor laughed, obviously enjoying the moment.

Brady marched up to him. "Woooooo!"

The head coach wore a smile as the seconds ticked away to a sixth straight victory.

"Game ten . . ."

Mr. Bridges was determined to be at Shiloh's last regular-season game. Earlier in the day, though, he'd felt minor chest pains, and his wife scolded him for even thinking of jumping into the pressure cooker of Georgia football.

Death and life, he told himself. *Nothing's stoppin' me.*

But the pain did stop him, before he'd even left the driveway. He sat in his vehicle, wincing as icy straps tightened around his ribs. The pressure was incredible. Slowly, the cold feeling turned into a numbness that spread from his chest, to his shoulder, and down through his arm.

My nitro. Where'd I put that stuff?

His fingers fumbled at his vest pocket, found the nitroglycerin pills, and shoved one between his lips. He sat back, eyes closed, and waited.

J.T.

J.T. ran fingers over his trimmed goatee and sighed. "Last game of the season, Coach. What we gonna do?"

"We're gonna win. That's the plan, isn't it?"

"No, Grant. I'm talkin' about Stanley. He's sittin' in that locker room, thinkin' he gonna play tonight. You remember, don'tcha? We said he could dress down, if he could find a piece of trivia for us . . ."

"The longest anyone's ever gone without talking."

"Tha's right."

"And he came up with an answer?"

"Yeah." J.T. crinkled up his mouth. "You believe that?"

Grant grinned. "C'mon. Let's go see what he has to say."

J.T. and Brady followed the head coach into the locker room. The team was gathered, tightening their laces, adjusting their helmet mouthpieces. And there was curly-haired Stanley, a gym bag in hand. J.T. had watched him fill the watercoolers, bring in towels and clean jerseys, and now the kid just wanted what he'd been promised: a chance to wear an Eagles uniform.

Why'd I ever come up with this? Kid's gonna get himself hurt.

"Stanley," Grant said. "You come ready to play tonight?"

"Yes, sir."

"First, we need to hear the answer to that trivia question."

"Lemme guess," Brady piped up. "The record belongs to a man."

"Incorrect," Stanley said. "Actually, a Miss Esposito went thirty-seven years, one hundred and eleven days without talking. She was in a coma."

"Nah. Thirty-seven years?" J.T. scoffed. "Man, that's a long time."

"It's not that long," Stanley said matter-of-factly. "If Shiloh's school files are accurate, you'll be thirty-seven next month."

Grant laughed out loud. "Wow."

"Hey, Coach, you the one goin' bald," J.T. shot back with a smile.

Grant was unfazed. "Sounds to me like we have an extra player tonight. I'll go clear it with the refs and the other coach. Exceptions have been made before, so I'm sure we won't have too much trouble."

"You wanna talk *trouble*? What position's he gonna play?"

"You tell me, J.T. He's part of *your* offense."

"Ohhh, no you didn't."

"You're a pretty big guy, aren't you, Stanley?" Grant asked.

"One hundred and eighty-two pounds. In kilograms, I believe that's—"

"Okay, okay," J.T. interrupted. "You wanna play, I'll let you play. We seen you cart those watercoolers around, and I bet you got a strong grip. One time, one down, we'll hand you the ball and you just hold on. You got that?"

"I got it, Coach." Stanley was beaming. "So what number am I?"

MR. BRIDGES

When his strength had returned, Mr. Bridges eased back into the house in hopes of still catching the opening kickoff on the radio. Martha was already snoring in their bedroom. That was good. He didn't want her fussing over him.

Not during gametime, anyway.

He set out his pad and pencil, then shuffled to the wooden cabinet in the corner of his den. He twisted the radio dial, but nothing happened.

"Don't fail me now, you persnickety thing."

He clicked it off and on again. The dial began to glow a lemon-yellow that warmed into egg-yolk gold.

After a brief whine, followed by a loud snap, the reception came in clearly. The announcers were right here, in his den, providing the details he'd been seeing in person the last three weeks.

Except for one.

"Shiloh's starting halfback goes out," the announcer said, "and in comes Number 00. This kid's nowhere to be found on our roster sheets, but we're told here in the press box that, uh, Stanley Gordon has been given a special waiver to play in tonight's game. On second and five, Zach Avery takes the snap. He hands off to Gordon, and the new kid lumbers forward for a gain of maybe a yard. Boy, judging by the fans' reaction, you would think they'd just scored a touchdown. They are ecstatic!"

Well, Stanley's a good kid. Bridges nodded. *Good for him.*

As expected, the football game came down to the wire. It was only in the last two minutes, with an onside kick and a hurry-up offense, that the Eagles eked out yet another victory.

Bridges clasped his hands together. "Thank You, Lord. Thank You."

Seven years after Coach Taylor first pulled into the Sonic Drive-In, Shiloh Christian Academy had a winning season.

The next day, Bridges picked up a copy of the *Albany Herald* and there was his own article, written under one of his pseudonyms. It was accompanied by a staff photo of Shiloh players kneeling on the field in prayer.

He used a pocketknife to cut out the section, which he then pinned beside the other clippings on a corkboard in his den.

The headline read *"Eagles Land in Play-Offs."*

CHAPTER 32
The Principal's Office

GRANT

Getting called to the principal's office was never a good thing, was it? Even as an adult, Grant wondered at the childlike fears it stirred in his stomach.

But I've got nothing to worry about, he told himself.

He had his first winning season under his belt. His team was going to the play-offs. The fact that Principal Ryker wanted to see him could mean something as innocuous as a question about the postseason schedule.

Grant smoothed his sweater. Adjusted his shirt collar. As he entered the reception area, he passed a blonde girl with a shoulder pack.

"Becka," he greeted her.

She nodded on her way out. One victim down. Would he be next?

Okay, stop it. Now you're just being silly.

"Hey, Sheila." He put his hands in his pockets.

"Grant." The receptionist looked up through her glasses. "How are you today?"

"Good. You?"

"I'm *so* excited about the play-offs. *Everybody's* talking about it."

Grant got a shy smile. "Well . . ."

"Let me get Mr. Ryker for you." She hit a button on the phone.

On the couch, another female student waited to face the principal. She bit her lip and fiddled with the sweatshirt on her lap. She was an SCA cheerleader, the one who seemed to have caught the eye of David Childers. She had a good reputation in the school. A nice girl, if not a bit feisty.

Was she in some sorta trouble?

Beside her, a statue showed an eagle in flight, with talons extended, as though it were about to snatch the poor girl away.

"Amanda."

"Hey, Coach."

The receptionist was speaking into the phone. "Mr. Ryker, he's here to see you . . . Okay." She addressed Grant. "You can go in now."

He glanced back at Amanda. "I'll try to warm him up for you."

She rested an elbow on the armrest and sighed.

Grant opened the door into the principal's inner sanctum and made an attempt at sounding casual, just two guys shooting the breeze. "Dan."

"Hey, Grant." Behind his desk, Ryker was selecting a book from his shelves. He turned to shake hands. "Good to see you. Have a seat."

"Thanks."

The principal leaned against his cherrywood cabinet. "I've gotta tell you, it's been fun telling people that we're in the playoffs."

"You got your 7 and 3 record." Grant lowered himself into a chair. "You know, God's been so good and the boys have worked so hard."

"Oh, in every area. The passion in the football team has

affected the whole school. You could argue that this is a different place. I'm excited about going to the game this Friday."

Grant grimaced. "Well, just keep in mind we're the lowest seed. I mean, Princeton Heights has not been defeated. They're the number one seed."

"I realize that. But something tells me that Princeton Heights will not be our last game."

"I hope you're right."

"Grant," said Principal Ryker. "It's obvious that God has His hand on you. I mean, what you have done with those boys. We are glad you're here."

"Thanks. Is that, uh . . . I guess that's why you called me in here, huh?"

"No." Ryker grew serious. "There's something else."

AMANDA

Amanda sank down into the couch, wishing for the cushions to swallow her. This was so embarrassing. The principal's office. She'd never been in much trouble—well, there was that time in fifth grade, for kicking that boy in the shin, but he'd been asking for it.

Ryker's door opened and Coach Taylor came out with a grin. He looked right at her. "You are awesome, Amanda."

"Uh, thank you?"

"And you, Sheila." He gestured to the receptionist. "You're awesome."

The lady wrinkled her mouth. "Well, that's not the *usual* sort of comment I hear from someone coming out of Principal's office."

Amanda figured she might have a chance. Maybe Ryker would have mercy. She and David hadn't meant to cause any trouble, but

it'd sure looked bad when they were caught together in the art supply closet.

*They won't be angry when they find out what we were doing,
right?*

She watched Coach Taylor leave. He seemed like a good guy. He'd
always greeted her in the halls, and he seemed to treat his players
with respect. She knew at least one who deserved it: David Childers.

She smiled. Okay, he was cute. But he was also nice and fun to
talk to, and he listened like he cared. He treated her with respect.
That was different from most guys she knew.

Even my parents like him. And now I've gone and ruined it.

"Amanda," the receptionist said, "Principal's ready to see you."

She stood and faced the door. There was only one way to do
this, and that was to tell Principal Ryker the truth. Maybe, just
maybe, he would understand.

Brooke

Light jazz music filled the air, and balloons swayed over buckets of
flowers. Brooke's boss was doing paperwork by the register, preparing to close out for the evening. The floral shop smelled sweet and
fresh. It was one of her favorite things about working here.

After ringing up a vase of roses for a kind black woman in a
cream-colored suit, Brooke went back to work on a wedding
arrangement. Behind her, the door chimed—probably the lady
leaving the shop.

So what now? Why's my boss wearin' that mischievous grin?

She turned, smoothing her baby-blue blouse and straightening her necklace. She broke into her own grin at the sight of her
husband. Grant looked handsome, but casual, in Dockers and a
sweater.

"Yes, sir," she said playfully. "Can I help you?"

"Uh, please." His eyes danced behind his dapper expression. "I'd like to buy a nice bouquet of wildflowers for my wife."

"Mmm, I see. That's awfully sweet of you."

"Oh, yes. Uh, I've got a special evening in mind for her tonight."

Brooke wondered how that was possible, considering they were running short on funds. Maybe he was planning a candlelit dinner at home. Whatever he cooked, she would make herself eat it. She owed him that much.

It's the thought that counts, she thought. *No matter how it tastes.*

Deciding to still play along, she said, "Well, in that case, you need a card to go with those flowers, don't you?"

"Oh, no. I've already got the perfect one. I'm gonna give it to her at her favorite restaurant this evening."

"Oh, really?" Brooke tilted her head. "I'm sure she'll be happy."

He nodded. "Oh, she will. So I need your nicest, largest flowers. And money's no object."

She raised a quizzical eyebrow. "Oh?"

"You see, uh"—Grant leaned closer—"I got a raise today."

"You did?"

"Six thousand dollars."

Brooke pulled her hands to her mouth in surprise. "Are you *serious?*"

"You know, that's exactly the way my wife's gonna respond."

"Oh, Grant."

Tears clouded her vision. This was too much—the truck, the raise, the things that'd been going on with the football team. For years, he'd served here without an extra dollar in his salary. He'd putted about town in a car held together with duct tape and cardboard, jumper cables and prayers.

It had seemed like nothing would change. Like they were stuck in mud. In concrete. Brooke had tried to encourage her husband and keep her own chin up, but some days it had taken all her strength to do so.

Six thousand dollars?

"Oh, Grant!" She went around to give him a hug. "That's *awesome*."

He swept her off the floor and spun around with her in his arms. She felt the tears spill from her cheeks onto his sweater. From the work area, her boss was watching them, but didn't seem to mind the affectionate display.

Grant set Brooke down, keeping his arms around her waist. "You know," he said to her boss. "You've sure got friendly service here."

"Go, you two lovebirds. Just go."

"Ohhh," said Brooke. "I can't do that to you."

"I'm your boss, and I say go. Do it before I change my mind."

"Thank you, thank you."

Brooke dashed to the back, clocked out on the computer, and grabbed her tan jacket. She slipped her arm around Grant's on the way out to the pickup.

"I guess we forgot something, didn't we?" he said.

"We did?"

"Your bouquet of flowers."

"Well, Mr. Taylor, I guess I will just have to take a rain check."

Two hours later, tummies full of Italian pasta and tiramisu, they followed West Oakridge Drive toward Old Pretoria. Almost home. Brooke reveled in the full moon, swollen and beautiful against the outline of pine and pecan trees.

CHAPTER 33
Clipped Wings

MR. BRIDGES

The den quivered with the radio's deep bass tones.

"Is that thunder?" Martha lifted a sleepy head from the arm of the sofa. "We got a storm brewin'?"

"Shhh. It's just the radio," Mr. Bridges said. "You can go on back to sleep, sweetheart."

She pulled her legs closer to her chest and groaned. He watched her mouth grow slack. After all these years, he saw beauty there that he'd failed to recognize when they were younger. He truly did love her.

She was an angel—his grumpy, favorite one.

"Hello again, everybody," the announcer said over the airwaves. "This is Lane Lavarre, along with my broadcast partner, Dale Hansen, coming to you tonight from Princeton Heights Academy, the site of tonight's opening round of the GISA football play-offs. For the first time in a decade, the Shiloh Eagles find themselves in postseason play. And Coach Grant Taylor's gonna have his hands full tonight as he takes on the number-one-seeded Panthers, who haven't lost a game all season."

Martha's right, Bridges thought. *Maybe a storm* is *brewin'.*

GRANT

Play-off football. So this was how it felt. Grant took it all in: the rows of field lights blazing from above, the anticipation of the crowd, and the clear brassy sounds drawn forth by the concise hand movements of the band director.

"Hmmm." J.T. raised an eyebrow. "Our band's actually getting better."

"An answer to *somebody's* prayers," Grant quipped.

There was a mid-November chill in the air, and he knew it was important for the boys to go through pregame warm-ups. They wore white helmets and white shirts with blue numbers. He was in a blue coat, with a white SCA cap. Soon enough, they'd be warmed by the action on the field.

An official blew a whistle, indicating it was gametime.

"All right, huddle up, huddle up." Grant took this last opportunity to solidify his players' resolve. He tried to look at each of them as he spoke. "Stay sharp, stay focused. Play hard, and honor God. Eagles on three . . . One, two, three!"

"Eagles!"

As the huddle broke, he grabbed his team captain by the arm. "Brock, be a leader tonight out there. Keep our defense unified."

"Yes, sir."

Princeton received the kickoff. They tried establishing a ground game, but when Number 21 attempted an end around, he was chased down and hit at the line of scrimmage. On fourth down, the Panthers had to kick.

"Good defense!" Brady barked. "That's the way we wanna do it."

Shiloh fielded the punt, obtaining decent field position on the return run of Number 50. Soon, though, it was fourth down. Shiloh's turn to punt.

The ball possession went back and forth. Neither team scored.

On a fourth-and-four, Grant decided to have his guys go for it. They could do this. Only four yards to earn another set of downs.

FACING THE GIANTS

Zach Avery started the play, but got caught in the backfield by a swarm of Panthers.

"We should've run one of my plays," J.T. said, only loud enough for Grant to hear. "A Double Sweep Wall, maybe."

"Trick plays, huh?"

"Only now and then, for shock value. That's all I'm sayin', Coach."

Princeton Heights took over the ball. Again, they went to their bread and butter—a hard-nosed, power-running game. Number 21 carried it on successive plays, chewing up yardage and the clock. Then, following his blocks, he cut inside and darted for the end zone.

The goal-line referee threw up his hands. Touchdown.

On their next drive, the Eagles moved the ball in close enough for a field goal. But the Panthers kept pouring it on, relying on their star running back. Another score. Answered by a Shiloh touchdown off a Zach Avery–Jeremy Johnson connection. Then another Panthers score.

Zach followed that with a misfired long bomb to Number 18, but the Eagles defense played tough and forced the Panthers into a punt with seven minutes left in regulation.

Grant could see the weariness in his boys. It showed not only in their slow jogs off and onto the field, but in their downturned mouths. Principal Ryker's words came back to him: *Something tells me that Princeton Heights won't be our last game.*

"C'mon, guys," Grant shouted. "We can still do this!"

This game was within reach. If they drove down and put seven on the board, they would go from 10-21 to 17-21.

Lord, You've brought us this far. Anything can still happen.

And anything did.

The punt wobbled through the air, and the Shiloh player mishandled the catch. The loose ball rolled on the ground, and the Panthers pounced on it. They controlled the tempo from there, marching downfield, and sealing their victory with another touchdown on the ground.

The battle was over. Finished just that quickly.

Grant dropped into a crouch, his head down. He looked back up and tipped his cap back. He'd believed and hoped for something far different.

We had a good season, Lord. I can't complain. Did this have to be our last game, though? After all their hard work, I wanted more for my players.

Bobby Lee Duke

Bobby Lee turned up the radio in his Hummer as he drove home from yet another victory. He pushed back in the driver's seat and rested his right arm on the passenger seat. He hated to gloat in others' failures, but he knew this life could be cruel. Knew it firsthand.

Nice try, boys. But this is no place for a few feathered cluckers.

From eight hidden speakers, specially fitted for this vehicle, the radio announcer gave a final recap: "So, after an impressive 7 and 3 record, the Shiloh Eagles fall short tonight in the first round of the GISA play-offs; 28-10 is the final score. The Princeton Heights Panthers take it to the Shiloh Eagles."

Bobby Lee shook his head. *'Bout time they got those wings clipped.*

Grant

Grant followed his players into the locker room. They dropped onto the benches, dirty, grass-stained, and exhausted. He pressed his lips together and tried to think of something wise and valiant to say, yet nothing came to mind. He knew this life could be cruel. Knew it firsthand.

But I've gotta praise You, Lord. Even in defeat.

Right now, it was hard to put that into words for these guys.

Number 35, Nathan Markle, threw his helmet to the floor. "I knew we were gonna get killed tonight."

Grant twisted his ball cap in his hands. Brady stood beside him, shaking his head. J.T. stood at his other side. After an awkward silence, Grant spoke. "Your effort was good tonight." He felt his throat constrict. "You've got nothing to be ashamed of."

"It shouldn't have ended this way," Brock mumbled.

"You played hard. Shiloh's had the best season they've had in a long time. God's been good to us this year."

"Guys." Zach Avery looked around at his teammates. "Coach is right. We're gonna praise God when we win; we're gonna praise Him when we lose."

Grant nodded. "Let's take a knee."

While his players joined him, he addressed heaven with thoughts he believed but did not feel. A blanket of disappointment hung over the room, and his words seemed trapped here, like stale air. He felt like he was suffocating.

And still he prayed.

After some hugs and backslaps, he headed to the parking lot. The temperature was dropping. He climbed into the truck and found Brooke there—as always, the faithful fan—waiting for him. She wore a blue SCA Eagles sweatshirt, and she had her chin resting on her hand on the center console. Her eyes were filled with sympathy and support.

"Hey," he said.

"Hey."

He pondered the game's outcome and bounced his palm once on the steering wheel. "I wish by some miracle we could've won tonight. They worked too hard to walk away with their heads down."

Brooke simply listened.

"You know, I was hoping God would give us just one win in the play-offs. They deserved it. Brock, Matt Prater, Jeremy, Zach, Jonathan, and all these kids who worked their tails off." He inserted the key. "Even David Childers . . . he's come a long way. One play-off win, that's all I asked."

Grant started the engine. Time to head home.

The season was over.

CHAPTER 34
In Trouble

BRADY

"Whoa, this stuff stinks."

"Nah." J.T. held up his spray bottle. "It's citrus cleaner."

"So it smells like stinky oranges," Brady fired back.

"Man, stop your navel-gazin'."

"Very funny."

It was Monday morning, and they'd collected all the players' uniforms in the Shiloh locker room. The laundry was done. The shirts were hanging in tidy rows. Now the assistant coaches sat across from each other, wiping down scuffed white helmets, preparing things for storage until next season.

"You know," Brady said, "if you'd have told me two months ago that we'd be playing Princeton Heights in the play-offs, I would *not* have believed you."

"Yeah. If you'd have told me our school was having a revival this year, I wouldn't have believed you either. But, uh, this ain't been a bad year."

Grant walked in. "You got all the jerseys?"

"All thirty-two of them," J.T. answered. His cap was turned backward on his smooth head. "I ain't ready to put them up, though. I'm ready to go another round."

"You and me both. Part of me wanted to get to state."

"To *state*?" Brady looked up. "Grant, are you serious?"

"Why not? As hard as they worked."

"Well, workin' hard is one thing. But to take this team to state? That'd take an act of God."

"Has He not been acting already?"

"Well, yeah, He has. But do you know who's gonna be waiting for whoever gets to state?"

J.T. threw his head back. "The *Richland* Giants."

"That's right, the Richland Giants. And Bobby Lee Duke will be there with his eighty-five players, ready to *spank* whoever made it to the state play-offs to kingdom come."

"I'm not afraid," Grant said.

Brady smirked. "I know you're not afraid. 'Cause you ain't going."

Grant considered that with a bittersweet smile.

"Oh. By the way, man," said J.T. "Some man called lookin' for you today."

"Who?"

"Uh . . . Stan Schultz."

"Stan Schultz?" Grant headed through the door to his desk. "Yeah."

"Stan Schultz," Brady echoed. "Isn't that a cartoonist?"

"That's *Charles* Schulz," Grant snapped from around the corner.

"No," J.T. said. "I thought Charles Schulz was that man that flew across the ocean in the *Spirit of St. Andrew.*"

"That's Charles *Lindbergh*. And it was the *Spirit of St. Louis.*"

"No," Brady said. "Lindbergh is a cheese."

"*Limburger's* the cheese. Lindbergh's the man."

Brady chuckled at Grant's impatience, while exchanging grins with his fellow assistant. Nothing like getting Coach riled.

"No," J.T. played along. "Lindberg was that blimp that blew up and killed all them people."

Grant rolled into view in his desk chair. "That's the *Hindenburg*." He looked at both men, shook his head, then rolled back out of sight.

"Nah," Brady said. "Hindenburg is where you go skiing in Tennessee."

"That's *Gatlinburg!*"

J.T. stopped his cleaning. "Gatlinburg? You mean like the country music group, the Gatlinburg Brothers?" He glanced at Brady as they both waited for Grant's reaction.

A helmet came flying through the doorway and rattled onto the floor. "You guys are crazy," Grant muttered.

He walked through to grab a phone jangling in the hall, while Brady and J.T. smiled and knocked fists. Mission accomplished. It was never a good thing to let a head coach take life too seriously. Brady figured he better remember that, because one day he would get his chance to lead—and he'd have a bunch of screwups trying to mess with his own head.

Well, bring it on. I'll be ready for 'em.

From the other room, Grant's phone conversation cut through Brady's thoughts: "Grant Taylor . . . Hello, Mr. Schultz. I was told you were looking for me . . . Yes . . . Am I sitting down? Why do you ask?"

Brady turned a questioning face to J.T.

J.T. raised an eyebrow and kept spraying that stinky orange stuff.

GRANT

Grant strode behind the school's football sleds and athletic equipment, and found a pair of officials waiting under the trees by the tennis court. They were here from the Georgia Independent

School Association. It was still early, with the sun spilling over the trees, warm and peach-toned.

What's this all about? Why the sudden need to meet?

One of the men stood in a button-down sweater, with a tie tucked underneath, while the other wore a suit jacket and thick glasses.

"Coach Taylor?"

"Yes."

"Stan Schultz." The bespectacled gentleman reached out to shake Grant's hand. "Executive director of GISA. How are you?"

"Fine, thank you."

"This is Barry Van Cleave. He's the athletic director for GISA."

"Good to meet you, sir." Grant shook the other man's hand. He was an austere fellow, tall, with serious eyes.

"Good to meet you."

"So, uh, what can I do for you?"

"Well," Schultz said, "we understand you've been working on this program for several years now."

"Yeah, seven actually. We were blessed this season."

"Blessed, huh?" Schultz exchanged a glance with his athletic director.

What's wrong? Grant wondered. *What're they hiding from me?*

"Coach Taylor, we want you to know that we've looked very carefully at your team. We've been checking the eligibility of all your players."

"Okay. But I can assure you we haven't played anybody that wasn't cleared to do so. Oh!" Grant felt his neck grow warm. "Wait. Is this about Stanley?"

"Who?"

"Our waterboy."

Van Cleave crossed his arms. "Waterboy?"

"During our last regular-season game, he dressed down and went in for one play. That was it. You know, just a way of thanking him for his hard work for the team. I got permission in advance, though. You can check with the refs."

"Ahh, yes," said Schultz. "I heard about it."

"Am I in trouble? I didn't mean for it to be a—"

"Please, Coach Taylor. Why don't you let us explain why we're here?"

Grant's mind was racing. Had the other team's coach reneged on their agreement and reported Stanley's involvement to GISA? Would Shiloh's seventh win be reversed? Ineligible players could lead to an automatic forfeit.

"I'm listening," he said. "Just give it to me straight."

J.T.

J.T. stacked red laundered jerseys in a plastic storage container. He and Brady were just about done with the morning's work, putting another season to rest. Their best season yet. With lotsa hope for next year.

Now, if J.T. could just get his friend to quiet down.

The big guy had his back turned, and he was bobbing on his feet, doing some sorta human beat-box thing. It wasn't half bad—for this brother from another mother. But see, it was wrong to be discriminating like that.

J.T. decided to join in, silently putting words to an old-school groove:

He ain't nuthin' but a white man, tryin' to find some soul . . .
Got these verses to reverse this . . .
Immerse us, is his goal.

Brady spun around and added shirts to the container, still making scratching sounds with his mouth. J.T.'s mental rhyme continued:

Like a peanut, gonna glean it,

Crush these words and make some butter . . .

Spread it thick, yeah, do it quick—this white boy, he's your brotha.

Approaching footsteps interrupted J.T.'s thoughts. In marched Coach Taylor. Instead of greeting them, he rifled through the jerseys in the container and said, "Okay, I need all these unpacked."

Brady's beat-box came to a stop.

"Coach, whatcha doin'?" J.T. said. "We just folded those."

Grant pointed at J.T.'s chest. "Go tell Mandy to make an announcement that practice *will* continue after school." He turned to Brady. "I need all the boys to meet me on the field at three thirty."

"What?" Brady demanded. "Why?"

"Just trust me."

J.T. watched Grant depart, then gave his fellow assistant a confused look. Now why did the coach have to go and break their flow?

MATT

"Hey, Coach." Matt looked over to Brady. "What's going on here?"

"Coach is on his way to let us all know."

"All right."

Matt figured this must be important. Still dressed in school clothes, the guys were milling around on the field—Brock, Zach, David and Jonathan, Bobcat, Jeremy . . .

Coach Grant Taylor approached from the edge of the track.

"All right, everybody, bring it in," he called.

The boys circled around, eyes full of questions.

"I want you to know I serve a big God," Grant started, with passion in his voice. "And He can do whatever He wants to do. He can open what He wants to open, and shut what He wants to shut. And a team that plays for His honor and glory will have His blessings following that team. Unlike those who try to cheat their way to the top."

Matt saw Brady's eyes narrow.

"Like Princeton Heights did in last Friday's game," Grant continued, "when they played two ineligible nineteen-year-olds."

What? Matt's mouth dropped. *Is this a joke?*

"The GISA directors informed me of all this earlier today: *They* have been disqualified, and *we're* advancing to the next round."

The next round?

Matt was suddenly unable to catch his breath. This was crazy. This was incredible. He wanted to holler at the top of his lungs. The season that'd been dead had just come wandering back from the grave.

Grant said, "Get your pads on for practice, boys. We're going to war with Tucker, Friday night!"

CHAPTER 35
Beginning to Rain

BROOKE

After work, Brooke caught a ride with Jackie to Friday's game. They drove by Arby's for a bite to eat, then rushed to the stadium, only to find a long line of cars being directed into the lot.

"They should be startin' any minute," Brooke fretted.

"Find it on the radio," Jackie said. "You won't miss anything."

Brooke tuned in the station and held the volume button till the broadcast filled the cab of the Explorer: "Welcome, ladies and gentlemen, to the GISA quarterfinals. Who in the world would've thought that we'd be seeing the Shiloh Eagles tonight in a contest against the Tucker Tigers?"

"Me." Brooke raised her hand.

"Well," said the other announcer, "with Princeton Heights' being disqualified, you could call this an early Christmas present for Shiloh. Folks, don't touch that dial. When we return, we'll be hearing the national anthem and preparing for the opening kickoff."

An attendant directed Jackie into a parking space. The muffled sounds of drums and the press of spectators heading into the stadium ratcheted up Brooke's pulse a notch.

"Hurry," she told her friend. "Yeah, that's good enough, that's fine. C'mon, we can still make it."

FACING THE GIANTS

Grant

The anthem had been sung, yet still no sign of Brooke. Grant peered back over his shoulder, searching the crowd, taking it all in.

Outside the field lights' glare, stars glimmered and the night pressed down with cold palms. If the team had done as instructed, they would have Thanksgiving leftovers sitting at home in their fridges. This was the big game. There would be time to eat turkey and stuffing later.

Along the track, the cheerleaders called out chants. There was David's friend, Amanda, with her hair pulled back in a French braid. On the top wall of the stands, banners showed support for the team.

So here we are, Grant thought. *Against the Tucker Tigers again.*

Last year, in his final shot at a winning season, Shiloh had lost to this very team. They'd also lost Darren, their star running back, to this school. Would the Tigers play spoiler a second time around?

A flash of blonde hair caught Grant's attention, and he waved at Brooke and Jackie as they made their way across the bleachers. Good. She'd made it from work.

"Hey, it's time," J.T. said. "We're receiving the ball."

"Let's do this." Grant blew his whistle and gathered the boys in their red jerseys. He decided to keep it simple. "Offense, put it in the end zone. Defense, build me a stone wall. This is the night we put it all together. Eagles on three. One, two, three . . ."

"Eagles!"

The kick went up, and the crowd roared. After letting the ball bounce into the end zone for a touchback, the Eagles started from the twenty-yard line. They set up over the ball, digging in their feet as they prepared to face the Tigers, outfitted in white jerseys with red-and-black numbers.

Tucker was a big team, well-coached, but they were also missing key players due to injuries. Grant's game plan was to attack those weaknesses.

For the next three quarters, the game remained scoreless. Both offenses kept stalling, knocked off their rhythms by stellar play on the defensive side. Then, going into the fourth quarter, Shiloh managed to gain three first downs in a row, marching the ball into Tiger territory.

Grant called a time-out. This was a crucial play.

While the team came off the field, J.T. turned to Grant. "I say we run Crossbuck 30. Ain't no way they expect us to try *that* again."

Last season, they'd lost the game on that play—the pitch back to Jacob Hall, who was supposed to have tossed it downfield to Jeremy Johnson. Instead, he'd been hauled to the ground as the clock ticked down.

"You sure?"

"Hey, do I look worried to you?"

Grant processed the idea as he turned to his players.

"What's the play, Coach?" Zach pressed.

"Crossbuck 30."

"What?"

"You hold on to the ball as long as you can. The linemen will buy you time, but as soon as the pocket starts to collapse, you pitch it back. You're gonna get hit hard, most likely, but just make sure Jacob gets that ball."

Zach's gaze hardened. "I can do that, Coach."

"I know you can."

The crowd was on their feet, sensing the importance of this play. As Zach lined up behind his center, the defense looked like they were ready to blitz.

"Blue 18. Blue 18. Set. Hut, hut!"

Zach took the ball. He dropped back and faked a pass to his left, waiting, waiting. The Eagles linemen dug in, keeping the Tigers away from their quarterback. Jeremy Johnson ran a short pass route, turned as though to catch it, then swiveled and sprinted toward the orange goal marker.

"Now!" Grant yelled. "Do it now!"

The walls of protection were crumbling, and Zach Avery knew it. He took one more step back and pitched it to Jacob Hall. Jacob rolled to his right and faced down the field.

Grant began to second-guess himself. Why had he agreed to run this play? Would it be a mere repeat of last year? If it failed, it would be a huge psychological blow to his team.

Please, Lord. Please, not again.

Jacob showed no hesitation. He drew back his throwing arm and flung the football forward with all his strength. The pigskin spiraled over the Tigers' coverage. Running beneath the pass, Jeremy let his fingertips cushion the ball and pull it into his arms as he finished his sprint for the goal line.

Grant's ears rang with the roar from the stands. People were high-fiving, hugging. He could see Brooke beaming with glee. He slapped his players' hands and shoulders as they bounded toward the sidelines.

The Eagles had struck first.

DAVID

Standing in shoulder pads and cleats, David Childers watched his team begin another offensive drive. They were still up 7-0, and the clock was winding down. Five minutes left. Three hundred seconds.

And then, to the semifinals.

David Childers had always thought of soccer as the more cerebral sport, but this duel between Tucker and Shiloh was like a real-life chess match. Each coach substituted players and mixed up his play calling, trying to outsmart the other. Grant Taylor was energized, yet intense.

Of course, soccer season never interfered with Thanksgiving.

Not that I minded skippin' green-bean casserole.

Yesterday afternoon, he and his dad had been guests at Amanda's house. Her parents were hospitable, and her father even came up with a makeshift wheelchair ramp for easy access into their single-level, cypress-sided home. After dinner, they watched an NFL game. Then, with plates of pumpkin pie and vanilla ice cream, David and Amanda played Scene It on DVD.

She won. Only because she was better at the word puzzles.

Despite David's fears—or maybe because of them—this had been a good school year so far.

He'd been afraid of moving to Albany, of trying out for the team, of making friends with a girl. All of these were now highlights in his life. Sure, he and Amanda had gotten into a little trouble at school, but that was behind them. Principal Ryker had extended grace, insisting only that Coach Taylor know the full story.

After this game we'll meet with him, David thought. *Or, I don't know, maybe if we make it to the championship.*

"Hey!" J.T. said. "You hear Coach talkin' to ya?"

David blinked. "What?"

"David," Grant called. "This is your field goal. It belongs to you. Put it through!" He punched David in the shoulder and then pushed him toward the huddle on the field.

David pulled on his helmet as he trotted out. The scoreboard said this would give them a 10-0 lead, with under three minutes left.

One hundred and sixty-six seconds.

He marked off the yardage in his head.

Thirty-nine yards? Thirty-nine! Even that NFL kicker missed from this distance yesterday. Why isn't Joshua out here instead of me?

From the bleachers, Brooke Taylor was watching. She'd been so nice to him at the house, feeding and encouraging him. This was just another kick. Another day out by the barn. And there, at the foot of the stands, his dad was also watching, nodding, with both arms raised.

David decided in that moment that he could do this. He *would* do this. No distractions. No pride. Nothing but a determination to put it through.

He lined up for the kick.

"Hut!" Jonathan called out. He took the snap. Set the ball.

David drove his leg forward and booted the pigskin between the uprights. The referee's whistle confirmed that it was good.

"Yeah!" Coach Taylor screamed from the sidelines. "*Yeah!*"

David held up both fists and saw his father do the same. In the stands, fans danced in celebration.

Stay calm, he reminded himself. *The game's not over yet.*

Mr. Bridges

Mr. Bridges had finished making notes on his pad. He was on his feet, his heart thumping with excitement. He could hardly believe this was happening. The school and these kids he'd interceded for, they were going to the state championship game as far as he was concerned.

Coach Taylor, you did as asked. You prepared your fields.

"With the clock running down," the radio announcer confirmed, "the Tucker Tigers are nursing their wounds as they face the end of their season. The Eagles, however, have a little farther to fly. They will take on Oakhaven next, to determine who'll face the Giants in the state championship game."

Bridges turned off the radio. Dizziness washed over him and he braced himself against the wooden cabinet, waiting for it to pass. Gingerly, he lowered himself to the sofa.

"Raymond?" Martha opened a groggy eye. "Everything all right?"

"More than all right."

"You look upset. Something wrong?"

He brushed a hand over his eyes, and it came away wet. "Not at all," he mouthed. "I think it's just beginnin' to rain."

FOURTH QUARTER: STONE WALL

CHAPTER 36
Thin Air

BROOKE

Brooke felt queasy. She stood over the kitchen sink as the teapot began to rumble on the stove. She hugged her stomach and rushed toward the bathroom. She'd done the same thing the past two days.

Was it something I ate? I feel awful.

She heard a knock at the door. Jackie was here, as requested.

"Thanks for stoppin' by." Brooke let her in.

"Well, isn't that what friends are for? You aren't lookin' so hot. You think maybe you should stay home from work?"

"I don't know. I just feel . . . sorta sick, you know?" They moved into the kitchen, where Brooke poured two cups of tea.

"Sugar?" she asked.

"Please, and lots of it."

"You're so bad. But I love you anyway."

"Somebody's gotta."

After they'd both sat down with their cups, Jackie leaned forward, dark curls brushing the shoulders of her jacket, and said, "All right. What kinda sick are we talking about?"

"I don't know." Brooke rested her elbow on the table, with her head on her hand. "I've just felt really nauseous the past two mornings. And then I feel fine again."

"And you haven't eaten anything weird lately?"

"Not unless fruit and cereal's weird."

"Are we talkin' papaya and bran? Or apples and Cheerios?"

Brooke's giggle seemed to trigger another stomach roll, and she closed her eyes until the queasiness subsided.

"Sorry." Jackie sighed. "You know, I don't wanna get your hopes up. You've talked like this before, and it turned out to be nothing. Still, Brooke, my gut says make an appointment with a doctor."

"I've been there three times this year. It's getting *embarrassing*."

"But don't you wanna know? Just in case?"

"Yeah, I . . ." Brooke felt her chin begin tremble. "I've wanted children since I was a little girl. I used to put a big blanket over the table and then make it into my little house underneath. I'd pretend I was the mommy, taking care of five or six kids, feeding 'em, giving 'em baths." She set her jaw and looked up. "I *do* wanna know, Jackie. But I don't think Grant can handle hearin' the bad news again. He already feels like it's his fault."

"Does he need to know that you went in?"

"I have to use the car. Or he'd have to drop me off. Either way, he's gonna ask questions, and I can't lie to him. We've never been like that with each other."

"Well, I'm just telling you what I would do." Jackie winked. "If you want, I'll help make the appointment and you can even use my car."

Brooke smiled. "You're such a good friend to me."

GRANT

Three days of rain had soaked the practice field at Shiloh Christian Academy. The boys slogged through mud, ignoring the cold and the deep aches it produced in bones and weary ligaments. They ran drills without complaint, and the offense worked with J.T. on integrating a few new plays.

Grant worried about wet grass and last-minute injuries. As the week progressed, he gauged the team's attitude. It'd been a long season. They were bruised and tired.

But they were also inspired.

On Thursday, he had them do light conditioning before corralling them onto the bus. Despite some questioning looks, they obeyed. Brady drove.

"Team, you've worked hard." Grant stood in front, arms braced on two seats. "You've pushed your bodies to the limit. Kept up your grades. You've stayed tough mentally. And spiritually, we've all seen the things the Lord can do when we focus our eyes on Him. Tomorrow, we're going into the game with one goal: to glorify God by giving Him our best. Our *very* best."

He gazed down the rows of seats.

I can't have my own kids. But, Lord, You've given me more than I could've imagined. These are my boys.

"For now, though, I think we need a little diversion."

J.T.'s eyes narrowed. "Coach, where you takin' us?"

"All American Fun Park," Grant replied. "Who's up for some laser tag?"

MR. BRIDGES

The weekdays had crept by, but at last the time had come.

Earlier, Mr. Bridges had shot nine holes with his golfing buddies, taking it slow on this brisk late-November day. At the tee on the seventh, Eddie had shared with him a quote by D. L. Moody.

Now how'd that go? "If God is your partner, make your plans big."

Well, here he was. Back in his den. And his plans were in trouble.

The big wooden radio crackled with what little life it had left, airing the next Shiloh play-off battle. Bridges felt stiff from his morning on the links. He regretted not being able to go to the game, but it would be a long drive. Plus, all that excitement, that adrenaline . . .

Just don't know if my ol' ticker can take it.

Alone in the lamp-lit room, he listened to the announcer call the final down: "With five seconds left in the game, the score still stands in Oakhaven's favor, 17-14 over the Eagles. Grant Taylor calls in the play to Zach Avery, who pulls the huddle together for their last shot at going to state."

Bridges leaned forward, his hands clasped in front of him. He tried to keep his blood pressure down, to stay composed. His wife was puttering about in the kitchen.

Lord, I'm still makin' big plans.

"It's third down and goal to go for the Eagles, and the crowd is going crazy. They line up in an I formation. This is do or die for the Eagles. Zach takes the snap and will give it to Jacob Hall for . . . No! Wait a minute, it's a *fake!* He's got Nathan Markle in the corner. The pass is up . . . *He's got it!*"

Bridges slapped his fist into his hand.

Thataway, boys. Thataway.

"Touchdown, Eagles! Touchdown, Eagles! Zach Avery *completely* faked out the defense and made a perfect pass to win the game 20-17. Can you *believe* this? The Shiloh Eagles are actually headed to the state championship. A team with only thirty-two players has made it to the big dance. *Ohhhh*, my."

With a huge grin on his face, he began writing the article that he would then e-mail to the paper before his midnight deadline.

The next morning, the *Albany Herald* arrived on the doorstep.

Bridges thumbed through the pages, found the Pigskin Review. He cut out a section of newsprint, then thumb-tacked it to his corkboard where the season's clippings overlapped one another.

His latest article read "Shiloh Will Face the Giants at State."

Last week, he and Martha had shared Thanksgiving with family, at their daughter's beautiful brick home on Nottingham Way. Now he had something else for which to be thankful—big plays and bigger plans.

BOBBY LEE DUKE

Bobby Lee eased into his Jacuzzi, a drink in his hand. Jeweled rings clinked against the glass. Ice rattled in the liquid.

He was getting annoyed by these little Eagles that kept flying.

From the wall-mounted TV, the Channel 10 sports anchor, Kevin McDermond, told the latest high school football story.

"On the eve of the GISA high school football state championship, the Richland Giants prepare to defend their three-year reign as lords of the gridiron. It's no surprise they've returned for this game. What *is* surprising is who they're playing. The Shiloh Eagles, who started the season 0 and 3, have come out of nowhere. And, through an almost *bizarre* set of circumstances, now face a team almost three times their size. We talked with both coaches today about their hopes for tomorrow's game . . ."

Bobby Lee sipped at his drink, watching himself on the screen. He looked comfortable, confident, wearing black as he stood before a long glass case. The news crew's lighting captured the rows of trophies at just the right angle.

Was the Shiloh coach watching this? What about his players? If so, Bobby Lee could bet they were quivering in their Riddell cleats.

"Well," he heard his own voice from the TV, "we've had a pretty good season. We plan on endin' it by putting another trophy right here in this case. We want Mr. Taylor to know that all eighty-five of my boys plan on getting *real* acquainted with his team. Our boys, they're fired up and they're ready. To be quite honest"—he pointed with his trademark sucker—"gametime can't get here fast enough." For dramatic effect, he planted the sucker back in his mouth.

The scene changed to an athletic field, with football players milling in the background. In the foreground, Coach Taylor stood in a red shirt and ball cap. He spoke softly into the mike, like he'd never done this before. "Uh, we're just excited to be here. Um . . . we've been blessed this season, and we plan on leaving our best effort out on the field."

What kinda talk is that? These Eagles look more like barnyard chickens.

The sports anchor wrapped up the segment with: "The game will be held at Wiersbe-Dunn Stadium. We'll have highlights tomorrow evening, directly following the championship."

Bobby Lee draped his arms along the outer edge of the Jacuzzi. He smirked.

Well, it was about time to push these little birdies out of their nests and see what they were made of. They may have got this far on determination and pure blind luck, but they were about to discover how thin the air was at the top.

CHAPTER 37
Negative?

GRANT

A dewy haze diffused the sunrise through the trees. Grant stared up past thick, hovering branches, at a sky golden and crisp.

Oh, Lord, this is it.

He'd spent another week of practice, of counting the minutes, of tossing in bed as defensive schemes played through his mind. Tonight, it would all come to a close at Wiersbe-Dunn Stadium.

Grant walked in from the orchard, his shoes wet from the tall grass. He kicked them off by the back door and found Brooke in the kitchen, still in flannel pajamas. With hair pulled back and no makeup on, she still looked good.

"Hey, sweetheart."

She gave him a smile in response, then settled into the seat beside him with her tea and a bowl of fruit. "Sleep at all last night?"

He shook his head. Cut into a green apple.

"Are you nervous?"

"It's a weird emotion." He stared off. "Part of me thinks we're gonna get crushed tonight. Part of me thinks God may do something awesome." He fed an apple slice into his mouth from the edge of the knife.

"Sounds like your fear's about to collide with your faith."

"Hmm. Something like that."

"When're you going out there?"

"I might leave early." He looked at her. "If that's all right."

"Just don't worry about me." She warmed her hands on her cup of tea. "I'll just meet you at the game."

"Okay."

"Either way, you're still playin' for a state championship."

That put a grin on his face. "Why, yes, we are."

BROOKE

Brooke had an afternoon appointment. She sat in the doctor's waiting room and fiddled with the beaded necklace over her ribbed turtleneck. The atmosphere was serene, with framed pictures gracing the walls beside brass lamps and padded chairs. Through the windows, she saw pillowy clouds drifting across a sky that was robin's-egg blue.

She wondered what her doctor would think. How many false alarms had they gone through already?

On the floor rug, a mother was reading to a darling daughter in her lap. Her son played beside her, while a second girl sat nearby with a red bow tied in her hair. Three children. Three precious little gifts.

"Where's the duck?" the mother asked her daughter.

The girl pointed at the book. "Duck."

Awww. Listen to that adorable little voice.

"Zebra?"

"Zee-ba."

Brooke shifted her legs, letting a middle-aged woman and her college-aged daughter pass. They settled into the chairs to her left.

"Don't worry, Breanna," the older woman said. "It'll be all right."

I wonder what they're here for? Brooke mused. So many lives. So many stories. She tried to imagine what it would be like to spend twenty years raising a child of your own. The cost of time, of emotion—but, of course, the rewards.

She believed God could do a miracle. Hadn't He already done so much for them this year? Was there room for just one more? Or had she already filled her cup of blessing?

Maybe so. Yet He could do as He pleased. He was God.

Even one child, Lord. You know the desires of my heart.

On the floor, the mom and daughter flipped to another page.

"Cat?"

"Caaack."

"Meow."

"Mee-oww."

Brooke rested her head on her hand. She wanted to be the one on the rug, cross-legged, reading out loud. She wanted to experience it all, the good and the bad—late nights, dirty diapers, and school plays. All of it.

The mother whispered. "There's the pig."

"Oink-oink."

Blinking, Brooke covered her mouth and bit down on her lower lip.

Nurse Laura

"Oh, no."

Clipboard in hand, Laura turned in her desk chair. "What's wrong?"

"Brooke Taylor's here again."

Laura ignored the chirping phone and followed the brunette nurse's gaze to Mrs. Taylor in the waiting area. She pulled in the folds of her light jacket, drawing together colorful stars, hearts, and moons. The pattern appealed to the younger children, many of whom considered her their favorite nurse.

So far, though, there were no Taylor kids.

"Ohhh," Laura said. "It's so hard to see her here."

"Maybe she'll be pregnant this time."

"I hope so. I really do."

LARRY

Larry Childers was dressed, van keys in hand, ready to go. His son, however, was pacing through the house. He'd been growing, maturing, but along with that had come a frequent forgetfulness. He couldn't keep track of his jacket. His shoes. His homework. The cordless phone.

"You ready, son?"

"I can't find my cleats."

"They're right here by the door."

"Oh. Thanks."

David rushed into the living room, nervous and out of breath. He was dressed in pregame attire, with a tie, a belt, and a dress shirt tucked into slacks. Coach Taylor wanted his boys to look proper, and Larry figured that was a good thing since it prepared them for the adult world.

"I hope I have everything." David propped himself on the recliner's edge and rummaged through his bag, like a soldier heading to war.

Larry smiled from his wheelchair. "Do you realize you're playin' for the state championship tonight?"

"I don't know why I'm so nervous. I'm not even gonna play."

"You know I'm proud of you, don't you?"

David gave a wry smile. "Yes, sir." He dropped his gaze.

"Look at me for a moment."

David looked back up.

"Don't ever doubt it," Larry said. "Whether you play or not, I'll be right there prayin' for you."

"Thanks, Dad."

Larry rolled forward. "Now let's go pick a fight with some giants."

Nurse Laura

Laura was at the keyboard, adding an appointment to next week's schedule, when an assistant came through the door behind her.

"Here's the results for B. Taylor."

"Ohh." She swiveled in her seat. "I'll take that."

Was Brooke pregnant? Finally? She glanced over the sheet on the clipboard and sighed.

"Negative?" asked the brunette nurse.

"Yes."

Laura could hardly say the word aloud. Her eyes were glued to the telling box that indicated there was no baby. Nothing to get excited about. This was her least favorite part of the job, breaking the bad news to her patients. And especially Mrs. Taylor. For years, she'd been coming in for checkups and pregnancy tests.

Some things just aren't meant to be, I suppose.

Laura stood and faced the waiting room. "Mrs. Taylor?"

Brooke's eyes lifted, blue and expectant.

"We have your results. If you'd like to take a seat in the room down the hall, I'll be with you in a moment."

Laura gathered herself. Tried to think of what to say. Still gripping the clipboard, she went to the small back office and opened the door. Brooke was seated, with a jacket draped over her lap and her purse on the floor.

"Yes?" She looked up with a hopeful smile.

"Listen," Laura said, "you and I have talked on many occasions, so I'm not going to sugarcoat this. I'm sorry, but the results are negative. You are not pregnant this time around."

Brooke's forehead furrowed and she dropped her chin. Blonde hair fell forward, covering her face.

Laura touched her shoulder. "I wish I had different news for you."

"It's okay," Brooke whispered. She rubbed a finger against her palm. "Really, it's okay. I appreciate you being honest."

"There's no rush to leave. I mean, if you need some time alone . . ."

"Thank you, Laura," Brooke said with a brave smile.

Clutching the telltale clipboard, Laura eased from the room.

CHAPTER 38
The Bigger Picture

GRANT

Grant arrived early for the game. The sun was chasing afternoon shadows across the empty parking lot, but he knew within two hours this place would be bumper-to-bumper with thousands flocking into legendary Wiersbe-Dunn.

Wearing his red SCA jacket and cap, he wandered past rows of blue bleachers into the middle of the field. White chalk marked freshly cut grass. The scene was set. The battle lines drawn.

He pushed hands into pockets. The December cold had arrived. He stood in the silence and let images from the season flash through his head. Then he jumped even farther back in time, remembering the day he and Brooke had left Statesboro and Georgia Southern University. He'd been so ready to change the world, to fly high with the Eagles in little Albany.

Just didn't know it would take me seven years to get to this spot.

"All right, God, You got us here," he prayed. "Whatever happens, may You get the glory."

He blew out a long sigh.

Ten minutes later, Mr. Cohen, the athletic director, led Grant to the locker room where they found Shiloh's red jerseys hanging beside white helmets. Along the upper wall, past champions were listed on white wooden shields.

"So, have you guys ever been here before?" Cohen asked. He

was holding a padded folder. Salt-and-pepper hair topped a friendly face.

"I haven't."

"Well, uh, we got restrooms"—the man pointed—"and ice machines down here. Um, is there anything else you think you guys're gonna need?"

Grant fingered a uniform. Looked around. "This is great."

"You seen Richland yet?"

"I know about 'em."

Cohen patted Grant's shoulder. "Good luck."

"Appreciate it."

"Oh, by the way." Cohen stopped at the door. "There's someone who's dropped by to see you. You mind if I send him in?"

BROOKE

Still sitting in the doctor's back room, Brooke gripped the jacket in her lap. She felt like she was dangling over a black chasm with only this thin material to cling to. She looked up. Was there anyone there? Anyone to keep her from plummeting down?

Lord, I . . .

She stopped. She had nothing to say. Nothing that wouldn't sound like a lie or a bribe or an empty promise.

In some nook of her heart, she'd been foolish enough to allow herself to hope. She'd wanted to give Grant the news. To reaffirm him as a man, as her husband. She'd even wondered what an ultrasound might show.

It was over now. Officially done.

Was there something she could've done to win God's favor? No, she didn't believe that. His gifts were by His choice, by His grace.

She buried her face in her hands as emotion welled up.

Don't do this, Brooke Taylor. Not now. She pushed back her hair. *Don't go fallin' to pieces where everyone else can hear you.*

With only a nod at Nurse Laura, she pulled on her jacket and headed out to the vehicle she'd borrowed from Jackie. Grant had already left in their Ford pickup for the stadium. There was no reason to even tell him she'd come here. This was just some silly notion that had got wedged in her head.

I shoulda known. What was I thinkin'?

Brooke reached into her purse for the keys as Grant's words from the pecan grove came rushing back: *"If God never gives you children, will you still love Him?"*

She'd been trying not to think about that. She'd found it easier to focus on the team and her husband's concerns. The question wasn't even fair in the first place. She loved God. How did this change anything?

Just because I can't have a baby of my own, just because I won't ever feel a child in my womb, just because . . .

Tears sprang to her eyes. They brimmed on her eyelids and trickled down her cheeks. They tasted salty and hot. How could she be asked to give love when her one hope to do so was being taken away from her?

Why?

She shook her head. No, she couldn't let this drag her down. If she wallowed in self-pity, it would only harm those around her.

But the tears continued, and something told her she had to decide now.

Right now.

"Will you still love Him?"

She couldn't put this off any longer. Without an answer, nothing would move forward. She could go through the motions. She could pretend to be alive. Yet, in the deepest part of her, things would begin to decay and die.

Her voice cracked. "I will still love You, Lord."

The words felt like moisture wrung from a cloth. Her entire being seemed to twist inside, and her brows knotted as her chin quivered. She pulled her eyes upward and found the strength to say it one more time. "I *will* still love You."

GRANT

There was someone here to talk to him? Grant waited with his back to the locker-room door. Who could it be? He heard the door squeak open and turned to see a man with combed-back hair, a tan, and an even smile. He wore a black sweater over a red shirt.

Coach Stephens? My former head coach at GSU?

Grant's heart caught for a second. Why was this man here? This was the guy who'd mentored him, taken him under his wing, and even ministered to him. And the same guy who'd demoted him to second-string quarterback.

Though it'd been eight years, almost nine, seeing Stephens's face was both a blessing and a reminder of a lost college dream.

"Coach." Grant smiled. "What're *you* doing here?"

"You're at the state championship." Stephens shook his hand. "What do you think I'm doing here? Anytime a former player would get this far, you know I'd be there."

"That blows me away."

Grant's words were sincere. Coach Stephens had never shown any animosity toward him—even after Grant had vented his frustration one particular evening eight years ago. Simply put, the coach hadn't let him play the position he wanted. That was all there was to it.

"Well, how're you feeling?" Stephens inquired.

Grant tugged on the brim of his cap. He glanced over the man's shoulder. He knew the coach was asking about his mental preparation for the upcoming game, but Grant needed to get this off his chest now.

Right now.

"You know," he said, "I, uh . . . I had a hard time those last two seasons at GSU. I wasn't real happy about standing on the sidelines."

"It was never personal, Grant. You were a good player."

"It was just frustrating for me to see someone else get the reward that I had worked so hard for."

"I did what was best for the team. That's what any good coach does."

"What about rewarding someone's faithfulness?"

"You were faithful, that's true. I mean, except for—"

"Yeah, that one night. That was just stupid of me. I was just mad and ready to vent."

"And I forgave you for that."

"But you still let the other guy play."

"I did." Stephens nodded. "I also let you stand beside me, hearing every coaching decision, every chess move of our games. I saw in you something no one else had."

"What's that?"

"The ability to train up others, to lead them. When Principal Ryker called about you taking the job at Shiloh, he was hesitant. You'd never coached high school ball. But I was more than happy to give a glowing recommendation. I knew you had it in you."

Grant swallowed. He'd always assumed that his decent college grades and charming interview had earned him the coaching job.

"Coach, listen. Thank you. I guess that . . . Well, I wanna say I'm sorry for questioning you. You were thinking longer term than I was. You were looking at the bigger picture."

"That's right." Stephens tapped him on the chest. "I envisioned you standing right here, fighting for this title."

"Wow. Please forgive me for the way I acted toward you."

"Apology accepted. Forgiveness granted."

"Thank you."

"Now enough of that. You have a game coming up." The former coach leaned forward. "Are you ready for this?"

Grant took a breath. "I am a little bit nervous. Uh, this championship, I . . . it's kinda surreal for me."

"Yeah. Well, I can promise you, I don't care what level of ball you're coaching, it's surreal when you make it to the championship game. And, Grant, I could just tell you, I'm so proud of you and what you've done. I've been reading about the team and where you've gone. And more than anything else, I'm just proud of the fact that you finally learned how to win the big one."

"Uh, we haven't played 'em yet."

"No, you won the *big one* when you accepted Christ. And now, as you're teaching these guys and ministering to them, I think it's just fantastic."

"I got it." Grant nodded. "These players got it."

"Well, I can promise you, win or lose this game, you guys are champions."

"I appreciate that."

"But hey, while you're here . . . you might as well win it, huh?"

Grant laughed. "I'm gonna try my best. You know this team we're playing, they're huge. Uh, they're fast. They're strong. I just don't want my players to be afraid."

"Well, in God's Word, He said 365 different times, 'Do not fear.' If He says it that many times, you know He's serious about it, don't you?"

"I would guess so. I needed to hear that."

"Well, look. You're going to do great tonight. I know you're busy. I'm going to go up in those stands and cheer you on."

"Good to see you."

"All right. God bless you, man."

"Thanks, Coach."

As Stephens departed, Grant turned and blinked in amazement. He felt like a weight had been lifted. He'd not only put off every encumbrance that might distract him from this moment in time, he'd been reaffirmed in his position as Coach, while also being humbled by Stephens's graciousness.

Grant couldn't wait to charge out there with his team, to see Brooke in the stands, and Coach Stephens, and all the others. There would be a cloud of witnesses, all gathered to watch them finish this thing.

We're gonna give it all we've got!

CHAPTER 39
To Be or Not to Be

NURSE LAURA

Laura was still reeling from her encounter with Brooke Taylor. She walked into the receptionist area, the functional backbone of this small private practice, and handed a clipboard to the brunette at the copy machine.

"Here you go. This one's ready to be filed."

Taking a seat at the computer, Laura wondered what it would be like to pack peanuts or stock groceries. Something to minimize the human element. The emotional toll of this place was getting to her.

"Hey, Laura."

"Yes?" She glanced back over her shoulder.

"This can't be right." The brunette wore a befuddled expression. She grabbed a second clipboard from atop a file folder and compared it with the recent arrival. "It looks like we had two *B. Taylors* in today. A *Breanna* and a *Brooke*."

"What?"

"Here, take a look. Maybe I'm the one who's confused."

Laura compared the paperwork, double-checked, then gave a muted cry. She snatched one of the clipboards and hurried out the front door, with her stars-and-hearts jacket flapping. Brooke had left only minutes ago. Maybe she could still catch her in the lot.

BRADY

Brady meandered into the locker room and found Coach Taylor sitting between rows of red-painted lockers. He had a clipboard in hand, going over the game plan.

"Coach."

"Hey, Brady."

Brady sat across from him. He pulled off his white cap and kneaded it in his hands. "You ready?" he asked.

"As ready as I know how to be."

A few months ago, that answer would have been unsatisfactory, when Brady had started doubting this man's ability to get the job done. Now his doubts were over. Coaching involved knowledge, discipline, confidence, and desire. As well as intangibles that could not be taught.

Do I have what it takes to fill this man's shoes? Maybe not. But he's been teachin' me how to walk in my own.

"You know," he said. "I thought this was impossible. But here we are."

Coach got a twinkle in his eye. "Pretty cool, huh?"

"You seen that crowd out there? The bleachers are already fillin' up."

"I bet there's a lot of Giants' fans."

"Bucketloads of 'em. I gotta tell ya, Grant, I was watching them come in off the bus. They are *huge*. Think we got a chance?"

"Not when I look at it on paper. But we're gonna fight like we do."

The intangibles, Brady realized. *It's time to get this done.*

BROOKE

Brooke craned around, checking her blind spot as she backed from the parking space. In her college days, she'd putted around in a

Honda hatchback, so now the Ford F150 and Jackie's Explorer demanded an extra effort.

Of course, bleary eyes didn't help. She could still feel the sting of salty trails along her cheeks. She'd have to stop somewhere along the way and wash up. Grant didn't need to see her like this before the game. Tonight was all about supporting him and the team.

Still looking over her shoulder, Brooke eased back into the lot. She faced ahead again, ready to straighten the wheel, but she was startled by the image of Laura running toward her. The nurse was waving her hands. She looked frantic.

What was wrong? What news could be any worse?

I will still love You, Lord. I will.

Brooke put the Explorer into park and climbed down, trying to make sense of Laura's sputtering sentences and broken syllables.

"The tests, they got mixed up. Brooke, I'm so sorry. I was wrong. It was wrong. There were two of you."

"Two of me? What?"

"I mean, two different files. There was one B, then another B. We didn't even catch it at first. See, we have another young lady who shares your last name, and you both came in today. We switched your files by accident."

"You what?" Brooke pulled quivering fingers through her hair. "Laura, what're you sayin'?"

"What I'm trying to say is, you're pregnant."

"I'm *what*?" Her hands dropped over her mouth.

"You're going to have a baby, Brooke. You're eight weeks along."

"Are you *serious*?"

"Never more so."

Brooke wrapped her arms around the nurse. This woman had always been there, caring and honest. Brooke tightened her embrace. "You're sure?" she reconfirmed. "This time it's not a mistake?"

"There's no question about it."

Brooke started hopping on her feet. "I can't believe this. I just . . . I can't believe this! Grant's gonna be so happy when he hears."

Matt

Matt Prater felt like he was watching a scene in a documentary. Except this was him and his teammates and the biggest night of their lives.

They filled the locker-room benches, quiet and attentive. Brady stood to one side, hands on his waist. J.T. looked on, his jaw set at a determined angle.

"In about five minutes," Coach Taylor said, "we head out for the warm-up."

Matt gave a sharp nod. *You better believe it!*

"I wanna say two things," Grant continued. "Number one, I love you and I'm proud of you. I wouldn't trade this season for anything in the world."

Brock Kelley and Zach Avery stared forward. Matt knew these guys had been rock-solid lately, carrying the defensive and offensive units.

"Secondly, you're about to play the biggest team you've ever faced. They're strong, fast, and undefeated . . . so far. But I want you to *remember* where God has brought us. I want you to *remember* how hard you've worked."

Matt looked over at Bobcat. Talk about a guy who'd worked hard, in class and on the field.

"We weren't supposed to have a winning season, but we *do*. We weren't supposed to advance through the play-offs, but we *did*. We're not supposed to be here, but we *are*." Grant's words reverberated between the walls. "So if there's anything in you that says this is a losing effort, then throw it out. 'Cause as surely as I stand here, I believe that as long as we honor God, nothing is impossible." He pointed his hat at his players. "Nothing."

Yep, I've found that out firsthand.

Matt thought about his dad out in the stands. About the old junker they'd rolled away together, to be replaced with something far better.

"Leave everything out on the field," Grant said. "Give your *best* to God tonight. And whether we leave the field the victors or not, we will give God the glory. Now . . . who will go fight the Giants with me?"

CHAPTER 40
We Belong

GRANT

Standing behind his players, hidden from the crowd, Grant waited. Ahead of them, SCA cheerleaders held clusters of red, white, and blue balloons while forming two pyramids on the field. Between them, a huge multicolored banner read "Go Eagles."

Fans filled the bleachers on both sides of the stadium. Signs draped the walls. On this crisp evening, beneath bright lights, armies were about to engage.

"Get ready, guys," Grant said. "Almost time."

Through the loudspeakers, a voice boomed across the field: "Ladies and gentlemen, let's welcome the Shhhh-*iloh* Eagles!"

Balloons rose into the night sky, and the players burst through the banner to the roar of the crowd. Grant, Brady, and J.T. followed.

A quick glance showed Neil Prater in the stands. And Coach Stephens. There was Mr. Bridges too.

"And now," the loudspeakers blared, "let's welcome the three-time defending state champions . . . the Rrrrich-*land* Giants!"

From the other end zone, the Richland cheerleaders held tight their team banner. Eighty-five black-clad players in red helmets charged through onto the field, causing the ground to tremble beneath their stampeding feet. And there was infamous Coach Bobby Lee Duke.

The Eagles players stood in awe of the other team's size. The Shiloh crowd fell silent as the Giants fans exploded.

"You've gotta be kiddin' me," Jonathan muttered.

Grant felt a chill set in, a sudden foreboding. As "The Star-Spangled Banner" played, he mouthed the words, but his mind was somewhere else. Had they bitten off more than they could chew? What were they doing here?

The song concluded to spectator applause. He spotted Brooke and Jackie settling into their seats. His wife was dressed for cold weather with a red wool coat and a scarf draped over her shoulders.

They caught each other's attention. Brooke's eyes were animated and gleaming, and Grant felt his heart rate kick up a notch.

He smiled, then turned back to the field. He was ready.

LANE LAVARRE

Lane took a sip of coffee. The stuff was nasty, but he needed his voice to stay supple in these winter temperatures. His voice was his job. He watched the On Air light, waiting to launch back over the radio waves.

"You want me to grab you a cup?" he asked his broadcast partner.

"Can't do it," Dale said. "Doctor says it's bad for my heart."

"Pretty soon, they'll be tellin' us we can't drink water."

From the press box high above Wiersbe-Dunn Stadium, he and his partner had watched the pregame festivities, the warm-ups, and the coaches gathering their players for last-second pep talks. It all came down to this. Another season of football was about to go into the books, with one team to be named top dog.

The On Air light flashed.

Lane spoke into his mike: "Welcome back, folks. The Giants elect to receive after winning the coin toss, and we're just seconds away from the state championship football game. Dale, I've gotta tell you something. It is impressive that Shiloh has made it this far, but the field tonight really looks lopsided."

"It definitely does. I'm looking at eighty-five players on the Richland sidelines as opposed to thirty-two for Shiloh. Even if the Eagles had great talent, they can't bring in fresh players like the Giants can. That's really gonna hurt 'em in the second half."

Lane took back over. "Coach Grant Taylor has sent his kicking team onto the field, and both stands are on their feet in anticipation. There's the whistle. The Eagles kick it off . . . and the state championship game is under way. Jerod House will receive the kick, and he'll head down the field. He gets a couple of blocks and breaks outside. He's got some daylight. The Eagles will give chase, and they'll take him down around the fifty-yard line. That's where the Giants will set up shop tonight, first down and ten, with good field position to start this state championship football game."

BRADY

"Let's go, let's go." Brady sent in his defense. "C'mon. Get out there."

The Giants were lining up for their first offensive play of the game, and the anticipation was tangible from the stands. Brady felt the hairs stand up along his arms. This was big-time football, or at least as big as he'd ever been a part of. Some day, he'd be doing this as a head coach himself. Everything until then was experience to build upon.

He studied the formations on the field. "Brock, watch it over the middle. All right, let's go, boys!"

Brady expected the Giants to pound the ball straight ahead through the defense, using size and strength to grind down their opponents. His stomach lurched, though, when the center hiked the ball and one of the Richland wide receivers sprinted full-speed down the sideline.

No, no, no! Are they goin' for all the marbles on the first play?

From the press box, it was obvious what was about to happen.

"Wes Porter will call the play for the Giants," Lane announced. "He steps back to pass. He's got Damien Fuller streaking down the sideline, and he lets it fly! The Eagles are caught *totally* unaware, with no one in position to break it up. Fuller will take the pass in, and he'll race into the end zone untouched."

Lane and Dale waited for the confirmation from the referees. No penalties on the play. Everything by the book.

"And the Giants strike early here in the football game with the first score."

Lane figured if this was a taste of things to come, it was going to be a long night at the mike. He took another sip of his bitter concoction.

GRANT

Grant couldn't believe this. A touchdown? Already? He looked across the field and there was Bobby Lee Duke, spreading his arms and taunting. He was Goliath, yelling across the valley at a smaller army of Israelites. He was a chess master, playing mind games over the board.

"Welcome to state championship football!" Coach Duke shouted before shoving that stupid sucker back in his mouth.

"Hey, man," J.T. said to Grant. "This is a whole new level."

"Yeah, but we fought our way to get here. We belong on this field."

"Well, we better start fightin' like we never fought before."

"I agree." Grant leaned toward Brady and gestured at the Giants' huddle. "They are quick off the line. We've gotta stay farther back."

"I know. I'll adjust."

"We can do this, guys. This battle's just starting."

MARTHA

Martha Bridges took her husband's position on the den sofa. Over her objections, he'd gone to the championship game. He was like Simeon, the old man who'd hoped and prayed for years at the temple, waiting to see prophecy fulfilled. Raymond had done the same for this school and these players, and far be it from her to keep him from seeing his reward.

Alone now, snuggled in her blanket and furry slippers, she listened to the game over the radio. She might not be able to handle all those people and the noise and the cold, but she would share the experience with her husband from here in his favorite spot.

"It's first down," said Lane Lavarre. "The Eagles will start this drive at their own nineteen-yard line. Zach Avery will drop back to pass; he looks, and he passes to Jeremy Johnson. But the pass is batted down by the Giants."

Martha turned up the volume.

"Second down. The Eagles line up, the ball is snapped, and Avery hands it to Jacob Hall, who tries to run it up the middle. But he gets *absolutely* nowhere as he is swamped by defenders. Coach Duke is yelling from the sidelines, jeering at his opponents. The man sure puts on a show, but he's got the trophies to back it up."

Frowning, Martha tugged her blanket tighter.

"On third and nine, the Eagles look to pass. But here come the Giants . . . and they're gonna get the sack! And that's gonna force the Eagles into a punting situation on fourth down. Look at this, Dale; have you ever seen Coach Duke clownin' around like this so early in the game? You've gotta wonder if he has *any* respect for his opponents at all."

"I don't think he does," Dale responded. "And at this point, Shiloh Christian Academy has done very little to change his mind. They have *got* to find a weakness in the Giants' defense, or this could be an ugly night."

BOBBY LEE DUKE

Bobby Lee watched his defense shut down the Eagles. Turning to his assistant coach and the players beside him, he brushed his hand back over buzz-cut hair and opened his eyes wide. "Wooo, baby, that's pretty! Wooo!"

They grinned. He knew they fed off his over-the-top attitude.

"Check it out, boys." He aimed his sucker across the grass. "Coach Turner is lookin' mighty worried."

"Coach *Taylor*," his assistant corrected.

"Awww, whatever. He knows who he is."

Shiloh punted the ball, and Jerod House fielded the kick. He turned, got a couple of blocks, then sliced to the outside. He accelerated past special-team defenders and found daylight. Making it look easy, he took it all the way down into the end zone.

Groans and cheers lifted from the bleachers. This game was over before it'd begun. These poor little eaglets had no idea what it was like at the summit of the football mountain. Bobby Lee folded his arms and spotted Coach Taylor's wife up in the stands. She had her hands over her mouth. Well, she would have a tough job ahead tonight, trying to encourage a deflated man.

End of the first quarter. The scoreboard showed 14-0.

After a few unsuccessful drives on both sides, the Eagles got a break when the Giants ran an option. The ball was pitched poorly, fumbled, and a Shiloh player fell on it.

"Nooo!" Bobby Lee vented.

The Eagles gained eight yards on a strong second-down run. On third down, though, the Giants dug in and came up with a big quarterback sack. Shiloh would have to punt it away again.

"Okay, time!" Coach Taylor frowned. "Ref, time out."

That's right, Papa Eagle. So far tonight, it's been all Richland.

CHAPTER 41
Plucked

During the time-out, Stanley circled the perimeter of the huddle and slipped cups of water into the players' hands. Grant appreciated the kid's work.

"Zach, that was my fault," Grant said. "I should not have called that play."

"Coach, they're all over us," Zach griped. "Nobody's open."

"They're knockin' us around out there," Brock added.

"I know they are. But they're getting cocky. We cannot let them play their game. Defense, I want you to blitz on first down. We've gotta get them off their rhythm."

"We'll do it, Coach," said Matt Prater.

Grant glanced over their helmets and spotted a banner on the other side that read "Pluck the Eagles."

Not if I can help it.

"One more thing," he said. "Offensive linemen, don't forget to protect Zach in the pocket. If he's gonna get off good passes, he needs that extra second. The Giants are doing all they can to pressure him into making a mistake."

Stanley pushed his freckled face into the huddle. "I'd like to note that Zach leads the league in his touchdown/interception ratio, and has gone without a single pick in the last three games."

"Good point. Thank you, Stanley."

"Anytime, sir."

On the next series of plays, Shiloh did show heart. They shoved the Giants back near their own goal line, but then the Giants started shoving back and manhandled the defensive line. Richland's star running back put down his shoulder and ran over an Eagle. His team looked strong, moving the ball near midfield in a hurry. With the first half almost over, they had a chance of going into the locker room ahead by three touchdowns.

"Hold 'em right here!" Grant shouted.

The Giants quarterback dropped back to pass and fired toward his teammate at the fifty-yard line.

With perfect anticipation, a Shiloh player, Number 20, darted into the path of the ball. He plucked it from the intended receiver and streaked the other direction.

"Interception!" Brady cheered. "Did you see that? Woooo!"

The Shiloh fans erupted as the Eagle player ran full-speed into the end zone. The Giants would have no shut-out tonight. Grant's smile felt like it would crack his face from ear to ear. He was going crazy with the rest of the crowd. He could see Brooke, Coach Stephens, everyone—all jumping and hollering. He high-fived his assistants.

Brady yelled, "That's what I'm talkin' about. There's my defense!"

"Let's go, let's go, let's go." J.T. was already rounding up the kicking team for the extra-point attempt.

"Good job, good job!" Grant congratulated those coming off the field.

Across the chalk-marked chessboard, his opponent was screaming and pointing at his players. "What universe are you in? Get in the game!"

Feelin' a little worried, Bobby Lee?

MARTHA

The doorbell chimed once, but Martha was glued to the radio.

"So," Lane Lavarre said, "with a few seconds left in the first half, it looked as if the Giants were going to take a three-touchdown lead. But after an Eagles interception, we've got a 14 to 7 football game."

Another chime. Longer, more insistent.

"Well, for cryin' out loud," she muttered, rising from the sofa.

A third ring.

"All right, I'm comin'. These ol' legs don't move as fast as they used to."

By the time she opened the front door, she was feeling indignant. Where was the respect for the elderly? Why were young people always so impatient?

"Hi, Mom."

"Grace? Oh my, you should've told me you were stoppin' by."

"I was listening to the game in the car, and I thought maybe we could sit and share it together," said Mrs. Carter. She draped her coat over a recliner. "Have you been tuned in? It's incredible. Shiloh just scored and—"

"I know, dear." Martha waved her off. "I may be old, but I'm not deaf."

"Is Dad at the game?"

"Against my wishes, I'll have you know."

"He's probably as happy as ever. Now, why don't you go rest your feet, and I'll pour us some sweet tea for the second half."

BROCK

Panting and tired, Brock followed the team into the locker room.

Grant pulled him aside. "Brock, how are you?"

"Honestly, I feel like I've played two games already. Those guys're monsters."

"I need you on that field. You're my leader out there."

"Coach, we're getting beat up. Every time we start to wear 'em out, they send in another set of players."

"That's when it's all heart. We've got twenty minutes to rest, but don't talk defeat around the other guys, okay? You've gotta help me keep up morale. We're not done yet."

"Yes, Coach."

He watched Grant move down a row of lockers to where Brady and J.T. stood in whispered discussion. Great. Even those guys were questioning Shiloh's ability to last another half. Brock eased along the aisle, hoping to catch a bit of their dialogue. He could see the assistants through a gap in the lockers.

"We can't keep runnin' our normal plays, man." J.T.'s arms were folded. "Their defense is killin' us."

"I agree. We can't outmuscle 'em, and we can't outrun 'em."

Grant paced as he weighed Brady's words. He stopped. "Then we've gotta outsmart 'em."

"Trick plays?" J.T. asked.

"Just enough to keep them guessing. You see another way?"

"We just can't use 'em too often, though. They catch on, and we toast."

"We're toast anyway," Grant noted, "if we don't put some points on that board. We have *gotta* make it through the fourth quarter—and they've got a deep bench."

"Coach," Brock said, stepping around the end locker.

All three men turned and stared at him.

"You mind if I tell the guys on the team something?"

"What're you thinkin'?" Grant asked.

"Well, Mr. Bridges—that old man who prays at the school—he said a couple of weeks ago that he'd thought of this Scripture for me. Now I think maybe it's supposed to be for the whole team. For tonight's game."

"Let's hear it."

"Here, maybe you should just tell 'em." Brock removed his white wristbands and relinquished them to the head coach.

Grant read over the scrawled writing. "This is good. I like it. But I think this task is all yours."

"What?"

"Remember, Brock, they look up to you. It's time to lead."

MATT

Matt plopped onto a bench with the other players. Despite the energizing interception and the late second-quarter touchdown, his teammates were dirty, sweaty, and huffing. Matt knew they had their work cut out for them.

Grant appeared in front. "First of all," he said, "I want you to know we're still in this game. Good job on the defense, getting us on the board. I believe they thought this would be a shutout. We're gonna keep surprising them."

Zach Avery nodded.

"You really think we got a chance?" one of the guys interrupted. "Coach, they're killing us. I can't even shake my guy."

"Man, don't you quit," J.T. said. "They only one touchdown ahead."

"Yeah, 'cause we got lucky."

"You ready to give up?" Grant asked. "We made a commitment to honor God with our attitude and effort, and we can't throw that out the window as soon as things get tough. You've figured out they've got power and speed. They're big, but they're also predictable. We have *gotta* stay together."

"I'm with you, Coach," Matt stated for all to hear.

"Good. 'Cause this is all about heart. Maybe we can't outrun 'em, but with a few plays J.T. has up his sleeve, I believe we can outsmart 'em." He turned to the side. "Brock?"

Matt watched his friend step forward. This was their workhorse, their team captain, the Master of the Death Crawl.

"Anybody know what these say?" Brock held up his wristbands.

"I *would*," Matt kidded, "if I could make as many tackles as you."

"Well, here ya go. It's from Isaiah 40:31. The first one says, 'They shall mount up with wings like eagles.' The second one says, 'They shall run and not be weary, they shall walk and not faint.' Guys, this is what Coach has been teachin' us all along, and it's what Mr. Bridges has been prayin' for." Brock's eyes glowed with intensity. "We've gotta go out and *give* it our all tonight. We've gotta *rise* up and face these guys. We've gotta run till they *can't* keep up!"

CHAPTER 42
Line of Fire

LANE LAVARRE

"One mistake," Lane mumbled, "and it's all over."

"You can say that again. I just don't think these Eagles can overcome the odds they're facing."

"Huh?" Lane glanced over at Dale Hansen. The press box felt more like an icebox, and he was huddled in his black leather jacket in an attempt to stay warm. Chattering teeth never sounded good over the airwaves.

For now, the On Air light was dark.

"No," Lane said. "I'm talkin' about the cheerleaders down there. I mean, how do parents handle watching them get tossed up like that?"

On the Richland side, a petite blonde girl balanced her right foot on the raised hands of her squad members, while stretching her left leg far behind her. She looked calm, extending her arms in a graceful pose. On the Shiloh side, in front of a banner that read "Go, Fight, Win," a brunette was flung high into the air and then caught by the others as though she were a mere feather.

"See, that's not right, makin' young women take those kinda risks."

"But it's okay for the boys to be smashing into each other, I s'pose."

"Well, yeah. I mean, they're . . . they're boys."

Dale chuckled at that, then gestured at the teams coming back onto the field. The fans turned loud and rowdy. Beneath the stadium lights, Lane saw a woman with SCA painted on her forehead. Others wore tinted hair for their team. This was what Georgia football was all about.

The On Air indicator lit up the press box.

Lane Lavarre took over in his radio voice: "With the Giants leading the Eagles 14-7, we get set to bring you the second half of this state championship football game. Unless the Eagles can find a way to solve Richland's size and strength, the Giants could very well be taking home their fourth consecutive state title tonight."

"Oh, there's no doubt, Lane, the Giants are the favorites here. For years, Coach Duke's teams have dominated their opponents. But how tough is Shiloh? What kinda stamina do they have? That's what we're about to find out."

"And here we go," Lane said. "Richland kicks, and it's a high, wobbly one deep into Eagle territory. Jeremy Johnson takes the ball and heads upfield. He breaks a few tackles and gets taken down short of the twenty-five-yard line. And that's where their offense will set up shop behind Zach Avery."

Dale jumped in. "I'll tell ya, this Avery kid's been impressive all year, but tonight he's seen nothing but Giants in his face. Let's see how he adjusts."

"Avery steps up over center," Lane said. "He takes the snap and pitches it back to Jacob Hall. The Giants close in on Jacob, and it looks like he's going to be . . . Wait a minute. Look at *this*. The Eagles come out with a little trickery, and they're just about to tie this football game!"

FACING THE GIANTS

DAVID

Grant yelled before the snap, "Make it work, Zach!"

Standing on the sideline, David knew Coach was going to try some trick plays, but this one happened so suddenly that it caught him off guard.

Even as Zach pitched the ball, it seemed obvious the Giants were going to smother Jacob Hall for a loss of yardage. Instead, Jacob lofted the ball back over the defenders' heads into Zach's arms. He caught it on the run and dashed along the far chalk line, aiming for the goal marker. Giants pursued him in force, but a nice block from his teammate allowed him to slip by unhindered.

No way! We can actually tie this thing?

David and Jonathan banged helmets as the crowd bellowed. The sound crashed over the stands and washed onto the players. To David, it felt cold, shocking, and thrilling all in one instant. He viewed his dad cheering from his wheelchair, in front of a banner that read "You Gotta Believe." In the bleachers, Brooke Taylor was hugging a fan next to her. Farther back, Mr. Bridges was gazing down with a smile.

This is like family.

The thought lodged itself in David's mind. He had left behind a network of church friends and soccer buddies in Athens, but he'd found a new community here with coaches, teachers, players, and fellow students.

Like Jonathan. And—he smiled—*Amanda.*

"C'mon, c'mon," Grant directed his kicking unit. "Let's go, let's go."

David decided he'd better keep his head in the game. He watched Joshua Webster move across the grass, preparing for the point-after attempt.

On the opposing sideline, Coach Duke stood with hands on hips, mouth hanging open. He looked like a statue. A crudely carved block of stone. Then he roared back to life, shaking his fist.

"Make 'em *pay*, boys," he barked. "Make 'em *pay!*"

What's that supposed to mean?

David turned to see Joshua send the ball through the uprights. That's when he spotted the defender barreling through the front line.

No!

The Giant careened into the Eagles kicker, nailing him into the turf.

"Hey! That was a late hit," J.T. said.

"C'mon," Grant reacted. "That was dirty!"

Joshua was rolling on the grass in pain, and Jonathan flagged the attention of his coaches.

"He's hurt, he's hurt," Brady said.

Grant rushed out with his assistants alongside. A team nurse joined them to check on their fallen player. Meanwhile, Coach Duke strolled his own sideline as though nothing had happened.

David glanced back at his father, whose face was knotted with worry.

Probably wonderin' if I'll be next in the line of fire.

Lane Lavarre

Lane informed his listeners: "Here at the state championship game, Joshua Webster's being helped off the field, with what we have been told up here in the press box is a broken collarbone. That came after a late hit by the Giants, after the Eagles tied the game at fourteen apiece."

"Yes," Dale said, "and Coach Taylor looks upset. A penalty will be accessed, but that won't bring back his starting kicker. This could play a major role in the game's final outcome."

LARRY

From the foot of the bleachers, Larry Childers could hear and relate to Coach Taylor's anger. What if that had been David out there? His son would've been crushed by a player twice his size.

"That was stupid," Grant vented. "That was dirty!"

"Hey, calm down," Brady said. "This is a new ball game. Joshua's gonna be all right."

Larry's throat tightened when he heard Grant calling his son's name.

Now it's his turn to be thrown out there?

"David, come here," Grant was saying. "You gotta cover for Joshua now. I need a hundred and ten percent, okay?"

David nodded. "All right, Coach."

"Be the man." He slapped David on the back. "Kickoff team, let's go!"

David jogged out as ordered, and Larry scolded himself for being afraid. How could he give in to fear when he'd been telling his son to do otherwise? No. This was an hour for courage.

Lord, please show Yourself through my son.

On the field, David stood with players flanking him. He raised a hand, then ran forward and kicked off. The ball sailed beneath a three-quarter moon, dropping into the hands of a Giant. Brock Kelley caught the guy and hauled him down.

From there, Larry watched the ball possession swing back and forth. Shiloh tried to run it, but got stuffed. Then the Giants failed to gain a first down. Shiloh again came up short. Richland switched tactics and used Number 88 to gain yardage with a straight-ahead, stiff-arm style. A little pitchout went upfield for another decent gain. Eventually, they worked the ball to the goal line.

You can hold 'em, boys. C'mon!

LANE LAVARRE

"Despite a good effort by the Eagles, the Richland quarterback holds the ball and dives over the middle into the end zone. He made that look too easy against this tired defense. Well, after a long drive, the Giants score, and now they'll go for an extra—"

"No, Lane, look at this," Dale Hansen interjected. "Coach Duke has decided to go for two. This could be a demoralizing blow for Shiloh. Richland lines up, snaps, and they try to hammer it back over the goal line on the ground. But the Eagles *prevent* the two-point conversion, leaving this a 20-to-14 football game."

"Folks." Lane leaned into this microphone. "Don't touch that dial. While the coaches talk to their teams before kickoff, we'll take a short commercial break. When we return, Zach Avery and the Eagles will hope to make something happen on offense."

BOBBY LEE DUKE

In his professional wrestling career, Bobby Lee had learned to ham it up, to put on a good show. But there was no acting now. He was livid. He'd expected to blow out this measly Eagles team, yet here they were, still clawing away. He looked up and shouted, "Why are they even on the scoreboard?" He turned back to his players with a fist in the air.

One of the boys flinched. Others retreated.

"What?" Spittle flew from his mouth as he shouted around the sucker in his mouth. "Don't tell me you're scared! They shouldn't even be in this ball game. They're like little dogs, nipping at your heels. Now get out there and *stomp* 'em!"

GRANT

"This is it. We're still in this. Most people thought we had no chance, but that scoreboard up there"—Grant gestured with his rolled-up play sheet—"says we're only a touchdown from winning this thing!"

Grant saw his players struggling to breathe. They'd been battling hard, many of them on both offense and defense.

But this was no time to let off.

"You think you're tired?" he asked. "Well, those Giants are sucking wind, I guarantee it. You've made them work. You've fought all year to get here, and you have only a few minutes left. Don't you give up on me now. Don't you back down. For the rest of your life, you will remember *today*! I want you to remember that you held *nothing* back. You did *not* lose heart. You did *not* stop fighting. You did *not* quit!"

CHAPTER 43
Dodging Bullets

MR. BRIDGES

From the bleachers Mr. Bridges observed the dismantling of his team, and it made his heart heavy. Shiloh was giving it their best, yet they were unable to make anything happen on the offense. Now the defense was back out there, feet dragging and chins down.

"'They shall run and not be weary,'" he whispered.

In the huddle, Brock Kelley seemed to be chiding his teammates, tapping at his wristbands as though they held secrets to the game of football. The boys stepped up to the line of scrimmage. The Giants tried an off-tackle run, but Brock was right there. He collided with the ballcarrier and threw him down hard.

"Tha's what I'm talkin' about," J.T. yelled from the sideline.

"That's my defense!" Brady joined in.

Brock got up slowly. He was grimacing. Exhausted.

The Giants set up again on third down, with their quarterback in the shotgun position.

"Let's *go*, Eagles!" Brady said.

Bridges noticed the Giants receiver accelerate as soon as the ball was snapped. He ripped past his defender, heading to the end zone.

"He's goin' for a bomb!" Coach Taylor warned.

Sure enough, the QB fired off the long pass. The wide receiver dived for it, but it dropped just beyond his outstretched fingers.

All around, Shiloh fans sighed in relief. The worried looks on their faces matched the sense of tightness in Mr. Bridges's chest. He knew they'd dodged a bullet, but they were simply waiting for the next one to come.

MARTHA

"Mom, would you like a refill on your sweet tea?"

Martha groaned and sat up in the den. Had she fallen asleep? She remembered a curtain of dizziness descending, and she felt more tired than she had in days. Was she coming down with something? Was it something she ate?

"Mom?" Mrs. Carter's voice issued from the kitchen area.

"No, I . . . That's fine, dear." She curled her legs on the cushions and tucked the blanket over her feet. "Why don't you come listen to the game with me?"

"I have something on the stove. I'll be there shortly."

The radio warbled from the corner: "With seven minutes left on the clock, the Eagles have shown the determination of a school twice their size. Unfortunately, they seem to be runnin' out of steam, and the Giants will now attempt a thirty-five-yard field goal to extend their lead. The kick is up . . . and it's good. The score is now 23-14."

Oh, Raymond, Martha thought. *Take 'er easy. I know how you get yourself worked up over these things.*

GRANT

Desperation rose in Grant's throat. Shiloh didn't have much time, and if they wanted to win this game, they needed two more scores.

Maybe I was wrong. Maybe we were too small to match up.

From across the field, Coach Duke's voice boomed. The man

was jabbing a finger at his assistant's chest, still upset about their offense's performance. "That is the *last* time we go for a field goal. We should be in the end zone *every* stinkin' time!"

Was Coach Duke actually worried? Grant allowed himself a grin.

"Okay, J.T., let's go with your Double Flex Long." He grabbed Zach Avery and gave him the play, then sent him onto the field. Grant leaned down, hands on knees, and watched.

This has gotta work. We need something right here.

Zach called out the snap cadence, looking over the defense. Jacob Hall lined up behind him, with Jeremy Johnson in the receiver slot to his left.

"And set. Hut!"

He took the ball, dropped back, and threaded a ten-yard pass to Jeremy through heavy traffic. Jeremy caught it near the forty and turned, but defenders collapsed in around him. Before going down, he lateralled it back to Number 11, who was racing along the sideline.

"You got it," Grant shouted. "Don't stop!"

Number 11 tucked the pigskin the way they'd practiced, and sprinted for the end zone while Giants players tried to catch him, diving but missing. The ref signaled a touchdown, and the crowd erupted. Players celebrated with backslaps and yells. Grant saw Brooke and Jackie hugging and jumping up and down. Coach Stephens was cheering too.

Grant gave him a nod. That play was similar to one they'd run at GSU.

Across the gridiron chessboard, Coach Duke's eyes bulged in disbelief as he roared at his players. "What're you *doing*?"

"Kicking unit." J.T. collected his guys. "Let's go, let's go, let's go!"

With just over five minutes left in the fourth quarter, Shiloh was down 20-23. David needed to make this extra point to bring them within two.

"Good job. That's my team." Grant patted players' helmets as they ran off the field. He stopped at the sight of his team captain. Sweat was dripping down the kid's face, and his breathing was ragged. "You okay, Brock?"

"Coach, I need a rest. I can't go much more."

Grant placed a hand on his shoulder. "Brock, I need you on that field. You have gotta stay in the game."

"I want to, Coach, but I don't know if I can."

"You can," Matt Prater said, stepping in. "I've got your back, man."

"I *need* you on that field," Grant reiterated.

"Yes, sir."

Grant watched Matt and Brock slog back into battle.

LANE LAVARRE

"Ladies and gentlemen," Lane called into his mike. "This is a one-possession ball game. The *surprising* Shiloh Eagles have scored, and now they set up for the point-after attempt . . ."

"*Who's the new kid?*" Lane mouthed to his partner.

Dale flipped through team roster sheets and jabbed at a name.

Lane continued. "David Childers is in to kick for Joshua Webster. We understand that this is his first season of football, and he's gone three for four."

"And looking at the stats, Lane, he's been limited to short-range kicks."

"Well, Shiloh can only hope that doesn't come back to bite them later."

MR. BRIDGES

Mr. Bridges's heart tripped with excitement against his rib cage. Despite the chill, he felt warm. Invigorated. Fans were scooted forward on bleachers watching a football game, sure. But this was a clash of wills. These boys were learning about endurance—on the field, in life, against all odds.

David measured off his steps for the kick.

"C'mon, David," Matt Prater called out. "You got this."

Bridges could see David's father, Larry Childers, parked in his wheelchair on the track with his arms raised, nodding at his son.

David stepped up and drove the ball through the uprights. The team celebrated as the scoreboard displayed a 21-23 ball game. Shiloh was now within a field goal of winning this war.

For the next few minutes, though, neither offense was successful.

Bridges watched the ball go back and forth. Four downs, and the Giants had to punt. Four and out for the Eagles as well, despite a nine-yard pass over the middle to Jeremy Johnson.

With time ticking down, the Giants began their final drive. The quarterback ran an option and swept right. Next, the fullback stiff-armed an Eagle and plowed ahead for yardage. Then Number 23 sneaked through a hole in the line and charged past Brock Kelley, carrying it all the way down to the one-yard line.

No, no! They can't lose it all now.

Bridges clutched his chest as a spasm shook him. He would have to remain calm. If his heart started acting up, Martha would only have more excuses to pester him, and he didn't need that.

Although secretly he didn't mind so much.

His own pain was diverted by the sight of Brock Kelley kneeling on the grass, wincing. Brock made a T with his hands. "Time out, ref! Ref, time out."

Please give these boys strength, Lord. They've about had it.

GRANT

Grant watched his best tackler stagger to his feet. Had he sprained something? Torn a muscle? They couldn't afford to lose anybody. Not now.

"Coach, I'm done," Brock said, removing his helmet. His hair was soaked with sweat. His chest heaved with each breath. "Someone else has gotta lead."

"Brock, *this* is when it matters most."

"But I let that guy get by me. I can't do it. I'm outta strength."

"I *know* you're tired. It's *easy* to lead when you're strong. But *now* is when you lead us, *right* now. Stop looking at where you are and what you *think* you can do, and you gimme your *very* best. Do you hear me, Brock Kelley?"

Brock's chin snapped up at his full name.

"Can you gimme *four* more downs? I just need *four* more downs."

"Okay." Brock drew in air and forced a nod. "Four more."

"All right." Grant called to the rest of the team. "Come here, come here! Look at me. We didn't fight this far to give up in the last quarter. You've *gotta* leave everything on the field. I need you for four more downs. *Who's with me?*"

BOBBY LEE DUKE

Bobby Lee shook a fist at his circle of players. He let his eyes widen, working it the way he used to do in the wrestling ring. He let his voice rise, fall, then turn hard and full of gravel. It was all about motivation.

"This is *our* time! And you've got to put the *nails* in the coffin. And field goals, they're *not* an option. We're not gonna let a bunch of scrubs come in here and take our trophy away, are we?"

"No, Coach."

"Are we?"

"No, Coach!"

He stabbed his finger at the field. "Now get *out there* and get it *done!*"

LANE LAVARRE

Lane shook his head. Though he was supposed to stay neutral in these skirmishes, he'd found himself pulling for the Eagles. They'd put up such a good effort. Yet now, down at the one-yard line, things looked grim.

"With less than two minutes left on the clock," he announced, "the Giants stand on the verge of their fourth straight consecutive state title. A tired Eagles team lines up to face 'em yet again."

CHAPTER 44
Staring Down the Barrel

BROCK

After the huddle, Brock watched his Shiloh linemen get set in three-point stances, with one hand down, the other cocked back and ready to thrust forward into a blocking position.

They were tired. Brock could see that in their trembling legs.

But the Giants were also depleted.

He gazed over the offense and tried to read what they had planned. He was sure they would run it, which meant the Eagles couldn't give even an inch. If the Giants scored, the game was over.

No! They cannot score. We have to hold 'em. We have to be a . . .

"Stone wall!" he yelled out. "Stone wall."

"Yes," Grant responded from the sideline. "Stone wall!"

"Stone wall!" Brock said, trying to fire up his guys.

The defensive line dug in their cleats, muscles flexing for the moment the ball was snapped. Even a split-second hesitation could open a hole in the wall and allow a running back to spurt through into the end zone.

Grant punched at the air. "Stone wall!"

"Stone wall!" Brock repeated. "Stone wall!"

LANE LAVARRE

"The Giants line up, first and goal. This score will solidify the state championship. The quarterback takes the snap, and he hands the ball off to his fullback, who barrels forward. The Giants are pushing forward and . . . No, wait a minute! He is *stopped*. He is *stopped*. Number 54, Brock Kelley, read that perfectly. He got *nowhere* on that play. The Eagles are still in it. They're still showing strong determination to fight this one out."

BROCK

Brock looked up as his guys formed a half-circle around him. "We *have* to hold 'em. If the Giants score, they'll be ahead by nine points. But if we can force a field goal, that'll still give Zach a chance at winnin' this thing with a touchdown."

"Three more downs!" Grant shouted from the sideline. "Three more!"

"I know it's getting tough," Brock said. "But you gotta hang with me."

"We're not goin' anywhere," Matt stated. "Three more!"

MARTHA

Martha lay curled on the sofa while her daughter stood in the radio's pale glow. They waited to hear the next play. Despite a great season and tonight's valiant effort, Shiloh was now staring down the barrel of the gun.

"It's second down and goal to go for the Giants," Lane called through the speakers. "The state title is within their grasp. Both of the stands are on their feet right now as they get ready to run this play. The quarterback pitches it back. Wes Porter will take it. He's gonna try to run it, and he has some momentum coming out of the backfield. He's . . . *No!* The Eagles have stopped him *again!* Matt Prater came up and put a big-time hit on him. Oh, my!"

"Just two more," Mrs. Carter said. "Anything can happen."

Martha started to reply, but her dizziness returned and she fell silent.

GRANT

Grant screamed support for his players. "That's my team, that's my team!"

He placed both hands on his head and spun around, trying to hold off the tension. He could hardly breathe. Behind him, the spectators were in a frenzy. Coach Stephens was grinning, cheering.

Across the gridiron, Coach Duke looked intense. And maybe a little worried? "C'mon!" he barked at his players. "Get it in the end zone!"

"Brock!" Grant caught his player's eye. "Two more."

Big Number 54 nodded.

MARTHA

"And here we go," Lane's voice boomed into the den. "They're gonna tee it up and try it again. Wes Porter will take the snap. He fakes the handoff, and he's lookin' to pass into the corner. He's got somebody there . . . But, no! The Eagles bat down the pass! And the crowd is going *nuts* here at Wiersbe-Dunn! The Giants have been kept out of the end zone by the Eagles on *three* straight plays. And now Bobby Lee Duke will have a *big* decision to make."

"What's there to decide?" Martha asked. "He's gonna try to win, ain't he?"

"Well, yes," Mrs. Carter said. "But he has two options. He can try one more time for a touchdown. If successful, it would essentially end the game."

"Nope, don't like that. What's the other choice?"

"It's not much better. He can kick a field goal, which would put Richland ahead by only five points. Still, Shiloh would need more than a field goal themselves to pull off an upset. They'd need a last-second touchdown."

Martha wrinkled her lips. Neither one sounded good to her.

"On the sidelines," Lane Lavarre announced, "Coach Duke and his assistant continue a heated debate. This could go either way, but Bobby Lee looks like he has his mind set. He's signaling in his decision, and it appears that he wants to win this game outright. It's fourth down, and the Giants are going for the touchdown. This crowd is going *absolutely* berserk right now."

GRANT

"He's not kicking it?" Grant realized.

This was the window of opportunity they needed. If they could hold the Giants here, Shiloh would take over the ball. With Zach at the helm, they'd have to move downfield in a hurry to get in field-goal range—but it was possible. Anything was possible. Wasn't that what this whole year had been about?

"Brock, Brock! One more down. One more down!"

His player motioned that he understood.

Grant's pulse pounded in his temples. Adrenaline coursed through his limbs. Here they were. Twenty-seven seconds left. And within a field goal.

If we can hold 'em. That stone wall has gotta hold.

BROCK

Brock's eyes scanned the offensive scheme, trying to determine where this play was headed. Surrounded by the screams, the banners, the waving flags, and chanting cheerleaders, he felt his attention start to waver.

Hold on, he told himself. *Stay focused.*

He flashed back to that day on the practice field, blindfolded. Crawling. Dying. Digging down and giving his heart. Giving everything he had.

I will not quit. I will not lose heart.

Brock blinked once and zeroed back in on the Richland quarterback. The guy's eyes flicked by, and Brock saw something there. He sensed it. The guy was marking Brock's position.

They're gonna run it. And they're gonna try to keep it away from me.

Brock angled his upper body, indicating to the opponent that he was geared to go one direction. He would wait, and the moment the center hiked the ball he would shift back the other way. He would fill the stone wall wherever it was needed.

LANE LAVARRE

Lane straightened his leather jacket and tried to suppress his own emotion. He needed his voice to stay even and clear for the broadcast.

It all comes down to this is. My, what a ball game.

He pushed aside his coffee mug and pressed his mouth to the microphone. "They line up at the one-yard line. Wes Porter's gonna take the snap. They're gonna run it. And Brock Kelley's gonna meet him head-on . . . And *there's a fumble*. There's a *fumble!* The Eagles have the football. Number 20 was right there to pick it up, and they're taking it back down the field! He's at the forty, he's at the fifty. Coach Taylor is about ready to jump out of his shoes. Number 20 is at the forty, and he'll be run outta bounds at the thirty-four-yard line. Are you *believin'* this? With two seconds left on the clock, the Eagles have got a *shot* at this football game."

GRANT

Grant was beside himself. His mind raced as he tried to think above the volume of the crowd.

"Two seconds, Grant," said Brady. "We've got time for a Hail Mary."

"No, no," J.T. countered. "The defense's too strong for the pass."

"No, we can't run it. That's our only option."

Grant stood between their dissenting voices, weighing his choices. He'd seen miracle plays before, but the odds weren't good. J.T. was right: All night long the receivers had been covered well by the Giants. Brady also had a point: A run was even less likely to work, one ballcarrier needing to carry it over thirty yards without being tackled and without any penalties.

What would Coach Stephens do here?

Grant could visualize the man in the crowd behind him. Stephens had mentored Grant along those GSU sidelines. All along, God had been preparing him for this job, for this opportunity tonight.

He knew what his old coach would say. He could hear it in his head.

"You gotta kick it, man."

That was it. That's what they would do.

"David." He turned and found his backup kicker. "I need a fifty-one-yard field goal."

"Coach, I can't kick it that far."

"David, they've been stoppin' the run and the pass all night. You're my best option."

The kid's face was a picture of doubt. "Coach, the farthest I've ever kicked is a thirty-nine-yarder. There is *no way* I can kick a fifty-one-yard field goal."

"I believe you can. Your job is to do the best you can and leave the results up to God. I need you on that field." Resolute, he slapped David on the arm and turned back around. "All right, field-goal unit."

"Grant, we've gotta throw it," Brady argued. "He can't kick it from there. It's too far."

"No, it's not."

"What're you doin'?"

Grant wasn't backing down. There was no room for hesitation. He stared into this assistant's eyes and said, "I'm preparing for rain."

CHAPTER 45
The Wind

LANE LAVARRE

Lane wanted to close his eyes. This was painful to watch.

"I don't understand this," he said, "but with two seconds left on the clock, Coach Grant Taylor and the Shiloh Eagles are putting the game in the hands of a hundred-and-forty-five-pound backup kicker."

"This is not a good move on Grant Taylor's part," Dale Hansen agreed. "That's a monstrous kick for anyone, and look at the way the flag's blowing up there. He even has to kick into the wind."

Well, let's just call the play and get this over with.

DAVID

David set up for the kick. He couldn't believe he was out here, late on a December night during his first football season, with the hopes of all these fans and players riding on the trajectory and strength of his right leg.

Fifty-one yards? That's too far.

In the field behind the Taylors' house, he'd managed to get it over forty only once or twice with Jonathan. He was supposed to believe. He was supposed to act on those beliefs. Yeah, he knew all that in his head.

But now I'm lookin' halfway down a football field.

He fixed his eyes on the ball. He had to focus. He'd just do his best, and hope it came close. Nobody really believed he could make this anyway.

J.T.

J.T. rubbed his goatee between his fingers. He appreciated what Coach was trying to do here, but he questioned the chance of success. Sure, some of the best high school players had been known to kick this far.

But a first-year kicker? Little David?

Out on the turf, the kid's shoulders were hunched and his chin was down. His entire body language spoke doubt and fear. In the wheelchair near the fence, Larry Childers had his arms raised, calling out to David, but the crowd was overpowering his voice.

Man, this ain't gonna work. We in trouble.

J.T. approached Grant. "He's not ready. He don't think he can do it."

"Maybe so, but I don't have any more time-outs." Grant stared hard across the field. "Call a time-out, Bobby Lee. Call that time-out."

J.T. followed Grant's eyes and saw the Richland coaches in discussion. Coach Duke was facing Grant, sucker in mouth. They were staring each other down like two fighters before a heavyweight bout. Would Coach Duke try to ice the kicker? If so, it might give Grant and J.T. time to encourage their player.

The Richland coach sent in the call, and a Giants defender flagged down a referee for a time-out.

The whistle blew.

Grant waved. "David, come here!"

LARRY CHILDERS

Larry knew his son was in trouble. For all these years, Larry had prayed for David to be strong, to be used in his weakness. He'd seen David excel at a new school, make friends, join the football team, and even get up the courage to befriend one particular girl.

Those prayers were not going to be wasted on this field.

Please, Lord, not tonight.

He stared at Grant as he tried to encourage his son, wanting desperately to help. But what could he do?

I can't just sit here. I have to act!

Larry unlocked the wheels on his chair and began advancing along the track. He saw Grant Taylor's wife in the stands. He knew how much she meant to David, almost a mother figure in some ways. She'd treated him kindly.

Right now she looked worried, as if that were her own son out there.

Larry continued his maneuver along the track, weaving past the line of SCA cheerleaders. Amanda was on the end.

Larry called out to her as he rolled by, "You just keep cheerin', Amanda. Keep cheerin'."

DAVID

David felt nothing but fear wrapped around his throat. Choking off his oxygen. How had he ended up in this position? All because he listened to his dad and went out for football.

Grant faced him. "Are you tellin' yourself you're gonna miss this kick?"

"Coach, it's too far."

"Listen to me. Do you think God could help you make this kick?"

David lowered his eyes. His helmet felt tight, like it was shrinking.

"Do you believe it, David?"

"Yeah. If He wants to."

"So do I. But you have got to gimme your best and leave the rest up to Him. Will you do that for me?"

He wanted to say yes, but there had to be a better option.

"Whether you make this field goal or not," Grant said, "we're gonna praise Him. But *don't* you walk off this field having done any less than your best."

He nodded. He went back to where Jonathan was setting up for the kick, and the teams were facing off over the scrimmage line.

He was still afraid to look up, to meet anyone's eyes.

I'm gonna try, though. At least I can say I gave it my best shot.

LARRY CHILDERS

Larry wheeled himself to the chain-link fence behind the goalposts. He faced the field. High above, the orange uprights rose into the night sky.

"Okay," he muttered. "I *will* do this."

He gripped the top of the fence and grunted as he pulled himself out of the chair. His arms shook and his muscles felt like brittle rubber bands in this cool temperature, like they would snap at any moment.

Nevertheless, he stood.

With elbows over the top of the fence, he let the chain-link support his weight. He might never be able to kick the ball, or run to scoop up his fallen child, or go on a trail hike in the woods. He might not get everything out of life he'd hoped. Instead, from this chair, he was learning to give.

I'm here, son, givin' you all I've got. Don't you ever stop believin'.

DAVID

David's mind raced as he waited for the snap.

He thought about his dad's words to him, about being weak so that God could get the glory. But even people who loved God didn't win sometimes. And trusting in God didn't automatically make you the best player. All season long, he'd had to practice and hone the skills he'd been given.

What about his namesake in the Bible? David was the youngest, but he cared for his flocks and fought off wild animals to protect them. He developed his skills and built courage.

And then one day he felled a giant with a stone.

Who am I foolin'? This is just a football. A pigskin.

David couldn't bear to look toward his father's position near the bleachers. He couldn't even look at his coaches. Instead, he glanced over at Coach Bobby Lee Duke, who simply folded his arms, shook his head, and sneered.

At least there was no pressure from that guy. He expected the worst.

Yeah, and he'll probably get his wish.

LARRY CHILDERS

Larry stared up the field, hoping to catch his son's eyes. The exertion of keeping himself up was almost more than he could bear.

I'm here, son. Right here.

A field attendant touched Larry on the arm. "Can I help you, sir?"

"Don't *touch* me." Larry forced the words from his lungs. He didn't need some busybody messing with him, and if necessary, he would fight to hold this position. "I'm *standing* for my son."

FACING THE GIANTS

DAVID

David looked up, facing the goalposts that seemed miles away.

And there was his father.

Dad?

Larry was standing, both arms lifted. David had never seen him on his feet for this long, and it caused something to rise up within him. This wasn't just about him and his inabilities. This was about all of them. Rising above.

"Dear Lord, help me make this kick," he whispered.

He inserted his mouthpiece and gave Jonathan a nod.

GRANT

Grant felt a shift in the wind. He looked up and noticed that the American flag high above the stadium was settling down. Then, it fluttered back to life and began rippling in the opposite direction.

He and J.T. exchanged a stunned look.

"Kick it *now!*" Grant bellowed across the field. "Kick it *now!*"

DAVID

Fifty-one yards. All or nothing.

"Set. Hut!"

The center hiked the ball, and Jonathan's steady hands were there to catch it. He set it in place. David took two steps, planting his left leg while bringing back his right. With every ounce of his strength, with no fear of the consequences, he swung his kicking foot through its entire trajectory. He connected and followed through, trying to give the ball as much lift as possible, as much distance.

The turf was loose here near the center of the field. The sheer velocity of the kicking motion dislodged his support leg and he went up in the air.

He came down hard on his back.

Now he was looking at nothing but stadium lights. Although he'd lost track of the kick, Jonathan was above him, staring off down the field.

His friend began to tense. That was not a good sign.

LANE LAVARRE

"The kick is up. It's on its way. It's *long* enough. It's *high* enough. Does it have the distance?"

In unison, Lane and Dale leaned over the broadcast table and watched the ball fly toward the end zone and scrape through the inside left corner of the goalposts.

"It does!" he yelled. "It's good, it's good, it's good! The Eagles have won. The Eagles have won the state championship. I *can't* believe what I've just seen. I *cannot* believe what I've just seen! A miracle has occurred here tonight! The Shiloh Eagles have defeated the Richland Giants, 24 to 23, to take the state title for the first time in their history. It's *incredible*. It's absolutely *unbelievable*!"

Dale Hansen came in on his mike: "The crowd here is screaming so loud, we can hardly think. The Shiloh players have lifted David Childers on their shoulders, and they're carrying him across the field. Who would've expected this? There's gonna be a lot of hoarse voices tomorrow in the fine state of Georgia, but the Eagles have *won*! This is a complete miracle!"

GRANT

Grant pounded the backs of several of his players before jumping up to high-five David, who was on his teammates' shoulders. He spotted Brock Kelley lying faceup on the ground, with fingers jabbing at the sky, and he dropped beside him. He thumped him on the chest. "*You* are a state champion! *You* are a state champion!"

He rose back to his feet and caught the eye of Coach Stephens in the stands. He pointed his finger at the man and grinned. Stephens pointed back.

Everyone was here, it seemed.

Brooke was cheering, along with Jackie. Mr. Bridges was higher in the stands, beaming with the joy of a dream fulfilled. Neil Prater was on the field, hugging his son. J.T.'s wife was bouncing up and down with a child in her arms, her smile as radiant as the sun.

On the far sidelines, Coach Duke was a man sleepwalking.

Grant headed in his direction. The coach was a three-time champion, and he deserved a measure of respect. As Grant grew close, he reached out his arm. No words needed to be exchanged. A simple handshake would do.

Bobby Lee's eyes swiveled onto him and narrowed. He ignored Grant's hand and said, "Coach Baylor."

"Uh, Taylor."

"You like yachts?"

"Yachts?"

"You know, nice boats with large sails."

"Sure." Grant moved his chin up and down, but he was thinking: *Is this guy loony? Is he tryin' to block out what just happened?*

"Good." Bobby Lee clapped him hard on the back. "We'll go out on the water sometime. I can always use a hand on deck, and you seem pretty good at readin' the wind."

"Thanks. I, uh . . . I just try to follow where it leads."

GRANT

Grant edged his way into the locker room through a bunch of rowdy Eagles. The team whooped and shoved, punched the air and one another. Some lifted their helmets over their heads, shouting out in celebration. J.T. and Brady were right there with the boys, taking it all in.

"Hey!" Grant barked. He lofted a tall, glistening trophy with both hands. "Who's the state champions?"

The players banged helmets and cheered.

Grant handed off the trophy to Brady. He didn't want to put a damper on the mood, but he did want to harness their energy and turn it in the right direction. He wanted them to remember this moment, these words, this gathering, for the rest of their lives.

Not all of their experiences would be bright—he knew that firsthand. Some questions would never be answered—he knew that too.

But none of that changes what God did here tonight.

"Okay, okay. I've got something to say." The noise quieted, and he pointed across the room. "David Childers."

David stepped forward. A hush fell over the room.

Grant said, "Don't you ever let anyone tell you that you're under-par, second-rate, or inferior. I just watched God do a *miracle* through you."

David listened, unblinking.

"I saw a field of Giants, eighty-five of them to be exact, fall in defeat. Now you tell me what's impossible with God."

"Nothing, Coach."

"You sound like you mean that."

"I do." David's mouth twitched with a grin.

Grant swiveled toward the others. They waited, seemingly eager to give witness to what had happened out on the field. Each had played a role. Each bore the aches and bruises of battle. Each had a story to tell.

BROOKE

Brooke slipped through a throng of reporters and Shiloh parents. She overheard Neil Prater being asked about his son's college football prospects, and she was pretty sure she knew his answer.

"Oh, we're longtime Bulldog fans," Neil verified. "And Matt bleeds Georgia red. That'd be his first choice."

She made her way into the locker room. Even though she'd be riding home with Jackie while the coaches took the team out to celebrate, she wanted to hear the words that would cap off this amazing victory.

Not to mention, I have a little secret to share. Judging by the pandemonium, however, that would probably have to wait.

As she stepped into the room, she found Grant with his back to her. He was addressing the boys, and they were soaking it in.

"How 'bout it, Zach?" he said to his quarterback. "I just watched you and the offense do what they said could *not* be done. Where other teams have *crumbled* under the Giants, you stood tall. Now you tell me what's impossible with God."

"Nothing, Coach."

"Brock?" Grant rested a hand on the team captain's shoulder. "How 'bout it? You built that stone wall, didn't you? And it *stood*."

Brock could barely contain his smile. He nodded.

"Now you tell me what's impossible with God."

"Nothing, Coach."

"How 'bout it, Scott?" Grant asked the next player on the bench. "What's impossible with God?"

"Nothing."

"Are you sure? 'Cause those giants are *big*. They outnumber us three to one. Are you sure there's nothing impossible with God?"

Brooke wanted to call out the answer herself. Oh, if only Grant knew that she was here, knew that his unborn child was in this room. He had no idea. And yet he was stating the truth to his team. Guiding them. Mentoring them.

"I'm sure, Coach," the player responded.

Grant still pressed them. "How 'bout it, Nathan? What's impossible with God?"

"Nothing, Coach."

"Jonathan?"

"Nothing."

"Are you positive?"

"Positive, Coach."

"So am I." Grant softened his voice. "So am I. God can do whatever He wants to do, however He wants to do it. And He *chooses* to work in our lives 'cause He loves us, 'cause He's good. I hope today's a *milestone* for what He can do for the *rest* of your life—if you trust Him." He removed his cap. "Now, why don't we spend some time thankin' Him."

Brooke slipped out the door as the guys kneeled as a team.

MR. BRIDGES

Mr. Bridges could hardly take all the excitement. He'd been part of an incredible evening. Back home, in his dark garage, he took a moment to acknowledge the Lord's goodness and faithfulness.

Thank You, Jesus, for lettin' me see this day. Thank You for the hearts and lives You've changed this year. May You be praised!

The smell of chicken and dumplings greeted him at the door. He found his daughter putting away dishes and wiping down kitchen counters.

"Grace, you're a welcome sight."

"Welcome home," said Mrs. Carter. "You did it, Dad!"

"The boys did it, not me."

"But all your prayers, your perseverance. You helped inspire them."

"I was just doing as I was asked, and waitin' for something to happen. I'm tellin' ya, I felt like Simeon, just an old man hoping and praying to see a promise fulfilled. Where's Mom?"

"In the den. You know, you must've passed on something to her, because I've never seen her so wrapped up in a game. She's probably asleep on the sofa. I haven't heard a sound from her."

Bridges looked down the hall. Lamplight spilled from the den.

Martha? Something in him jumped.

He rushed along the carpet, as fast as his shuffling feet would permit. He rounded the doorway and found his wife huddled and motionless under a blanket. The material wasn't even covering her feet.

"Martha?"

No response.

The old radio hummed and crackled in the corner. That ancient thing had done its job, serving faithfully for years, but it couldn't last much longer.

He moved closer. He wondered what his life would be like without her. Of course at their age they'd talked about that sort of thing. With Social Security and his Cooper Tire retirement, either one could make it financially. Plus, Grace lived close by, along with her young'uns.

But he still didn't like the idea. He was an old man. In so many ways she was stronger than him. He couldn't live without her, he really couldn't.

"Martha?"

She snorted and lifted one eyelid. "Huh? Oh, Raymond."

He swallowed. His pulse was at a near standstill. "Hi."

"You won."

"We won."

"You got to see it for yourself. Well, that's a good thing." Her eyelids closed again. She looked peaceful.

He adjusted the blanket so that it covered her feet. He whispered, "I guess I don't tell ya enough, but I love you, Martha. Now more than ever."

Her mouth twitched and her face relaxed.

It was best to let her rest. Time to turn off this old radio. Mr. Bridges scooted to the corner, but the radio's lights began to flicker before his hand could find the knob. The big wooden cabinet emitted a loud pop, and the flickering continued, followed by a high-pitched whine.

It's time, Bridges thought. *This ol' boy has run his course.*

And then he felt something in his own rib cage pop. His vision blurred and wavered as numbness spread from his chest through his body. He tried to resist it, but it continued with inexorable certainty.

Not an unpleasant sensation. Not entirely. A bit of pain and tingles, but manageable.

He staggered onto one knee. "Oh," he cried softly.

The clamps tightened around his heart. He thought about his nitro pills, but he couldn't feel much of anything now. He could hear only the pulse roaring in his ears. He reached forward with gnarled fingers and brushed the radio's polished surface.

You done good, you ol' thing. You done good.

He crumpled onto the carpet, looking up one last time as the lights on the radio dial began to fade.

GRANT

Grant had scarfed down pizza with the guys and felt overwhelmed by the events of the past few hours, not to mention the past few months. He didn't understand why it had taken years for a break-through in their school, on their team. He didn't understand a lot of things. But he did know that he believed every word he had said to the boys in that locker room.

On the pickup seat beside him, a gift waited to be unwrapped.

"What is it?" he'd asked David Childers.

"I'll explain it after you open it."

"Right now?"

"No. Uh, you and Brooke can open it together."

"We'll do that."

Grant parked the Ford truck in the driveway. A light was on in the living room, indicating Brooke was home. He moved through the door into the dining room, where a bouquet of wildflowers sat on the table. He'd picked them up for her earlier in the week, making good on that rain check.

He set down his ball cap, his jacket, and the wrapped gift.

"Well," said Brooke. "Look who just walked in this house."

He turned to see her on the living room sofa. She was painted by soft lighting, wearing jeans and a dark shirt, with a beaded cross necklace.

She folded her hands beneath her chin and gazed up at him. "Couldn't be the state champion coach, Grant Taylor, could it? 'Cause he's not supposed to live here. He's supposed to be out lookin' for a job."

Grant leaned against the doorframe. He put his hands into his pockets. "God did it, Brooke. He did it. He gave me this job, provided for our needs, took away my fear. And throws in the state championship just because He can." He knelt in front of her. "It's been one of the best days of my life."

She smiled and shook her head. "The day's not over yet."

"Whaddya mean?"

"Grant Taylor." Her voice began to crack. "I just want you to know . . . that you've made the team."

"What team?"

She cupped his face with both hands and stared him straight in the eyes. She said, "The daddy team."

Grant stared back at her, stunned. His brow furrowed and his heartbeat quickened as he processed her words. "We're gonna have a baby?"

"We're gonna have a baby." She held out the sheet from the doctor's office. "I just found out today."

Grant looked down at the paper, then felt a wave of emotion begin to spill out of him. He'd already witnessed a miracle today. He'd already praised God for doing the impossible. And he'd determined to be content with the Lord's plan for his life, for his job, for his family. Now God was doing something more, something only He could do.

Grant dragged a hand over his head as his eyes began to fill with tears.

Brooke reached forward again and held his chin. "You tell me, Coach Taylor . . . Tell me what's impossible when God's on your side."

"Oh, God." He let himself crouch forward so that his head was on Brooke's lap. She draped her arm over his back and laid her head on his as he began to sob. "Oh, God," he said again. "I'm overwhelmed."

END OF A SEASON

CHAPTER 47
Two Years Later

GRANT

Grant was on his knees in the pecan grove. The dew pressed through his pants, but the day was already warming up. All around him, beams of sunlight set the orchard on fire with gold and green hues.

He raised his hands in thanks.

God had been good to them. Grant and Brooke had a beautiful son, and another on the way. Of course, he was still making thirty thousand a year. With Brooke now staying home with little Caleb, they were minus her part-time income. In other words, they were making no more now than they had in his last losing season.

Plus, they had kids to provide for.

And the dryer that still cut out every now and then.

Not to mention the—

Stop right there, he thought. *The point is, I'm learning to be content.*

A car was coming down Old Pretoria. It slowed and turned into the Taylor driveway. Grant stood and waved at David Childers.

The kid was no longer a kid. He'd graduated from Shiloh Christian Academy last month. After a trip to Statesboro with Grant and Larry Childers, he'd decided to enter the Sports Medicine program at GSU. It was the end of a season, with new opportunities around the bend.

For David, though, it was a tough decision. Amanda had received an academic scholarship to the University of Kentucky, and they would be a day's drive apart.

"It's not that far," Grant told him.

"But far enough," David shot back. "I, uh . . . I just wonder if I'm gonna lose another woman in my life."

"The road ahead's gonna have a lot of dips and turns, David."

"I can already feel myself pullin' away from her."

"You're going into a protective mode, and that's normal. But let me say this. You follow where the Lord leads and trust that His plan is best. You don't have to go wanderin' off through the thorns to find the path of your future wife. Your paths will come together, if you stay within God's will."

"You're sayin' I should just trust Him, in other words."

"When it all comes down to it, yes. You won't always understand. Some days it'll look dark and you'll wrestle with doubts. But trust Him."

DAVID

David settled on the Taylors' living room couch. Most of the time he didn't say much when he stopped by. He just liked being around a family, seeing them interact. Maybe someday he'd have one of his own.

He glanced at pictures of the Shiloh football teams in the scrapbook on the coffee table. So many memories. A picture of Mr. Bridges caught his eye. Had it been two years already since his funeral? Hundreds had attended, and his legacy had sparked a weekly prayer ministry of both students and parents. They even had plans to name the new education wing after him.

"Look at all these guys," Grant said. "It's the title game."

He had blond Caleb on his lap, at a low table cluttered with plastic football figures. Caleb's thirteen-month-old hands gripped the toys and banged them on the wood.

"Daddy would've run a different play," Grant said. "Someday I'll teach you football in the backyard, but we need your little brother to get here first."

Caleb swept his hand through the plastic troops.

"Hey, guys," said Brooke, coming in from the dining room.

"Hey."

"Hi, Mrs. Taylor," David responded.

She rested a hand on her swollen belly and watched her husband and son playing together. She was wearing a loose pink-striped blouse.

A fraternity shirt? David wondered. *No, I think it's maternity. I can never keep those straight.*

Behind Brooke, on a mantelpiece, a pair of trophies represented Shiloh's back-to-back state championships. His favorite part, though, was the framed Scripture on the wall between them.

It read:

> *With God all things are possible.*
> Mt. 19:26

Amanda had done a great job on the calligraphy. All he'd done was come up with a frame. Of course, they shouldn't have tried to borrow the school's art supplies without asking—which had gotten them in trouble two years ago—but it was meant to be a surprise.

"Grant," Brooke said. "I've been thinkin' maybe we should get a cat."

"What? You mean, like a pet for the kids?"

"No, to take care of our rodent problem."

"Our what?"

"I found another rat."

"What'd you do with it?"

"I bagged him up and threw him in the garbage."

"Are you serious?"

"Didn't think I had it in me, did you?" She winked. "Well, he was just a little thing anyway. He just had a big stink."

"Speakin' of which, I think your son needs a diaper change."

"He's all yours."

"He's *my* son when he needs cleaning up, is that how it works?" Grant stood, holding Caleb at arm's length and wrinkling his nose.

"Don't tell me, Grant Taylor, that you're afraid to face your fears, 'cause I know you better than that."

On the couch, David tried to stifle his chuckle.

"Oh." Grant turned his way. "You think that's funny, do you?"

"Uh, no, Coach. Well, maybe just a little."

ACKNOWLEDGMENTS

FROM ALEX KENDRICK AND STEPHEN KENDRICK TO:

Eric Wilson (writer)—You are a gifted writer and a joy to work with! May God bless you as you have blessed us.

Larry and Rhonwyn Kendrick (Dad and Mom)—You led us to Christ and have been a faithful model for us. Thank you for honoring the Lord with your lives! We love you dearly!

Christina and Jill (our wives)—If there's one thing we did really, really well, it was in choosing our wives! Your support and love are priceless! We love you.

Allen Arnold and Amanda Bostic (publisher and editor)—Thank you for your belief in this story. Doing this novel was a dream come true!

Michael Catt and Jim McBride (pastors)—Your counsel, encouragement, and friendship have made our time at Sherwood a blessing. We love and admire you.

Sherwood Baptist Church (home church)—God has blessed us with one of the best churches on the planet. Your faith and love as a body of believers are amazing!

FROM ERIC WILSON TO:

Alex and Stephen Kendrick (screenwriters)—It's been a joy to collaborate. You guys not only made me laugh, you made me cry.

Allen Arnold and Amanda Bostic (publisher and editor)—Who would've guessed this would be our first project together? Thanks for giving me a chance at a fifty-one-yarder.

ACKNOWLEDGMENTS

Carolyn, Cassie, and Jackie Wilson (wife and daughters)—
Through one storm after another, you make this family a beautiful place to be.

*Coach Fisher, Vince Young, and the Tennessee Titans (NFL football team)—*You showed how it could be done, and gave me the encouragement to keep fighting.

*Coach Peter Russell, Coach Ralph Perry, and Coach Red Crabb (mentors in my school years)—*Without your training, I may have never learned the perseverance for this job.

*Downtown Nashville's FedEx Kinko's team (my coworkers)—*Your patience and flexibility continue to make my writing possible. You guys rock.

*Readers Everywhere (yeah, you!)—*I write with you in mind. I pray that you'll come to know Jesus deeper than ever, no matter what life throws your way.

Alex and Stephen with their dad

HOW DAD TAUGHT US TO FACE OUR GIANTS
By: Alex and Stephen Kendrick

In the fall of 2006, hundreds of movie theaters across the nation projected a scene of a football coach daring his blindfolded team captain to attempt his most difficult drill. The "death crawl" required him to cross the field on his hands and feet while carrying another player on his back. After pushing his body to the limit, he begged the coach to let him stop short of the goal. "It's too hard! My arms are burning!" he yelled. But the coach's passion to see him succeed surpassed the boy's desire to give up. "Don't quit! Don't quit! Don't quit!" the coach screamed with more intensity as every additional yard only increased the pain.

If you turned toward the audience at this point in the film *Facing the Giants* you would see more than a few men with tears in their eyes as they questioned their own level of commitment. But as the coach's impassioned voice echoed between the theater walls, his message "not to quit" actually originated years before in the hearts of the screenwriters as they watched their own father's life.

OUR DAD

When my brother Stephen and I were writing the script for *Facing the Giants* in my living room, it was seemingly impossible not to let our dad's influence effect what we wrote. So many lines came from things he said to us. So many of the lessons were things he taught us. God blessed us with Larry Kendrick as our dad, and in many ways, he has become a hero to us. Proverbs 17:6 says, "The glory of children are their fathers", and that is certainly true of us.

As kids, when we began making movies in our backyard with the family video camera, our parents weren't sure what to think of it. Most of our movies had the same plot, "chase 'em down and beat 'em up!" In our versions, however, James Bond was baptized into "Savings Bond," and Indiana Jones became "Alabama Jones" in his quest for the Biblical sword of Ehud.

"Dad, when I grow up, I want to make movies," I would say. And Stephen was sure he wanted to be a stunt man. This did not necessarily thrill our mother, Rhonwyn, who hoped our current dose of piano lessons and church camps would persuade us otherwise. But the camps became new story locations and piano translated into movie scores. Over the years, our passion was only getting stronger.

At first, our interest in movie making was foreign to our father. He grew up battling his share of insecurities and fears. His seven-foot-tall father, who drank alcohol in his early days, was an imposing presence in his childhood. (We used to hug his knees.) And although Granddad lived for Christ later in his life, our dad's formative years were marked by a lack of confidence that kept him away from athletics, music, or social activities. But somewhere along the way, he began to sense a call into the ministry. Although he had accepted Christ in his youth, he reasoned his best option was to pursue education and become a teacher. However, God's gentle voice kept calling. One day he knelt next to a creek and surrendered to the ministry. As part of his commitment to Christ, he resolved that when it came to passing fear and insecurity to another generation, the "buck" would stop with him. He committed to be faithful to his wife and to the Lord. He resolved that his children would know the love and acceptance of their father and would see him live a godly life before them. If God gave him the opportunity to give his children wings to fly,

he would support them the best he knew how.

Our parents were married in 1965, and two years later, our brother Shannon was born. I arrived in 1970, followed by Stephen in 1973. Our parents dedicated all three of us to the Lord and begin praying scriptures over our lives. As we grew, we were kept in church, given the chance to play instruments and participate in sports. Dad didn't demand perfection, he was just glad we were out there trying. We were kept in line by loving discipline and were encouraged to seek the Lord in our teen years. On several occasions, we stumbled upon Dad early in the morning, sitting on the side of his bed as he read his Bible and prayed. We found Mom doing the same. As teenagers, we would sit in front of their mirror, parting our 80's hairstyles down the middle while they read passages of scripture aloud. It seemed sufficient to hear a little scripture each day to feel good about our spiritual walk as young men. But that was before Dad got sick.

THE FIRST GIANT

In *Facing the Giants*, there's an older character named Larry Childers. He's confined to a wheelchair with a disease called Multiple Sclerosis (MS), but his outlook on life and level of faith are stronger than most men. He encourages his son not to give up when things get tough, and believes that God can do the impossible. That character is our dad.

In 1984, we can remember getting ready for school and noticing Dad still in bed. It was unlike him to be the last one up. He normally was ready to head to work at the church. "Dad needs to get some more rest," Mom said. But the next day was the same, then the next week. We then learned Dad was diagnosed with something called "MS." He soon slipped into depression and we began to understand just how serious it was.

Over the next few months, Dad struggled to understand what God was doing and why this was happening. His body began to break down, and before long he was experiencing everything from severe numbness to burning pain. Doctors gave him a number of experimental medicines, but no cure. He was told he may be blind, deaf, or paralyzed in the near future. It not only scared him, it scared us. While our mom prayed and tried to keep us busy, Dad silently spiralled into darker depression.

When a man realizes he can't protect or provide for his family the way he wants, it does something to him. His self-esteem takes a dive, then his attitude towards life. Apathy and depression soon take over and hope is slowly stripped away. We know now that the deepest test of faith is when you feel like God has abandoned you.

After 16 months of struggling to understand his pain, Dad hit rock bottom. One day while we were in school and Mom was at work, he knelt down beside the bed and let his frustration and confusion pour out like water. He wept aloud before the Lord and told God he was done trying to understand. "Either take me home or heal me, but don't leave me here! I can't live in this personal hell anymore! Jesus, You are my Lord and You can do anything, but I don't know where You are in this nightmare! I have confessed every sin I can think of and waited on You, but You are silent! Why, Lord? Why won't You help me? Are You not the God Who heals? Can You not reach down and take me out of this pit?"

He had resolved to serve God with his life. He had determined to love his family with everything he had. He had walked in integrity and honor, but here he was, wilting away in pain. But that wasn't the end of his prayer. Through his tears and trembling, he also made a deeper commitment. "Jesus, though I do not understand, I will praise you whether you heal me or not! I will not walk away from you!"

When tested, most men don't cling to the Lord. Most men give up. But our dad is not most men. He clung in amazing faith to an amazing God Who wants us to live our lives in total reliance on Him. It was there on our father's knees that God manifested His presence to him after months of silence. He peacefully reminded Dad that He loved him, was with him and had never left him. Dad got up, got dressed, and began the rest of his life.

HOW OUR DAD TAUGHT US . . .

A RENEWED FAITH

Over the next few months, the doctors were amazed. Although Dad was not completely healed, his regression slowed. He still experienced burning and numbness, but his attitude changed and his spirit lifted.

We all noticed. Something was different about Dad. He did whatever it took to attend our school and church events. He prayed with new zeal, and told us of his renewed commitment to God. We were amazed.

Others noticed too. "What happened to Larry Kendrick?" they asked. "I thought he was supposed to get worse, not better." But the healing was more internal. His faith in God was no longer based on the blessings God provided, but on the fact that God deserves worship and praise because of Who He is, not just for what He does for us.

Dad began preparing for God's next assignment when he was asked to teach at the Christian school Stephen and I were attending. Right after I graduated, the school folded, leaving hundreds of students not knowing where to go. God birthed in Dad a vision for a new school, and he shared his hope with us. "We serve a God Who opens doors that no man can shut," Dad would quote (Rev. 3:7). But it didn't make sense on paper! He needed teachers, facilities, and funding, and he had little to nothing! But he believed God was in it and was determined not to give up. We saw Dad do what we now call "preparing for rain." As he prayed, he moved forward in faith.

In 1989, he founded Cumberland Christian Academy using the facilities of a local church. Several teachers and 81 students came aboard, and though many thought it impossible, the new school set sail.

Over the next few years, attendance grew to over 400 students and several campuses. Many students came to Christ and were challenged to live with a persevering faith. As Dad's body continued to get weaker, his faith only got stronger.

Today the school is in its 18th year, and Larry Kendrick is still the Headmaster as he travels across the campuses ministering to students, teachers, and families from his motorized wheelchair. Dad cannot stand anymore, but he stands in intercession for us and his 13 grandchildren daily. When people watch his physical struggle, then see his commitment to God and positive outlook, they get a new perspective on their own problems. We now see how his bodily limitations afford him a greater spiritual impact on everyone he touches.

DAD'S ARROWS

During Dad's years at Cumberland, Shannon, Stephen, and I graduated from college. Shannon went to work for IBM, and Stephen and I attended seminary and accepted God's call into full time ministry.

Over the next few years, the Lord gave

each of us godly wives. At our request, Dad performed all of our weddings, and gave us each a special gift. In front of our family and friends, he gave us a father's blessing. He spoke of his strong love for us and unconditional acceptance of his new daughters. He committed his life-long friendship and prayer support to us, and said he was releasing us as arrows from his quiver into the world to do God's will. Every young man should hear those words from his father. It was one of those unforgettable moments that completely filled our hearts!

PRODUCTION BEGINS

Shannon would go on to become a church deacon and Stephen and I led student ministries at Roswell St. Baptist in Marietta, Georgia. The desire to make movies never left us, and we often produced short videos for ministry illustrations or events.

Those videos opened a new door in 1999, when I became the Media minister at Sherwood Baptist in Albany, Georgia. Two years later, Stephen came on board as a preaching assistant to Michael Catt, the Senior Pastor.

Michael is a courageous "out of the box" leader, and somewhat of a renegade. If he believes a ministry idea can reach people with the gospel and is not contrary to scripture, he is willing to try it. After reading a survey indicating that movies and TV were among the greatest influencers in our cul-

ture today, I pitched the idea of producing a low budget feature to him. He prayed about it . . . then told us to proceed. So in 2002, Sherwood Pictures was born with no initial funding, scripts, or movie equipment. But we had seen that scenario before. Our dad had followed God toward a vision on faith, but he never gave up and it became a reality.

There's a big difference between a "good idea" and a "God idea." If God is in it, it will work. So we prayed for a movie plot and enough money to produce it. The result was a $20,000 movie called *Flywheel*. The cast and crew were all church members, and the movie was completed and scheduled for a spring 2003 release at our local theater in Albany. We finished it the day it premiered and were praying it wouldn't be cheesy.

The response shocked us! During a six week run, *Flywheel* became the second highest grossing movie of the theater's 16 screens. Blockbuster then released it in 4,500 stores nationwide. Numerous television networks aired it, and it picked up seven awards at film festivals. But the most important response was the hundreds of emails and phone calls from inspired viewers who had made new decisions for Christ after seeing the movie. God had done it and we were ecstatic!

FACING THE GIANTS

We almost immediately began praying for another movie plot. Looking back through our lives, we noted how God had worked in our family and church. We remembered the struggles and commitments Dad had made to the Lord. A scene idea was sparked of a dad in a wheelchair trying to support his fearful son from the sidelines at a football game.

We coupled this with inspiring stories of answered prayer from friends around us in Albany, and began writing *Facing the Giants*. Each night, Stephen and I would begin with prayer asking for scene ideas, humor, and Biblical truths to communicate in the script. We begged the Lord to develop the story into something that would impact hearts, communicate authentic Christianity, and honor the Word of God and the name of Jesus. We also began praying for the money to fund it, better equipment to shoot it, and the people to make it happen.

Once again, our pastors and incredible church family at Sherwood Baptist stepped up and volunteered to give, act, pray, and work. With no fund-raising, the Lord prompted people to give tens of thousands of dollars so the project could move forward. Having been inspired by *Flywheel*, David Nixon productions from Orlando, Florida put together a team of five professionals and joined the adventure to help Sherwood tell the story of *Facing the Giants* with production excellence. After dedicating the project to the Lord, the church began shooting on Tuesday, April 27, 2004. Director of Photography Bob

Scott, Assistant Director David Nixon, Gaffer Keith Slade, Sound Mixer Rob Whitehurst, and 1st Assistant Cameraman Chip Byrd were present on set training our volunteers and operating the equipment for the production.

Bob Scott had just worked on the set of a major Hollywood movie and said he believed that God had been preparing him through 20 years of professional football photography to shoot our movie.

Because of their unique availability, retired men, stay-at-home moms, and home-schooled teens primarily compiled the working crew during the six weeks of shooting. Though none of the actors were paid and the majority of the cast and crew had no prior experience, we all moved forward in faith. Locations for the movie were donated by local residents, businesses, and schools and over 500 volunteers from all ages got involved. Sunday school classes cooked meals for the crew each day. The entire movie was shot with one high definition Panasonic Vericam Camera and edited on a PowerMac G5 computer using Final Cut Pro HD software.

By the spring of 2005, the first edited version of *Giants* was completed. God had gotten us through production, but we had prayed for a wide theatrical release. So far nothing seemed to be coming over the horizon.

We were told by numerous people that it would take a miracle for a distributor to take a low budget movie with "no name" actors made by volunteers from a church. It just wasn't realistic. But since when is a miracle ever realistic?

Our last piece to the movie was a popular song we wanted to use from the group Third Day. After contacting their label, Provident Music Group, in Nashville, they told us they needed to see the movie first. We sent a DVD, and then prayed for favor.

Isn't it like God to set up unlikely odds so that He can intervene for His glory? Can He not do more than we could ever hope or imagine?

Provident loved the movie, and not only granted us permission for the song, but sent it to their parent company—which happened to be Sony, the largest movie distributor in the world. They liked *Facing the Giants* enough to release it in 441 theaters across the nation. We had been praying Ephesians 3:20 —that God would do more than we could ask or imagine and He was answering in flying colors. We were blown away! On September 29, 2006, our feeble "five loaves and two fish" were multiplied into a 17 week

run that impacted 1.7 million people from Tampa, Florida to Anchorage, Alaska! God's $100,000 movie grossed over $10 million and we began receiving thousands of emails and calls about changed lives.

With over 3,000 reported professions of faith in Christ, we were humbled again by God's amazing habit of being glorified. The DVD has now been translated into 10 languages and released in 56 countries. This little movie made by a church in South Georgia is now reaching the world with a message of hope and faith.

Its message was first written in our hearts while watching the Word of God being lived out in our church and in the life of our father. Dad could have given up when his MS diagnosis showed no cure, but he didn't. He could have given up on God when he suffered in the midst of depression, but he didn't. He could have given up when starting a new school seemed impossible, but he didn't. That resolve gave us a foundation to trust God for the impossible and to praise Him whether we win or lose!

LESSONS ABOUT FATHERING THAT WE LEARNED FROM DAD:

1. LOVE GOD PASSIONATELY: Fathers are commanded to love God wholeheartedly and teach their children to do so as well (Deut. 6:4-9). A child will figure out whether God is first in his dad's heart. Go beyond taking your kids to church and praying before meals. We saw Dad serve in church faithfully, give sacrificially, and worship sincerely. It was a love relationship rather than a religious duty.

FACING THE GIANTS

2. WALK IN INTEGRITY: God promises to "bless and make mighty" the children of a man with integrity (Pr. 20:7, Ps. 112:2). Our dad was the same man in private that he was in public. You can't fool God. Don't compromise and God promises to bless your parenting.

3. LOVE YOUR SPOUSE: Fathers are to love their wives as Christ loved the church (Eph. 5:25). Children are best raised within the soil of a healthy marriage. Dad has been faithful to mom for 42 years. We watched him love her, defend her, and apologize to her when he blew it. It brings amazing security when a child knows his parents are devoted to one another. You are establishing their future marriage model.

4. BE A MENTOR: It is a father's responsibility to daily pour God's Word and life lessons into his children (Deut. 6:7). We would hear Dad talk about the Lord on the phone, around the table, and as we traveled in our amazing green torpedo station wagon.

5. DISCIPLINE YOUR CHILDREN: Fathers are commanded to train up their children with Godly nurture and discipline (Eph 6:4). Dad would lay down the rules, but use Biblical discipline when necessary. Although we were assured of his love for us, he still applied one of those thick, leather 70's belts to our constitution. That did not feel "groovy." But we needed it and thank God for it now.

6. BLESS YOUR CHILDREN: Children tend to develop their identity and sense of security from their father (Prov. 17:6). God commanded Israel to bless their children. It means "graciously speaking success" over their lives. God the Father also blessed Jesus at His baptism. They phrase "You are my beloved child, in whom I am well pleased" should flow from the lips of dads throughout their kids' lives. Learn how to bless your children using Num. 6:22-27, Deut. 28, and Mt. 3:17.

7. CULTIVATE THEIR DESIGN: God has uniquely pre-wired each child for His purposes with specific gifts, talents, and passions (Eph. 2:10). Wise parents will discover Heaven's blueprint within their child and cultivate it. Dad gave us lots of opportunities, but also gave us permission to fail. He never forced us to be what God had not designed us to be. He taught us to seek the Lord and commit our abilities to Him (Prov. 16:3, 1 Cor. 10:31).

8. PRAY WITH YOUR KIDS: The prayers of a righteous man are powerful and effective (Jam. 5:16). Children can learn to fearfully and humbly approach the throne of grace by watching how their fathers pray. We saw God answer prayers in Dad's life in amazing ways.

He and mom would often pray Psalm 91, Psalm 1, and Isaiah 54:13 over us and they still do today. Dare to pray with your kids to the God of the impossible!

A PERSONAL MESSAGE FROM
THE KENDRICK BROTHERS:

We want to challenge you in your own spiritual journey. If you do not have a relationship with Jesus Christ, we want you to know that He is the Real Deal. We're not talking about religion . . . we're talking about a relationship with Jesus. He alone has proven to be the link to God that people are longing for . . . and desperately need.

His entire life demonstrates this. His virgin birth, sinless life, powerful teachings, amazing miracles, unconditional love, sacrificial death, miraculous resurrection, and impact on the world all are unique to Jesus Christ alone. Read Matthew, Mark, Luke, and John in the Bible and see for yourself. He is not only qualified to forgive your sin, but He can change your heart and make it pleasing towards a holy God. Quit trusting in yourself to get into Heaven.

Scripture says that all of us have fallen short of His righteousness (Romans 3). That's why God lovingly sent Jesus. His death on the cross was necessary to make things right between sinful people and a holy God. He didn't have to do that. That's just love in action . . . personified.

Regardless of where you are, let us encourage and challenge you, on behalf of Christ, to surrender to God today. Romans 10:9 says that if you confess with your mouth—Jesus as your Lord (Master or Boss), and you believe in your heart that God has raised Him from the dead, then you will be saved.

If you are already an obedient follower of Christ, then we want to encourage you further in your spiritual walk. We challenge you to start putting feet to your faith—to "prepare for rain" by praying radical prayers and living a life that demonstrates your trust in God.

We encourage you to refocus your passions toward the higher purpose of glorifying God and not just for your own temporary fulfillment in this life.

Don't let anything to cause you to stop loving Him—whether its infertility, losing your health, your job, your spouse, or anything else. Resolve in your heart that you will praise God when you win and when you lose. Find a group of believers at a local church that share this passion and that will join you in facing your giants!

May God bless you!

Alex Kendrick and Stephen Kendrick

BEHIND THE SCENES

COMMISSIONING SERVICE: The Sherwood Baptist church family prayerfully dedicates *Facing the Giants* to the glory of God.

SHOOTING THE FANS: Director of Photography, Bob Scott, guides the Panasonic Vericam HD camera during a crowd shot.

HUDDLE ACTION: A team of volunteers were guided by professional, Keith Slade, who designed the lighting for this outdoor huddle scene.

THE SOUND OF REVIVAL: Pro Sound Mixer Rob Whitehurst captures the audio of a pivotal scene with volunteer actors Alex Kendrick and James Blackwell.

GAME DAY FANS:
Sherwood church members were strategically positioned in the stands during games scenes.

DEAD CAR SHOT:
The camera is prepared for the broken car scene when Brooke sinks down into the floorboard.

ALEX AND STEPHEN KENDRICK:
Alex (left) functioned as the director and an actor on the set while Stephen worked as the producer behind the scenes.

PRODUCTION LEADERSHIP:
L to R: Rob Whitehurst (Sound), David Nixon (Assistant Director), Alex Kendrick (Director), Stephen Kendrick (Producer), Keith Slade (Lighting), Bob Scott (Director of Photography), Chip Byrd (1st Assistant Cameraman)

BEHIND THE SCENES

REVERSE RED CARPET:
The Albany premiere had church members face the red carpet while the actors stood on the sidelines and cheered.

MAIN CHURCH MOVIE CREW:
The primary crew of *Facing the Giants*.

In the summer of 2007, Alex and Stephen began working on the script for Sherwood's next movie *Fireproof*, which focuses on covenant marriage.

"BROCK, YOU WATCH HIM!"
Grant Taylor (Alex Kendrick) coaching the Shiloh Eagles from the sidelines.

FACING THE GIANTS

"YOU'D MAKE A BETTER HEAD COACH." Brady Owens (Tracy Goode) listens while Alvin Purvis (Mike Garner) criticizes Coach Taylor.

"WE'RE GETTING KILLED." Jonathan Weston (Tommy McBride) and David Childers (Bailey Cave) watch their Shiloh Eagles get hammered on the field.

"YOU CAN DO IT, DAVID." Larry Childers (Steve Williams) supports his fearful son, David, from the sidelines.

"WILL YOU STILL LOVE THE LORD?" Brooke Taylor (Shannen Fields) and her husband Grant struggle with the news of infertility.

BEHIND THE SCENES

"PREPARE FOR RAIN."
Grant listens while Mr. Bridges (Ray Wood) challenges him to put his faith into action.

"DON'T GIVE UP!"
Coach Taylor yells at Brock Kelley (Jason McLeod) during the grueling death crawl drill.

"MY MAMA CAN KICK IT WIDE LEFT." Assistant coach J.T.Hawkins (Chris Willis) encourages David Childers to change his kicking philosophy.

"A UNIFIED TEAM."
Matt Prater (James Blackwell) and Brock Kelley listen to Coach Taylor's challenge.

"FACING THE GIANTS."
The Richland Giants charge onto
the field at the onset of the State
Championship game.

"PUT THE NAILS IN THE COF-
FIN!" Richland Coach Bobby Lee
Duke (Jim McBride) orders his
team.

"WHAT'S IMPOSSIBLE WITH
GOD?" Brooke and Grant share an
answer to prayer.

About the Authors

Alex Kendrick and Stephen Kendrick helped Sherwood Baptist establish Sherwood Pictures in 2003. They have co-written *Flywheel*, *Facing the Giants*, *Fireproof*, and the upcoming film *Courageous*. Both live in Albany, Georgia, and serve in leadership positions at the Sherwood Baptist Church; Alex is associate minister, and Stephen is associate teaching pastor.

Eric Wilson is the *New York Times* best-selling writer of *Fireproof*, the novelization, as well as the novelizations of *Flywheel* and *Facing the Giants*. He lives in Nashville, Tennessee, with his wife and two daughters.